KILLING MEMORIES

THE LOSER MYSTERIES #2

BY

PEG HERRING

ISBN: 9781944502232
© Peg Herring, 2nd Edition, 2018

First published in United Kingdom by LL-Publications 2013
Edited by Leslie Brown
Printed in the USA

For Shelly, who loved the Loser books. Gone too soon, my friend.

CHAPTER ONE

If you're pretty sure someone you like a lot killed somebody you didn't like at all, what are you supposed to do about it?

LOSER
I stood near the window in Bert's office, a little nervous about being inside without a job to do, especially in such a nice place. Using the sleeve of my flannel shirt, I removed a light film of dust from the windowsill, a small service that made me feel a little more worthy.

"You own the place." Bert pointed his unlit cigar at me and clamped it between his teeth. "You can hide out there as long as you need to."

The office, like the man himself, conjured a sense of old money and Southern charm. It smelled of books and lemon wax, and the studded leather chairs opposite his desk invited ladies to be seated but offered a woman of dubious parentage and no style no welcome whatsoever. No doubt my appearance would have kept me out of the building if Bert hadn't escorted me in himself.

As I considered my lawyer's suggestion that I go into hiding, I looked down two floors to the parking lot. An expensive assortment of cars waited below for their well-heeled owners, which was not unusual. Having two news trucks parked end to end outside the dignified office building was unusual, however, and I imagined the horror the inhabitants must be feeling. A newscaster sat in the cargo deck of each truck, one male, one female. Modern architecture shut out the sounds from below, but they chatted idly in what appeared to be pantomime, microphones set beside them in case I should suddenly appear. Smoking nearby were a couple of cameramen and a guy in a bad suit, probably a print journalist. They all looked up occasionally at the window where I stood, and I moved back a little, making sure they couldn't see me.

Hiding out sounded good to me. Very good.

"When your foster mother died," Bert spoke around the cigar with practiced ease, though it was as thick as my thumb, "you were...indisposed." A true Southern gentleman, he chose the nicest possible word for my condition at the time. "Her lawyer contacted me to report that—" He consulted a paper on his mahogany desk. "Marta Baer left everything she owned to you." He smiled. "It seems you were her favorite."

Shaking my head, I gave up two of my precious store of words. *Thirty a day. No more.*

"Her last." *Twenty-eight left.*

Bert frowned. "Don't minimize it, Beth. Ms. Baer had many foster children over the years. She left her place to you."

I knew Marta had loved me, though I often wondered what she'd found to love. I'd loved her too, and I was grateful for the six years we'd spent together. But her love and the bequest, for that matter, surely came from pity. Marta must've known I was a loser before I actually was Loser. I was glad she'd never seen what I became after her death: a homeless, friendless wreck on the streets of Richmond. Loser, who cried silent tears and barely spoke, who slept in a city park or along the James River or behind a gas station, but never inside. When I tried to sleep with walls around me, the voices of the dead prevented it.

"The house has been maintained for you." Bert shuffled through papers to find the specifics, licking his finger to separate them as he went. "I asked the lawyer to see to it until you were prepared to make a decision. He put the house and property in the care of the local real estate agent, who, in turn, hired a man to maintain it for you."

I amended my earlier thought about being friendless. Bert Suggs was my lawyer, but he'd also proved himself a good friend. Almost two years ago, he'd prevented my arrest for murder. In the time since, he'd looked after my interests when I refused to look after them myself. And now, he was offering me a chance to escape the notoriety that had found me a second time. Although I was getting positive press this time,

10

it was no less terrifying for me to be interviewed, examined, and publicized. Losers avoid notice. It's how they survive.

Watching members of the press waiting below, I considered Bert's idea. Had I been told after Marta died that I'd inherited her house? If I had, I'd ignored it. My foster mother's death had been the last blow in a series that had turned me from Beth Lousiere into Loser. I didn't recall even seeing Bert after Marta died.

As if to prove he was telling the truth, Bert set a copy of my foster mother's will on the desk, turning it so it faced me. I moved forward and picked it up, feeling the thickness and texture of the paper. Marta had died of a heart attack. That was my fault. She'd left her entire estate, a large farmhouse outside Beulah, West Virginia, and a modest sum of money, to me. To be specific, she'd said, "to my beloved foster daughter, Beth Lousiere." My eyes got misty, but I pushed thoughts of the past away.

"I thought of the property when they said you'd be released from the hospital today." Bert laid the cigar in a silver ashtray, carefully placing the soggy end so it overhung the edge. "I thought you might want to leave the city for a while."

Bert's suggestion made the muscles at the back of my neck tense. Leave the places I was used to? Make decisions? I was used to living in the present, accepting whatever came, and for a long time, my future had seemed unfathomable and of little consequence. The thought of change was as terrifying to me as talking to the reporters downstairs.

"...new start," Bert was saying. "You're big news here in Richmond, but in Beulah, you'll simply be a former resident returning after living in the city for a while."

Several folders lay on his desk, each thick with paper, and I guessed they all concerned me. One had newspaper clippings sticking out of the edges. Some clerk in Bert's office, charged with keeping track of my most recent press coverage, had stuffed them in any which way, and I felt my old urge to neaten and organize kick in. They should be organized by date and—I stopped. The point of the file wasn't its messy state. Those clippings made leaving Richmond a good idea, if I could make myself do it.

Bert's thoughts ran parallel to mine. "If you're gone for a while, the public will forget the Homeless Hero who saved a little girl and her daddy. Reporters will stop digging up your past and move on to someone else." He leaned back in his ergonomically-designed chair. "You still own the house in the Fan, of course. If you decide to come back here, you can sell the one in West Virginia."

Could I sell Marta's house to strangers? I wasn't sure, but I couldn't imagine going back there to take up my old life, either. What exactly would a former street person do in Beulah? Go to church on Sundays in stained sweatpants? Help out at the craft show with grimy fingernails? Get elected to the village council in duct-taped running shoes? The whole idea was ridiculous.

Bert seemed uncharacteristically ill at ease, and his next words revealed the reason. "Beth, I think it's a good idea. Right now, you think like this street person, Loser. I'm no psychiatrist, but when you suffered such terrible tragedy, Beth couldn't handle it anymore, and Loser took over. Going home won't bring the old Beth back, but Loser is a creature made of sadness. You need to get back some of Beth—some ability to see purpose in your life—in order to recover." His lips kept moving when the speech stopped, and I guessed what he wanted to add. He knew his next piece of advice, "Get some counseling," would go unheeded. It was impossible. For one thing, counseling requires talking. To strangers. *Like that was going to happen.*

Was it possible I could step back in time and forget the last few years? What if people back home asked, as they're likely to do, *What have you been up to, Beth? Where have you been all these years? Who died as a result of your selfishness, Loser?*

"They'll leave you alone, I think." Bert spoke as if he'd read my mind. "Small-town people aren't as meddlesome as they're portrayed."

I remembered the people of Beulah, who were like people everywhere: some good, some not so good. I was the problem.

"Gotta go."

Bert had taken up the cigar again, and he rolled it between his fingers. "I've reserved a hotel room under my secretary's name," he said with attempted nonchalance. "You can stay there until you decide what you want to do."

I shook my head and backed away, giving him a wave and a tight-lipped smile. Bert opened his mouth as if to argue but closed it again. He'd known me long enough to realize I don't respond well to logic. "Skittish" he'd called me once when he didn't think I could hear. I admit it: I'm skittish and a whole lot worse.

I left Bert's office, taking the stairs to avoid the tiny space of the elevator. My battered tennis shoes sounded dully on the metal stairs, and I took note of the duct tape that held them together. A month ago I hadn't cared. Now, I was embarrassed, at least a little, by my shabby appearance: dusty black T-shirt paired with faded blue sweatpants and a black knitted toque pulled down around my face.

On the ground floor, I stopped, recalling the news crews outside. I couldn't leave by the front doors if they were still out there. Standing well back, I peered through the glass. One truck had gone, and I couldn't see the man in the cheap suit. One die-hard reporter between me and freedom, a woman of brittle beauty who probably had no idea anymore what her natural hair color was.

Toying with the splints on my fingers, I considered my options. In my time on the streets, the biggest choice I'd had each day was whether to stand in front of the drug store or wander through the Fan, an area of Richmond known for historic, stately homes and the magnificent statues along Monument Avenue. I didn't belong there, but I was tolerated because I behaved myself, picked up trash from lawns and sidewalks, and did odd jobs for those who did. I wanted to go there, but how would I avoid the news crew with their Homeless Hero crap?

Because I'd helped a man accused of murder, I could no longer be just plain Loser. Because of sensational, often untrue stories in newspapers and on TV, my life was no longer my own. People who wouldn't have told me what time it was a few days ago now wanted to help me, reform me, re-educate me. What that meant was they wanted to force me to make choices normal people make every day.

Where did I want to live? What would I like to do? A reporter who'd sneaked into my hospital room the day before had insisted it was my moral obligation to "do something" for the homeless of Richmond, since I was now their spokesperson.

Right, I thought. *A spokesperson who counts her words, terrified that something awful will happen if she exceeds her daily quota. That should work.*

The nurse who'd helped me dress for release had called my experience with murderers a blessing in disguise. "Your fingers will heal, and I think you should get back to a normal life," she'd said. "Time you got off the streets and rejoined society."

Who says so? I'd wanted to ask her. *Who says it's time?*

Even Bert, who mostly left me alone, had mentioned I had money to manage, insurance money he'd invested for me that had grown to an alarming sum. And I owned not one but two houses.

I glanced out the door again. The perky blond reporter waited patiently, ready to stick her microphone in my face. I had news for her and for the rest of them too. I was not ready for a normal life. Despite the good intentions of others, I couldn't snap my fingers and become Beth Lousiere again. I was Loser, at least a big part of me was, and for Loser, normal's not all it's cracked up to be.

Turning away from the front door, I headed back through the lobby, down a corridor on the left. I found an exit there, but it was marked *For Emergency Exit ONLY—Alarm Will Sound.* I touched the smooth metal bar briefly, considering if it was worth setting off the alarm to get away from the press. Probably not.

Retracing my steps, I headed down the next corridor, ignoring the suspicious look I got from the security guard on duty. This one led to what I wanted, a secondary exit probably used by employees. I stepped outside, exhaling in relief at leaving the confines of the building behind.

I hadn't gone three steps when a voice sounded at my elbow. "Ms. Lousiere, would you answer a few questions?" It was the reporter in the bad suit. I should have guessed not all of them would give up easily.

Shaking my head vigorously and holding up a hand, palm out, in the classic "Go away" gesture, I kept walking. He followed anyway. "Ms. Lousiere, the only way your story can be told correctly is if you talk to the press. Now, I'm not here to give you a hard time. I just want to help you get the truth out there."

The guy had *barracuda* written all over him, and he was circling me, hoping for blood.

"Beth, is it true you sustained your injuries protecting Nick Saraff's daughter from her aunt's lover?"

I kept walking.

He tried a different approach. "Police are talking about re-opening the investigation into the murders of your husband and child two years ago, Beth. Since you were their main suspect back then, can you point them in a direction that might help them find the real killer?"

I walked faster, but he kept up, loping along beside me like an elderly beagle. "I don't believe you killed your family, Beth, but how can people be convinced if you won't tell what you know?"

I broke into a run, feeling the strain in my recently traumatized leg muscles. Living on the streets had kept me fit, and the reporter was no match for me. When I turned the corner, he was still shouting questions, his breath coming in gasps. "Are you going back to your house on Grace Street, Beth?"

If he and his buddies expected me to go there, it was the last place I'd go. Slowing to a walk, I searched my mind for places I could hide. I'd have to avoid my usual haunts and most of my friends, many of whom would tell everything they knew for the price of a hot meal or a bottle of wine.

Beulah, West Virginia, was far away from Richmond. Marta's house was isolated and familiar. I could be by myself there, at least for a while. I might find a purpose, something small, something even Loser could handle. I circled back, made sure I'd lost the poor man's Anderson Cooper, and went in the same door I'd left by a few minutes earlier. Climbing the stairs to Bert's office again, I bypassed the secretary and leaned into his doorway. "I'll go."

Bert seemed relieved. "You need a car, and you'll have to renew your driver's license."

I hadn't thought of that. We'd had a car, Darrin and I, but I had a vague memory of giving it to someone, a church, maybe, or one of the shelters.

Bert went on, "We'll close up the house on Grace Street until you decide what you want to do with it."

I used the rest of my daily store of words in honor of Bert's concern for me. "I'll get the license. Buy a car and sell the house on Grace Street."

EDDIE'S SECRET BLOG, JUNE 5

I'm not sure where we are exactly. It's a motel, a real crappy one. When I said the place smells bad, my mom got mad. "You have a nose like a bloodhound, Eddie, always smelling something nobody else does. Deal with it, cuz we have to stay where they take cash."

I shut up then, cuz there's no sense talking to her, but still. The carpeting's covered with sticky spots I don't want to know about, there's no Wi-Fi, and the TV remote works about one time in eight. Crap City.

Mom's in trouble, but she won't tell me what's going on. She doesn't call her friends. Her nails are all chipped where she chewed the polish off. She never mentions Dickweed's name. The first night we were here, I woke up around two. She was in the bathroom, cleaning something off her shoes. I couldn't see very well cuz the door was just open a crack, but the water in the sink ran red. Real red.

It's crazy. Two days ago, I'm sitting in algebra class, all normal, and the principal's secretary comes to get me. As we're walking up the hallway, she says my mom is there cuz of some family emergency.

When we get to the office, Mom's sitting on the edge of a chair, chewing her lip and staring out the doorway like she hasn't seen me in a decade. When I left for school that morning, she was all wrapped up in Marie's purse party at noon. Now, she acts totally different.

"Eddie!" She comes to meet me, putting her hands on my shoulders and digging her nails in till I wince. She's got a funny expression that seems like a warning. "Your Uncle Bob died, dear." She turns to the secretary and bats her eyes. "We didn't even know he was sick."

She babbles on while the secretary purrs those sympathy noises people make when they're supposed to care. I know Mom well enough to see she's giving me time to catch on and play along. I never had an Uncle Bob, or any uncle that I know of. Bob might be Dickweed's brother, but he never mentioned one. In fact, he never talked about any family at all. Not that he speaks to me much, but I'd remember a brother. It would be sad if there were two like Dickweed in the world.

I play along. My mom's a little weird all the time, a lot weird some of the time, but we've always supported each other. When I got caught in the girls' locker room and the principal called her in, she acted like she totally believed my story that I wandered in by mistake. And when she talks to Dickweed about my father, supposedly killed in Iraq, I keep my mouth shut. We've only got each other. It's what you do for family.

When we get out of the school building, things get even weirder. Mom hurries to the car, where I see her gray rolling suitcase and my biggest duffle bag, both stuffed full, in the back seat. "Come on," she says. "We have to leave." She gets in and turns the key. I notice her fingers are shaking.

17

"What?" I stand there staring at her like an idiot. "Why?"

"Eddie, don't ask questions. Please." She turns the key a second time, causing that grinding noise the ignition makes when it's already on.

I glance back at the school. "I've got finals tomorrow—"

She leans over, reaching out a hand like she's going to physically pull me into the car.

"You don't understand! We've got to leave now!"

When she gets like that, it's better to do what she says. I get in and shut up.

LOSER

The morning after my release from the hospital, I left my hiding place behind some low bushes in Monroe Park. The night had been warm, and the promise of real heat hung in the humidity already present in the air. Bert had been upset when I'd refused his offer of a hotel, but I'd been desperate for real sleep, with no roof over my head, no soft bed under my body, and no people.

Leaving the park, I made my way to the house on Grace Street that I owned, at least for now. I'd agreed to meet Bert's assistant there, hopefully early enough that no reporters would be around. I approached with caution, using trashcans as cover. I was in luck. My former home was clear of bothersome pests.

In the parking space at the back of the house was a silver Buick Envoy, not too new, not too fancy. Bert had guessed exactly what I'd want. When I stopped to look it over, a man got out of the car. He was tall, with long arms and legs and a frame that was muscular without being ripped. His hair was a little darker than mine, and he had those high cheekbones that are supposed to guarantee you'll never look old. He looked very young, in fact, and his crisp suit, white shirt, and discreetly striped tie suggested a kid dressed for church on Easter

Sunday more than a newly minted lawyer. "I hope this is okay," he said, indicating the car with a wave. "I'm Alex Bronson. After Bert told me a little about your requirements, I picked it out."

I saw him checking me out and imagined the thoughts in his head. *This is the woman so damaged by life that she dropped out, the woman so crazy we have to babysit her. She can't speak to the press. She can't pay her own bills. Wealthy but more than eccentric. A loser.*

I reached out a hand for the keys. "Thanks."

He held on to them, but his smile was non-confrontational. "I'm to drive you," he informed me. "Mr. Suggs' orders. One should not drive to the DMV office with her license expired."

This from a guy who looked like he still had a learner's permit. Accepting his argument, I climbed meekly into the passenger side. As Bronson started the car, I watched to see if anything had changed since I last drove one. Possibly reading my mind, he pointed to a screen on the dashboard. "GPS," he said. "You type in the address you want, and it tells you exactly how to get there." He demonstrated. "It can be annoying at times," he said with a grin, "but you'll seldom get lost."

Bronson drove to the DMV office as the car told us where to turn and how far ahead the next turn was. The ride in a quiet car was quite different from my last, which had been in an ambulance, where EMTs had talked about me as if I were deaf: "Broken fingers on both hands." "No obvious internal injuries." "Awake but unresponsive."

Now I watched as Richmond passed around us: the Children's Museum, the university, the post office, and the turn we didn't make that led to VMH, the hospital where I'd spent the last few days. When the calm voice announced we'd reached our destination, I sat in the car for a moment, gathering the courage it took for me to face society's hurdles. Being respectable meant talking—speaking to strangers. Though I would try to act like a normal person, they'd know. Resolute, I put my hand on the door handle. Time to get it over with.

"Would it help if I went along?" Bronson asked. I'd almost forgotten he was there, and my sweaty hand slipped off the handle as I started in surprise. When I turned to assess the reason for his offer, his expression was friendly. "Mr. Suggs said you don't like doing things like this, and I can relate. For me, it's dental cleanings—all that scraping!" He shuddered, letting the idea of our shared apprehensions sink in. "I could go along and play your overly chatty boyfriend. That way you won't have to say much."

I didn't want to owe this guy anything, and I didn't know what he stood to gain from helping me out. Was he trying to score points with me so I'd tell his boss what a great guy he was? Being nice to the crazy client? Maybe he was curious to see how I'd handle myself in the stressful world of the DMV. He might find humor in watching me turn into a gibbering idiot when they asked my date of birth.

Support of any kind was better than none. "Yes."

Bronson hurried around the car to open my door, but I was out before he got to me. I gave him a look, and he shrugged comically. "I'm a Southern male. They beat it into us."

I hurried up the steps of the imposing Richmond Central Customer Service Center, which felt a little like storming a castle. Inside, my steps slowed. As I opened the door, the muted hum of a busy office made me flinch. The dozen or so people waiting in the rows of chairs turned to look at us, most scowling with impatience that said they'd been there a while. The clerks paid us no mind, and Bronson stepped ahead of me, took a number, and said, "Let's sit over here, honey."

We waited twenty minutes. Bronson passed the time by telling me about his great aunt, a woman convinced that driving a car was an inalienable right despite advancing macular degeneration and dementia. The people around us were soon chuckling at her antics and Bronson's comedic delivery, which was worthy of a nightclub act. When my number came up on the screen overhead, I rose from my chair, swallowing hard.

Bronson stood too and followed me to the counter. "Hi, I'm Trent Dilfer, and this is my fiancée, Beth—" He gave the clerk an engaging grin. "I mean, Elizabeth Lousiere. She needs to reinstate her license, which expired a year or so back."

The clerk I'd drawn was neither friendly nor belligerent, which is all one can hope for, I suppose. I handed her a photocopy of my old license, hoping she'd use the information and not ask a lot of questions. After examining it through half glasses suspended on a chain and set low on her nose, she looked at me over the specs, her expression indicating that someone who let her license lapse was not on her list of good little girls. "She'll have to do the vision screening, take the knowledge test, and—" She raised her brows before adding, "—take the driving test."

Bronson waved casually as if that would be a breeze. "Is it okay if I ride along on the test?"

The clerk frowned behind long, straight bangs. "I don't think—"

An arm circled my shoulders, and I was pulled into Bronson's embrace, where I smelled something light and manly. "It's a temporary thing," he said glibly, "but Beth's likely to throw up under stress." He leaned over the counter and lowered his voice. "We just found out we're pregnant."

The woman's expression changed from blank to interested, and she turned to me. "How many weeks?"

I searched my mind for a time when throwing up was likely. "Five."

"Awww!" She leaned toward me. "When's the worst time of day?"

I saw Bronson's forehead furrow, but I had this one. "Mid-morning." I'd been sick only a few times during my real pregnancy, but it had always been around ten o'clock.

"Awww!" Turning to her monitor, she became businesslike. "I'll give you Dan. He won't have a problem with your boyfriend riding along."

I took the knowledge test, which was easy enough. Once my clerk had explained the answer to the one question I missed, she took me to one side, where I passed the vision test and had my picture taken. Excited about the baby, she never got around to asking why I'd let my license lapse.

Bronson kept up a running patter, answering questions about when I was due (April fourth), if we had plans to marry (we apparently did), and whether we were going to find out the baby's sex. (We weren't. We liked surprises.) It worked better than I could have hoped. Our clerk hardly noticed that I only spoke a few words. If she thought of us later, she'd no doubt remember the chatty boyfriend whose girlfriend was too mousy and way too poorly dressed for a charming guy like him.

The driving test wasn't as bad as I'd feared. I hadn't forgotten how to drive, and the guy who took us out was about as lackadaisical a judge as I could have hoped for. Bronson immediately engaged him in conversation about the upcoming college football season, and I became a secondary consideration. Beyond, "Turn right," and "Back up," and "Follow those lines," Dan ignored me completely. In the end, I got a temporary license without exhausting my daily limit of words. I even had a few left over.

When we left, Bronson opened the car door for me and went around to the driver's side. "Where to?"

"Home." I used a word he'd understand, though the word had no meaning for me.

"All right." He put the car into gear and backed out of the lot. We drove for a few minutes before he said casually, "We could stop somewhere for lunch if you're hungry."

Great. He was feeling sorry for the crazy street-person client who no doubt needed a square meal. "No." I made myself add, "Thanks."

"Okay." Apparently, he wasn't bothered by my refusal, because he went off on a different topic. "I hope I didn't offend you with the whole pregnancy thing."

I shook my head. I almost had to smile, first at the memory of the clerk's excited reaction to our "news," and second at the thought that someone like me would be offended by anything. I'd been called names. I'd been ordered to stay away from homes and businesses or get my head beaten in. I'd been talked about like I wasn't there. Why would I mind a few lies told in a good cause?

Bronson skirted a bus that coughed to a stop in front of us. As we reversed our earlier route, mid-morning traffic buzzed around us. He chatted on, telling funny stories about work and traffic and his landlord, the kind of stuff people use when conversing with a stranger. He probably found it odd that I didn't warm up, as even shy people usually do after a few minutes and some shared experiences. I wasn't like that.

When we got to the house on Grace Street, Bronson parked in the dirt square behind the house. There was barely room for two cars to pull in next to each other, but I knew that space would increase the asking price of the house considerably. *Off street parking*, the ad would boast. *Six fireplaces, five bedrooms and a possible sixth. Charming original woodwork. Fenced garden area.*

Those things had drawn Darrin and me to the house as a young married couple. We'd worked hard on it, renovating most of the rooms in line with the rules of the Fan's historical committee. I'd thought we were a happy family until I learned my husband was cheating on me. That's when Darrin had ended up dead.

"Nice place," Bronson said as we got out of the car. "Bert says you're planning to sell it?"

I nodded, and he craned his neck, gazing up at the Victorian roof trim. "Wish I could afford it, but I've got student loans to pay off before I can consider any house, much less one in the Fan." Still looking up, he said, "I'd like one like this someday though."

I looked at the house I could not enter without hearing the voices of my murdered husband and infant daughter. "Not like this one," I advised. That made twenty-nine words I'd spoken today. One left, and it wasn't quite noon.

Bronson seemed to understand he shouldn't pursue the subject. "What are those flowers I smell?"

I could have told him, but that would have led to chitchat about my garden and my past. I shrugged as if clueless.

"Well," he said briskly, "here are the keys."

I took them, and he backed away a few steps before turning. I had one word left, and I gave it to him. "Thanks."

"It was a pleasure," he said gallantly. He walked away, and I wondered how he'd get back to the office. Maybe I should have offered him a ride, since he'd been so helpful. It's what I would have done back when I was Beth Lousiere. But Loser wasn't Beth.

Alex Bronson probably thought when he was gone I'd go into my house and do whatever people do in their homes. Instead, I took a seat in the corner of the garden, leaning my back against the board fence and crushing some weeds that had taken over where begonias used to grow. I spent the rest of the day there, thinking about what I would do. The afternoon waned and then the evening. When a light rain began to fall, I moved to the porch, where I curled up on my side and listened to the night until I was able to fall asleep.

CHAPTER TWO

EDDIE'S SECRET BLOG JUNE 2

Another town, another ratty motel. This one smells like that stuff they use to cover other smells, and it's so strong it's hard to breathe. We're still in West Virginia, but I'm not sure where we're headed. I think Mom's laying false trails, going one direction for a while, staying overnight, and then taking off in a different direction. She'll wake me up at three a.m., make me get dressed, and we sneak real quiet to the car and drive away. She left her phone at home, she won't use the GPS, and she threw everything I had with Internet access into a trash can. She let me keep the little digital recorder she bought me for school, so I'm using it right now, taping over my history lectures so I remember all this when it's over. I'm gonna write a book about living on the run, but I'll use an alias and change the names and all that. Even if Mom did something bad, no one will know it's her the book's about. And if they arrest her, I'll use the advance money for lawyer fees.

Yesterday Mom stopped at a Wal-Mart and bought two disposable phones. She says I can use mine to call her if I need to, but that's all. I'm not to call anyone in Romulus. That's not a real big deal. I mean, I liked some of the guys back there, but there's nobody I need to talk to. Ten different schools before fourth grade is pretty much guaranteed to make a guy into a loner.

I kind of liked Romulus, maybe cuz I lived there longer than anywhere else. After Mom married Dickweed, school got a little easier. When I didn't get thrown in somewhere new every few months, I started getting pretty good grades. Not A's or anything, but I did okay.

Home was okay too. We had a house with a pool, which was great, and an awesome entertainment system. Dickweed's a tool, but he ignored me unless there were people around he wanted to impress. Then I was "Mr. Ed." I know about the talking horse from watching *TVLand*. Dumb.

I still don't know why we had to leave Romulus. I can't get Mom to talk about it, even when I give her Smile #1, (Love You, Mom). All she'll say is that it'd be dangerous to go back. She won't say what the danger is, but she's real serious about it. If I bring up the town or school, she always makes me promise one more time I won't contact anyone from there. "Nobody!" She puts her face real close to mine like she really means it. I asked about Dickweed once, but her expression got all weird, and she said real harsh, "He's in the past."

One day when she went out to get us something to eat, I looked through her suitcase. The clothes she brought along are her plainest jeans and shirts, no fancy designer tunics or leggings or silk scarves. There was a wad of cash in the zipper pocket, almost five thousand dollars in hundreds and fifties. In the left side pocket was a plastic bag with a white blouse of hers inside, all wadded up. The front was stained a rusty red color. I'm pretty sure the money came from my stepdad's safe, and the red—it was blood.

LOSER

The morning I left Richmond was sunny, and the whole gang was at the All-Aid, basking. That was good, because I wanted to see them one last time. I didn't plan to announce my departure. There were only a few people I intended to tell, and only one of them was here.

My friends stood, sat, or leaned in various spots around the building. Some of them were truly homeless. Others were semi-homeless, meaning they had a place to live, but standing on the street all day was preferable to being there. Some were physically handicapped; others had mental, chemical, or emotional issues. Most I considered friends, though friendship is different on the streets than it is in the houses that line those same streets.

Everyone here had helped me out at some point. Most were generous with tips on how to survive and alerts on what to watch out for. Like people everywhere, some of them could be treacherous. A few wouldn't hesitate to sell me out for a dollar.

"Hey, Loser!" Bubba yelled as he noticed my approach. "How you doin', girl?" I waved, and Bubba launched a loud introduction for the entertainment of anyone within half a mile. Grabbing my shoulder and sending a cloud of malodorous breath in my direction, he shouted, "Here she be, the toughest lady on the streets. Loser take on a guy with a gun, slap him down, shoot him dead, and then beat up his girlfriend."

None of it was strictly true, but the rest of them loved it, and I saw that Bubba, a born entertainer, would use it as his new shtick for weeks to come. No one could argue him out of what he chose to believe, and even if someone could, it wouldn't be me. Even a guy with a 70 I.Q. can win an argument with someone who doesn't talk.

Each of the others reacted to my appearance in his or her own way. Aisha ignored me entirely, lost in her own world. Waving in my direction, Penrod uttered his favorite phrase, "Choose an awkward moment." Howard punched my arm as I passed his wheelchair, and Lewis bowed in exaggerated admiration.

Seeing my discomfort, Mabel stepped in. "Y'all hush now," she ordered, wiping her mouth in a habitual gesture. "Loser already heard what you got to say a million times." She came to meet me, pulling her bad hip forward with a grimace of pain. Mabel was one of the world's great hypochondriacs, but even hypochondriacs can have real ailments

Ignoring comments from the group, Mabel and I moved around the side of the drug store. It was cooler by only half a degree, but in Richmond's summer, we take whatever relief we can get. Hobbling to the wall, Mabel turned her back and let it take some of her weight, heaving a sigh as the pain eased a little. I knew her pain must be bad today, because she wasn't out in the street, waving at passing cars. A jaunty wave is Mabel's way of cheering a dark and lonely world: a smile, a little kindness a driver doesn't have to pay for or even return. The locals know her and wave back. Others stare at her off-kilter face and malformed body. Mabel doesn't mind, or at least she doesn't appear to.

"You look different, Loser." Mabel's good eye was bright with curiosity. "Like you got something to say for once."

"I'm leaving." No wasted words for me.

Mabel's head tilted to one side. Whatever she'd expected, it wasn't that. After a moment she said, "Goin' somewhere nice, I hope."

I nodded. My memories of the town of Beulah, West Virginia, were mostly good. There'd been a few people in the town who didn't take to "Marta's brats," but that was to be expected. One of her boys had been a peeper; one of the girls had stolen an old truck from the guy down the road and disappeared. The community had respected Marta, though, so when I did my homework and behaved reasonably well, the people of Beulah accepted me. Many were even kind.

Mabel looked across the parking lot, where there was nothing to see. "I'm glad." To my surprise, she wiped a tear from her eye. "We been good friends, though, Loser. Good-good friends."

I didn't know what to say—did I ever? I gave her a quick hug, feeling the rough surface of the skin of her arms, burned from hours in the sun. I felt my own tears forming and became aware that I would miss Mabel. Eccentric as she might be, she was more real than the friends I'd had on the police force who, when my hour of need came, believed the worst and left me in despair.

Mabel took my hand. She obviously wanted to add something more. "Loser," she said, looking into my eyes, "feel this bump I got on the back of my neck. Do you think it might be a tumor?"

After listening patiently to Mabel's complaint-of-the-day, I slipped away, a little sad that from now on she'd have to find someone else to lend an ear to her many aches and pains.

That afternoon, I drove the car around the block a few times to familiarize myself with its features. Once I felt reasonably capable, I couldn't think of anything more I needed to do. I recognized that I was dragging my feet. I had decided to leave Richmond. Now, I had to actually do it.

With sudden resolve, I stuffed the tote bag I'd carried for months into a trash bin in the alley. A new life required nothing Loser had once owned. After that, I walked all the way around the house once, twice, three times, feeling the soft grass underfoot and occasionally touching a flower on one of the many bushes I'd planted and lovingly tended back when I was Beth Lousiere. I'd read somewhere it was a charm for good luck, but I'm not sure I believed that. It felt more like a solemn and final goodbye. I'd said goodbye to Verle, the restaurant owner I'd often worked for in the past, and Jake, my old partner on the police force, in emails sent from the public library. I knew both of them would reply, wishing me well, but neither would be mushy about it. I guessed they thought it was high time I became a contributing citizen again.

There was nothing to do but leave. I punched Marta's address into the GPS system the way Alex Bronson had showed me: 12 *Post Road, Beulah, West Virginia.*

Set as new destination? The screen asked. I nodded and then smiled at myself. *Can't even talk to a machine!* But the device, a minimal talker like me, accepted my gentle touch and ordered, "Now turn left!" We were on our way.

Beulah, West Virginia, is a last-stop kind of place. Beyond it is only mountaintop, where there are lots of animals and trees and not many people. I arrived without incident, and the drive was actually relaxing. There were things to see as I drove, but with one exception, I didn't have to interact with a single soul. When I stopped at a gas station for fuel and food, the bored clerk tried to make conversation about the weather. It was somewhere near the bottom of topics that might be considered threatening, and all I had to do was make agreeable noises.

A few hundred miles of westward freeway passed quickly, and I traveled north for almost a hundred more. Leaving the main highway, I turned east. At a thousand feet above sea level, I rolled down the window to feel the cool, unpolluted air and smell the pines. The twisting road slowed my pace, and the day was dying. The real estate office that managed the property would be closed by the time I reached Beulah. I hadn't planned on a bed anyway.

I drove through the tiny town around six. The streets were empty: not just nearly so, but completely empty. Anyone with business there had long since done it and gone home to supper. The place looked like peace itself, and it smelled like the sawmill on the outskirts. Leaving the town behind, I traveled half a mile and turned up a sharply twisting road that clung to the mountainside. It was narrow, with room for only one vehicle at a time. There weren't any others, so that wasn't a problem.

I found myself looking at the roadsides for flowers whose names I knew. Many had come and gone by now; the red bud trees were green, not magenta. I saw starry little chickweed tufts and fluffy-headed coltsfoot ready to spread its seed for next year. Green and gold shone in the clearings, and long-lived columbine showed white against the greenery.

I drove by Kathy and Mort Dahl's house as the road twisted again, passing through a tunnel of trees before coming to an open space where it ended. Before me was Marta's house. My house.

Turning its back on the road, it faced the mountains, so the driveway led to what was actually the rear entrance. It was as I remembered: a rambling two-story farmhouse with a chimney at each end and a verandah on the front and west sides. On cool evenings, we'd sat there, catching the last rays of the sun. On warm days, we'd sat wherever there was shade. Marta had always had a basket of something in her lap: peas she was shelling, beans that snapped under her strong fingers, a garment she was taking up or letting down, or even a pistol that needed cleaning. Marta had taught me to shoot, which served me well when I got to the police academy.

Getting out of the car, I stretched then turned in a circle, surveying the whole place. The split-rail fence that lined the driveway was in good repair, but it needed a coat of sealer. The apple trees in the side yard hung low with fruit, and I found myself wondering if I remembered how to make an apple pie. There were several outbuildings to my left, most of them no longer used for their original purpose. The building Marta had called the chicken coop was, as far as I knew, filled with old saddles and tack. The two granaries hadn't held grain for years, though they still smelled of it. And the barn might or might not be filled with hay. I was hoping there was at least enough for a bed.

I took a plastic bag filled with simple groceries out of the back seat of the car and stood for a moment, trying to decide what I wanted to do. In the end, I took a slow walk around the house, starting on the verandah and continuing along the west end, peering in every window. On the east end were two bedrooms, one of them Marta's, but the blinds were drawn. Moving to the front of the house, I cupped my eyes to look through French doors into the living area. What I saw was familiar and comforting, as if Marta had merely gone to town on an errand. Her chair, slightly indented from where she'd so often sat, had a small table beside it where a half-completed afghan lay, partially covering a basket containing skeins of yarn in blues, greens, and creams. I knew how that basket felt in my hands, the smoothness of the handle and the roughness of the woven bottom.

The rest of the room was furnished with well-maintained but slightly dilapidated furniture, exactly what a person should expect from a place where eighteen teenagers had come and gone. Their pictures, often several versions of each, filled the wall opposite Marta's chair, where she'd been able to look up to see them as she worked.

Even from outside I could pick out several pictures of a smiling teenager who was the once-upon-a-time Beth, happy with Marta and gaining self-confidence little by little. That Beth had wanted to become a cop in order to help people. She'd wanted to become a mother to

31

prove she could be a good parent despite her own parents' weaknesses. Marta had helped Beth believe she could do those things, that she was as good as anyone else.

All of that had fled when Beth's—when *my* husband confessed infidelity only months after our first child was born. I'd been trying to cope, trying to give him another chance, when he and our baby were murdered in the house on Grace Street, the home we'd dreamed of and worked for. That house was no longer home.

I wondered if this house could become home for me. Once I'd been happy here. Could I recapture that happiness and forget the pain that followed? Could I learn to accept and ignore the fact that my colleagues on the police force in Richmond thought I'd smothered Kara and stabbed Darrin more than a dozen times?

Put that into some deep crevasse in your mind. Concentrate on now.

Forcing myself to move on, I looked in the kitchen and dining room windows. Everything was as I remembered it; Marta was not one to idly rearrange furniture or change her colors. The four bedrooms upstairs were probably unchanged as well. Mine had been the last one down the hallway. Would I be able to sleep in that room? I hadn't slept inside a house for almost two years, but returning to a safe place, a place where no voices would accuse me of neglecting loved ones: would that help to heal me? *Maybe someday*, my mind whispered.

I left the veranda for the softer ground of the flowerbeds along the side of the house. It was harder to see in the windows from ground level, especially since I'm not what anyone would consider tall. Jumping a little, I saw that the main-floor bathroom was exactly the same, right down to the stain on the sink basin from a drip that would not stay fixed.

Once I'd rounded the house, I returned to the front porch and the view. The ground cut away steeply from the base of the house, the porch floorboards supported by a cantilevered framework that bit into the hillside below. My footsteps sounded hollow as I walked along them.

The view was breathtaking: treetops as far as I could see. Places below me were populated: the town, some housing developments, scattered cabins, homes, and a few businesses. Here, the forest screened them from view, and I felt completely, utterly alone.

It was the best feeling I'd had in two years.

CHAPTER THREE

I can tell Mom wants to talk about why we left Romulus, but she just can't do it. When I asked if we could eat at this nice Italian place I saw near this week's fleabag, she said we don't have a lot of money, so we have to watch our spending. I offered to get a job, but she said no, we probably won't be here long. When I said I'd do odd jobs, she got all teary-eyed.

"You shouldn't have to," she says. "I had things all figured out and now look at us! I didn't know he was—" She stops, putting her fingers to her mouth to cover her lips, but I see them quivering.

Something bad happened to split her and Dickweed. She used to defend him, saying I should be grateful for the roof over my head and the nice clothes on my back.

I tried. I never said what I thought of his treating me like I wasn't there or of him thinking he was always right, no matter what. And then there are his goofy TV commercials where he does this fake Rambo thing wearing camo and face paint and—I'm not making this up—an olive green headband. ("Hunt yourself a great deal, now, down at Hopgood Motors!") I was careful to always call him Rich, not Dickweed, in front of Mom, but I'm pretty sure she knew I hated the guy.

Honestly, I think she did too.

I don't know what the final straw was, but the blood on Mom's clothes and her break with everyone in Romulus makes me scared that for Dickweed, that straw really was final.

LOSER

My first morning back home, I was awakened by the sound of tires crunching up the graveled driveway. If I were a talker, I might have uttered a curse word or two. I wasn't ready for company.

I'd slept in the hayloft. Marta's barn had large, open spaces at either side for ventilation, which meant I didn't feel closed in. There was hay enough for a soft bed, and I'd found an old horse blanket in the chicken coop that made a decent underlayment. The night had been typical of summer nights in the South, so a covering wasn't necessary. I slept better than I had in months.

But now, here I was: hay in my hair and on my clothes, coming from the barn when my first visitor arrived. Not the way I'd intended to start my return home. I peered out the window at the car below. It stopped and a woman got out, her attention focused on the house. I saw her lean back into the car and get something out of her purse. The metallic ring told me what it was. The real estate agent was bringing the keys to my property.

I made the best repairs I could to my appearance, brushing the dust off my clothes and running my fingers through my hair. Luckily, it was short these days. Due to the fact I had several broken fingers from the struggle that brought the whole "Homeless Hero" nonsense on, Bert had sent his personal stylist to the hospital to "take care" of me. Horrified at the wild mass of hair I mostly covered with a knitted hat, she'd obeyed my one-word command: "Short." She'd been pleased with the results and left me with a tube of mango-scented "product" I could use to "get that separation you want with this look." The stuff was at the bottom of my tote bag. I didn't plan on using it, but street people don't throw anything away. It might be worth a trade to someone. Remembering that I'd ditched the tote, I felt momentary regret. Had I thought I could leave Loser behind in the trash?

Ordering myself to focus, I climbed down the ladder and left the barn, coming up behind the woman. She jumped in surprise when I said, "Hi."

"Goodness!" she said, putting a hand to her chest like she had the vapors. "Beth?"

I nodded. She was familiar, but I couldn't make a connection. She was too old to have been a friend or classmate, but her voice, her face, even her breathy manner, were familiar.

Without warning, I was hugged, clasped in one of those embraces I know is going to last longer than I want it to. "Beth, it's good to see you again. Welcome home."

I was still searching my mind for her identity. "I used to ask Marta how you were doing," she said, finally releasing me. "I'll never forget that speech you gave on condoms in tenth grade. The visual aids were, um, memorable."

Mrs. Wayans. Teenaged Beth re-appeared momentarily with a mental *Oh. My. God!* My real estate agent was my former speech teacher.

Flustered, I managed a smile and a little grimace. "Sorry."

"Oh, don't apologize, dear. It was exactly what your classmates needed to hear, and Lord knows the school board would never have let a teacher get away with presenting that sort of information!" She waved the topic away with a sweeping hand. "Now, I'm sorry to have missed you yesterday. I didn't know you were here until Kathy called me this morning."

Small-town telegraph. The Dahls must have seen a car go past their place and, knowing there was no one else on this road, concluded when it didn't return that I was at Marta's. No doubt word had gone around town that one of Marta's foster kids had inherited the house and was coming back to do something about it. I wondered if most residents of Beulah even recalled which of us was who.

"You should have swung by the house," Mrs. Wayans was saying. "Come on. Let's see if Calvin's been earning his keep." She led the way to the house, heels clicking on the flagstone walk. I opened my mouth to object, but three things stopped me. First, of course, my practice of not speaking unless absolutely necessary. Second, I didn't have a good reason why she shouldn't go in with me, and finally, now that I'd placed her, I remembered Mrs. Wayans' personality. She pretty much did as she liked, nicely, but with determination. So it was that I entered Marta's house for the first time in years with a constant stream of chatter for backdrop. Maybe that was a good thing, distracting me from the fact that my foster mother was gone from here forever.

"I retired from teaching a while back," Mrs. Wayans was saying. "Thirty years in the ninth grade was enough." I searched my mind for her first name. I couldn't keep thinking of her as Mrs. Wayans. Jean? Jackie? Genevieve! I thought that was right. Did her clients call her Jenny? Another reason to stay silent.

"Frank died two years ago." I made an appropriate noise of sympathy, but she went right on. "I needed something to do, so I got my real estate license. I know everyone in the county, had most of them in school, so people know I won't cheat them."

"Um."

She turned to me, apparently noticing I hadn't said much yet. "I know you were sick after Marta died." Her eyes said she either knew or guessed my disease had been mental, not physical. "After Harlan Fitch talked to your lawyer in Virginia, he asked me to manage the house until you decided what to do with it." She licked her lips. "If you decide to sell, I hope you'll work with me. I've got some ideas."

I tried for a look of thoughtful consideration. "Good."

"I know, you need time to think about it, but I've learned in this business that it doesn't pay to be shy." She smiled. "Kind of like speech class."

I looked at the door, willing her to leave. I liked her, or at least I had liked her when I was fifteen, but I didn't want company right now. And I certainly didn't want to chat.

I didn't know if she noticed the look, but she turned around slowly, taking in the condition of the room. "Well, Calvin hasn't done too badly,

I guess, for a man." She ran a finger over the top of the bookshelf. "There's a little dust, but I suppose he thought he'd get more notice of your arrival."

I pursed my lips, refusing to feel guilty for failing to give advance notice. I looked at the door again, and this time she noticed. Licking her lips again, Mrs. Wayans held out the ring of keys. "The two silver ones fit the front and back doors. I'm not sure what the others are for."

I knew them all. I took the ring from her, feeling the weight of the glitter-filled acrylic #1 figure I'd bought for Marta one year for Mother's Day. It was a little battered from use, but it felt good to know she'd kept using it all those years after I left.

"Calvin has a key to the house," Mrs. Wayans said, "but if you like, I'll have him bring it back."

"Please."

Her forehead narrowed briefly. She was probably figuring out I wasn't the carefree girl who'd once giggled her way through speeches. Putting it together with my being too "sick" to come home for Marta's funeral, she'd no doubt conclude things about me that would travel through Beulah with the speed of cyberspace. I didn't like it, but I couldn't worry about it, either.

When she was gone, I explored the house, letting my memory wander as I took stock of what I'd need to buy. Food, for one thing, since there was nothing to eat in the place. The unknown Calvin had seen to that; no sense attracting rodents and bugs when the house wasn't occupied.

Noticing the empty wood-box next to the fireplace, I recalled the snap of burning logs and the display of sparks when Marta added fuel. I felt an urge to try my hand at fire keeping. Should I ask Calvin to fetch firewood?

No. There was no need now. It was summer, and even if I stayed on, the house had a furnace if I needed warmth. The luxury of heat on command seemed slightly alien to me, but I knew I'd be grateful when the time came. I checked the electricity. It was on.

I went on, exploring rooms and closets. It occurred to me that I'd need clothing. In normal life, people change their clothes from time to time to fit the weather and the occasion. Marta's clothes were still in her bedroom, all hanging or folded neatly in place, but Marta had been taller than most men and square-built, where I was shorter than most women and small of frame.

Anyone but a loser would have thought of clothes before leaving Richmond. I remembered there was one of those dollar-something stores in Beulah. I could get a couple of outfits, sweats or maybe jeans to wear when working around the place. I didn't plan to become Beulah's fashion plate, just someone who looked fairly normal.

I drove to the store that afternoon, my jaw tight with apprehension at my first appearance in town. Two clerks, one at the register and another putting greeting cards into a rack near the front, were no more than seventeen. There was a man stocking shelves who might have been around when I lived here, but he ignored me, totally focused on Fritos and Doritos. One of the girls tilted her head and rolled her eyes at the other as I came in, and after I passed, I heard snickers that almost certainly concerned my shoes. Hating myself for caring what two babies thought, I added footwear to my mental shopping list.

Taking a cart with the obligatory bent wheel in front that squealed objections each time it moved, I filled it with cans of stew and soup, cereal and milk, and M&Ms for dessert. It felt strange to buy whatever I wanted, and I fought the feeling I should put some of it back and save the money. Bert insisted I was financially secure despite the lousy economy. I pictured him shaking his head upon learning I'd done my shopping at the Dollar Dynamo. Baby steps.

On a rack in the clothing section, I found thin cotton pants, some not-too-disgusting shorts, and a couple of t-shirts that didn't have rhinestones. I bought underpants, two sports bras, and several pairs of socks. With more interest in comfort than style, I tossed a pair of sandals and some tennis shoes into the cart. Moving to an isolated part of the store, I sat on the floor to try them on. If your feet aren't happy, you aren't happy, which is one reason I'd stuck with my old shoes so long.

The bell over the door tinkled a tinny alert. I glanced up at the convex mirror in the corner. The man who entered the store was probably not a local. The cowboy hat he wore hid his face, but I heard the smile in his voice as he greeted the girls. As I returned to trying on shoes, I heard the door to the cooler at the front of the store slide open and thump shut. I heard the clerk say, "That'll be a dollar, sir."

I heard the plastic seal break, followed by a soft sigh as the man apparently took a long drink of a cold beverage. He spoke then, his voice friendly and casual. Too casual, it seemed as I sat there, suddenly wary. "Either of you ladies know Marta Baer?"

There was a moment of silence, and I pictured the two girls looking at each other blankly. After a moment, one of them had a thought. "She old, like sixty, maybe?"

"About that, yeah."

"She used to go to my church, but she died."

"Oh. I'm sorry to hear that." He didn't sound sorry.

"It's been a long time," the girl said in the tone of one who doesn't yet know time is not the healer people claim it is. "Maybe a year."

"I see. Anyone living in her house?"

"I don't think so." If I'd had illusions of everyone in town talking about my return, they were shattered. These girls hadn't heard of me, or maybe they had and paid no attention. What interest would they have in the return of a former resident who left when they were in middle school?

The other girl asked, "What you lookin' for Marta for?"

40

"Nothing important." The man's shoulders moved in a shrug of dismissal. "I used to know one of the foster kids she raised, and I wondered what ever happened to her."

"Oh." His answer destroyed the tiny bit of interest the girls had felt. Again, ancient history.

The manager, done with one re-stocking task and on his way to the next, passed the spot where I sat listening and looked at me doubtfully. I smiled at him, removed a shoe, and tossed it into my shopping cart. He moved on, but I noticed that he hovered nearby.

I put on my old shoes and pretended to consider the home decorating shelf, which was ninety percent Jesus-in-Our-Home and I-Love-America kitsch. Finally, I heard his box cutter slice through packing tape as he went back to stocking shelves. When I checked the mirror again, the man who'd asked about Marta was gone.

Paying for my purchases with cash, which I will always prefer to credit, I stowed them in the back seat of the car and started for home. Something about the stranger's interest in Marta made me cautious, so when I passed the Dahl's place, I pulled off the gravel road onto a two-track I remembered that traveled into the woods a way and petered out at the spot where an old cabin had burned before I was born. As a teenager, I'd found it a great place for private time with my boyfriends. It served my current purpose too, hiding my car from view of the road. I got out, closed the door quietly, and headed through the woods, cutting off the last corner before my driveway. I stopped a few feet back from the clearing where the house sat, looking at what I'd suspected I'd find. There was a black Hummer parked in the driveway. The man I'd seen in town was doing as I'd done the day before, circling the house and peering in the windows. I tried to recall if I'd left any sign of my presence, but I didn't think so. I hadn't been inside that long. There were tire tracks in the drive, of course, but the house still looked abandoned.

Looking for one of Marta's foster children, he'd said. A female. Was he a reporter who'd trailed me all the way from Richmond? Probably not. His license plate indicated he was from West Virginia.

As he came back around to the front of the house, I saw his face clearly. He looked like an outdoorsman, the kind who can handle whatever Nature throws at him. He was handsome, his face deeply sun-tanned. Wide shoulders filled out his jacket in a way his tailor must have appreciated. Hearing his steps on the wooden porch, I noted expensive boots with square heels and narrow toes.

For some minutes the man surveyed the yard as if taking in details of the closed outbuildings and the unbroken quiet. His gaze swept the tree line, and I froze as it seemed to stop at the spot where I stood. *No, I told myself. He didn't see you, and if you keep still, he won't.* It was hard to fight the urge to run, to avoid trouble, whatever this particular sort of trouble was. Beth urged calm, but Loser wanted to escape to the anonymity of a big city with a park for sleeping and alleys for hiding.

In the end Beth won, or maybe she delayed action long enough that it became unnecessary. The man made a move that signaled decision, pushing himself away from the porch post and heading for his vehicle. He drove onto the lawn to turn around rather than backing down the driveway. His tires spun ruts in the grass as he accelerated and disappeared from sight.

I waited until the dust cloud he'd made settled and then turned back, making my way quietly through the trees until I reached my car. I sat in it for a while, wondering who the man had been looking for. If it was me, I couldn't think of a reason. Reporters from Richmond were unlikely to travel this far for a story, and even if they sent someone to find me, the stranger didn't seem like a media type. All Marta's foster children were at least a decade gone. What had brought him to the little town of Beulah and beyond it, to my front door?

Chapter Four

For the next two weeks I was a ghost in my own past. The man in the Hummer didn't return, and Marta's place began to feel familiar again. I tried to pretend I was seventeen and none of the terrible things had happened. Marta wasn't there, of course, but her things were. I listened to her tapes sometimes: the Beatles and the Kingston Trio, Brenda Lee and Buffy St. Marie. Other times, I listened to the silence, which was just as good.

Having survived my first shopping expedition, I tried the grocery store the next time I needed food. It had been a long time since I'd been inside such a place, and I felt ashamed at the ease with which I chose melons, grapes, ice cream, fresh-baked bread, and several different kinds of meat. Many of my street friends lived for a month on less than I bought in one trip.

I rediscovered cooking, and, while it wasn't much fun to create complicated meals for one, I counted it as reintegration. I was learning to be Beth again, and Beth loved to cook. The house filled with smells of simmering soup or stew, baked rolls and cookies, and homemade applesauce spiced with cinnamon.

I'd arrived too late to plant a garden, but Marta had long ago invested in crops that need no help from humans to keep going. I weeded her berry bushes, choked with thistle but still producing. My reward was sun-warmed berries that burst with juicy flavor in my mouth.

Calvin, a man Marta would have called "a long, tall drink of water," showed up at the door one day. He was no more interested in talking than I was, but we managed to agree that he would continue to mow the grass. I'd take over the house and other yard work.

He handed over his key with no apparent reluctance, wished me "Afternoon," and left. That was the only interruption for days.

In a shed, I found pruners and went to work on the fruit trees that lined the driveway. I was no expert on such things, but I fell back on my old resource, the library. I learned that real pruning was best done late in the year, so I contented myself with removing only dead or damaged branches. I was interested to hear myself thinking I'd finish the job in a few months. Was I planning on staying?

I went to bed—actually to barn—each night with aching muscles and a need for rest that was welcome. Work truly is its own reward. Waking with a sore back or crampy legs reminded me that I was a living, breathing person who contributed something to the world, even if I only rescued distressed trees and overgrown bushes.

After a week of solitude, I had two visitors in one day. First was Jen Wayans, whose first name I'd found in a pamphlet she'd left on the end table in the living room ("Call Jen—we can deal!") Before she was fully out of the car, she was apologizing for showing up unannounced. "I know you like your privacy," she said, implying she didn't understand it but was willing to be tolerant, "but I wanted to make sure everything's okay here."

"Fine," I said, leaning on my rake and massaging my lower back.

"That's good. Calvin says you two talked out an arrangement." Well, *talked* wasn't exactly the word for it, but I nodded.

She tilted her head a little. "Does that mean you've decided to stay?" I shrugged. It wasn't that I didn't want to tell her. I simply didn't know.

Her smile dimmed a tad, but she stepped forward and gave me a hug anyway. "I'm glad you're happy here, sugar. You could do the town a lot of good, you know."

I must have looked uncomfortable, because she hastened to add, "Oh, not right away. I know you need time to rest up first. But someone who's lived in the city would be welcome in just about any organization we've got. I'll bet you know how things should run in the twenty-first century." She pushed a wisp of hair off her high forehead. "Young people with anything on the ball usually leave Beulah and go to the cities, where they can make good money. Mostly what we've got is the young ones who didn't have the gumption to leave and retirees who come back after thirty years someplace else. Besides being *re*tired, they're just plain tired!"

She laughed at her own joke while I tried not to let my expression reveal the terror her confidence in me brought. Would the denizens of Beulah start ascending the mountain to demand I serve on the town council, the library board, the hospital auxiliary? Not only did I not want to do any of those things, I didn't have the words to explain why.

As Jen wrapped up her visit, I managed not to give up another word, though I wasn't sure what I was saving them for. She gave me a second hug I didn't want, got into her car, clicked her seatbelt in place, clamped the strap out of her way with some sort of made-for-TV miracle device, and backed out of the drive with a wave any pageant queen might envy. I had twenty-four words left for the day. Old habits die hard.

That turned out to be a benefit, because a car came up the drive that afternoon, a black BMW, although it wasn't black by the time it got to me. It was more dust-colored, at least two-thirds of the way up. The car itself was no surprise. Working at the end of the drive, I'd heard its tires crunching on the gravel road long before I saw it. The surprise was Alex Bronson, who stepped out, grinning like a teenager at my confused expression.

"Not expecting me, were you?"

I shook my head. Richmond in Beulah was definitely odd. Sharp suit, blindingly white shirt, perfectly-razored hair. I'd only been away from the city a few weeks, but it felt like he'd arrived from outer space.

Bronson approached the spot where I stood with paintbrush in hand. I'd covered most of the rail fence with sealer, and there was a clear line between the old and new finishes. It gave me satisfaction to see the improvement as I moved along the drive.

"Hope I didn't get too much dust in your paint job."

I waved a hand to dismiss that little problem. I had all the time in the world, and if it needed to be done again, I could handle it. Setting the brush across the top of the can, I wiped my sticky hands on an old dish towel, waiting for Alex to explain the reason for his visit.

"Mr. Suggs wanted to know how you were doing up here," he said, looking around with lively curiosity. "The lawyer in Beulah didn't have much to say on the subject, so I volunteered to make the trip."

I imagined Harlan Fitch had been polite but uncommunicative. Professional courtesy or no, a hometown girl would not be spied upon for a city slicker. I had a flash of gratitude for the people of Beulah, who, though they undoubtedly found me odd, were still willing to protect me from outsiders' prying.

I stopped myself before I got too sentimental. However protective the citizens of Beulah felt toward me now, they'd change their minds if they learned the truth. Would they want Loser, who'd wandered Richmond's streets for more than a year, suspected of murder and out of her mind, among them?

Bronson looked toward the house. "Don't suppose you have any iced tea in there."

A real Southern woman would have said something like, "Oh, my goodness, where are my manners!" I simply turned and started for the door.

In a few minutes we were seated on the front porch, sipping freshly made tea and looking out at some major beauty. The trees below us were still green, but fall was foretold in an orange or reddish branch here and there. I found myself anticipating the brilliant colors to come: ash leaves turning yellow, dogwood purplish, hickory golden, oak red, and maple scarlet. The vista before me would become an oriental carpet of color, and I wanted to be here to see it.

Bronson seemed willing to take on the bulk—pretty much all—of the conversational burden. He talked about Bert a little and brought me up to date on other news from Richmond. The papers were full of stories about my disappearance, but Bert had told the press I'd gone out of state seeking privacy. Bronson commented on the view. He mentioned a couple places in the town of Beulah he'd noticed as he drove through. He told me what the Suggs Law Firm had going that was of interest. When he finally ran down, I turned to him with raised brows. He laughed, raising his palms in mock surrender. "I know, I know! You're wondering why I drove all the way up here."

I nodded but couldn't help smiling back. The kid was engaging. I could see why Bert had taken him on. It seemed one of his jobs for the law firm was keeping track of me lest I revert to my old ways. Bert was hoping I'd turn back into what he considered a normal person.

Reaching into a pocket, he pulled out a shiny black rectangle. "Bert wants you to have this."

It was a phone, a fancy one. Bronson spent a few minutes showing me how part of it slid outward, revealing a keyboard. I'd seen them before but hadn't used one. "With this you can text, so you don't have to talk." He demonstrated, putting his own number into the memory and linking it to a ringtone. Taking out his own phone, he called me, and I heard a few bars of a vaguely familiar tune.

"That's 'The Caisson Song,'" Alex explained. "I did a stint in the army." Closing the phone, he handed it over. "Now, you can reach me if you want something." Pointing a finger at the device I held rather gingerly, he added, "In fact, that little critter can do about anything you want it to."

I forced a smile, unwilling to seem ungrateful. The modern phone, at least to me, is a double-edged sword. It can do amazing things, but it tells people where you are. It connects you to other people all the time, every day. Despite its amazing capabilities, I couldn't think of anything I wanted a phone like that for.

Bronson apparently read the lack of enthusiasm on my face, but he took a charging cord from his pocket and handed it to me anyway. I imagined Bert insisting he talk me into accepting the phone. "It's got a good battery and range," he said, as if hopeful that would help.

I looked at the phone doubtfully. As if to underscore my reservations, it rang in my hand. Without thinking, I tossed it to Bronson, who caught it, glancing at me with wry humor as he checked the caller I.D. and answered.

"Hello, Mr. Suggs. ... Yes, I made it. ... She's doing well. ... Oh?" Bronson looked at me briefly. "Yes, I think she would." He listened for a long time. "All right. I'll pass that along."

He ended the call, his expression troubled. "Mr. Suggs is glad to hear you're okay. He's received a request that he isn't sure about, but I think it's something you'll want to know."

Curiosity mixed with dread rose in my mind. News Bert didn't think I could handle couldn't be good. Quickly my Loser half imagined the worst: cops after me, someone dying, something awful.

Bronson didn't keep me in suspense. "A friend of yours, Mabel Carter, was hit by a car last night." He held up a hand when I gasped. "She's alive, but her hip is badly broken. The doctors had to do some pretty extensive surgery, but they think she'll recover."

I sat back a little. Poor Mabel! I thought of all the times she'd been at my elbow when it seemed I couldn't go on. Her method for keeping me going was odd, but it had always worked. Whenever I was close to despair, Mabel talked nonstop, turning my attention to her many ailments until my black moods of self-pity were replaced with something else. Irritation sometimes, but it did the job.

Bronson was waiting for some sort of response from me. "Bert knows Mabel?"

"No. Apparently, Mrs. Carter knew Mr. Suggs was your lawyer. She wanted him to sue the driver of the car and make her 'a bundle, like the lawyers on TV always promise.'" He grinned as he quoted Mabel directly. "Mr. Suggs declined to pursue the case, since Mrs. Carter was standing in the street when she was hit."

Waving. As some had predicted, Mabel's passion for making others happy had, in the end, brought disaster for her.

"She'll have to go to a nursing home for rehab. It will be a while before she can walk normally again."

A nursing home? Mabel's voice sounded in my head as if I could actually hear her tirade. "Ain't no real nursing, and it ain't nobody's home! Holding pens for folks waitin' to die! No privacy, no dignity, no McDonalds! I'd rather die on the streets!"

Mabel didn't know for sure how old she was, but she remembered Eisenhower's inauguration, so she was no spring chicken. Street people help each other out, but no one I could think of was capable of giving her the care she was going to need. I told myself there were good nursing homes if a person had money—or a friend with money. I could ask Bert to see that Mabel was well cared for. I could check them out myself on the Internet and choose one that seemed reputable. Or—

"Send her to me."

Bronson looked confused for a moment. "You want us to bring Mabel here?"

I nodded. "She's my friend."

EDDIE'S SECRET BLOG, AUGUST 26

We're staying in a trailer court, for god's sake, and it's awful. It reminds me of places we used to live before Mom met Dickweed. There are bratty little kids all around, and they scream pretty much all day. Happy or unhappy, the screams sound the same.

It's a furnished rental, and Mom took it for a month. She still won't tell me what's going on, but she says we might be able to stay here for a while. She talks about getting me into school next month. When I tell her not to sweat over school, she just rolls her eyes.

As bad as this place is, it's kind of nice to be just Mom and me again. Not that I was always at the top of her list, but lots of times when I was little, I was all she had to talk to. Now, we're back to that, and we talk a lot about the way things used to be. A lot of it was bad, but some was good, and I'm not sure it wasn't better than what came after.

As a kid, I didn't know you were supposed to have two parents. Nobody I knew did. Mom and me lived in rundown apartments and moved a lot. The main thing I remember about them is they were all painted the same almost-white color, and the carpets always smelled.

There were guys who came around and even stayed for a while, but they didn't usually make the mistake of trying to be my parent. Each one was just Mom's Boyfriend, and my job was to learn the guy's name, remember what kind of cereal he wanted for breakfast, and stay out of his way as much as possible. In a situation like that, a smile is a kid's best friend. As long as people think you're okay they ignore you, and a smile goes a long way toward making them comfortable. I built a little "smile set," practicing in front of the bathroom mirror and putting them into categories so I could use the right one when I needed it: the Sad Smile, the Embarrassed Smile, the Honest Smile, and so on. I got pretty good at calling up the right one when a teacher, boyfriend, or stranger was trying to decide if I was going to be trouble. With the right smile, they usually decide not.

So we learned to get along. We never had much money, and there were times when the boyfriend of the month turned out to have a problem or be a problem, but I thought we did okay. But when I was eleven, Mom decided she was sick of it. Some guy named Brad knocked her around, and we had a third visit from the cops. One of them, a nice enough guy for a cop, took Mom aside and told her to get away from the guy or plan on spending time in intensive care. So we moved—again—so Brad wouldn't know where we were when he got out. As usual when we moved, we had to leave some stuff behind. Mom's friend Gerald loaned us his truck for one afternoon, so everything we couldn't get in two pickup loads went to the Salvation Army store.

That time, Mom didn't bounce back like she usually did. She didn't promise me we'd find somebody better. She didn't even go out looking. For more than a week, she just sat on our lumpy old couch, staring out the window at the dirty, empty alley three stories below (no elevator, of course). I kind of tiptoed around her, not sure what was going on.

If I brought her mac and cheese (which is all I'm real good at in the cooking department), she ate it and set the dish down without even looking at it. At bedtime, I'd remind her that she needed to sleep, and she'd go to bed, but I had the feeling she just stared at the ceiling in the dark, waiting for sunrise so she could go back to watching the alley. I worried about her, but then she came to some sort of decision, and things started to happen. Our lives changed, big time.

I think Mom needed a plan for the rest of her life, and I learned about it in bits and pieces. I suppose some of her thoughts must have been about me, but even if they weren't, I was expected to go along. She decided to bet everything on getting a husband who could support us, and she went about planning her campaign kinda like the Allies planned the D-Day Invasion. It was a little scary to watch.

Mom talked to me some, telling how she was sick of being poor and depending on some guy or some minimum-wage job for grocery money. She'd get up from the couch and look at her face in the mirror like it was real important to see it again. A couple times she asked how old I thought she looked. Now, to me, adults fall into two categories: old and real old. I gave her #6 (Love You, Mom) and said she didn't look like a grandma yet.

Next thing I knew, we up and moved to Romulus, where we knew nobody. To get us there Mom went online and sold most of the stuff we had left, including all my video games and a lot of my CD's. With barely enough money for first and last month's rent, we moved into an apartment over this old lady's garage. The house was real nice. The apartment, not so much. It smelled like gas, and it was cramped, even for two people. It was okay though, because we were down to just a TV, the lumpy couch, and appliances. Besides, Mom said it was the address that was important, not what was inside.

The first week we lived on ramen noodles and Pepsi. Mom got a job waiting tables in a place close enough to walk to, so after while there was money for groceries, at least the basics. She sold our junker car to a scrap metal place, and with the money, we went shopping for what she called "decent clothes." She'd been looking through magazines in the store (They were too expensive to buy) and showed me pictures. "This is how I need to be," she told me, "at least how I have to pretend to be." I didn't get it at the time, but I always told her the ladies looked cool.

In a shop where the clerk brought whole outfits to my mom in the dressing room, I watched from a wicker chair while she bought clothes totally different from the Target/Wal-Mart stuff she'd always worn. It was something to watch.

I knew my mom was pretty, real pretty, but the clothes she chose (with lots of advice from the clerk) added something. It's hard to explain it, but she went from looking like a girl in a reality show to looking like the women in the pictures in mall shop windows.

The big hoop earrings she liked got replaced with tiny studs made of real gold. She took the rhinestone out of her nose and the pin out of her navel and let the holes close.

"Thank god I was always leery of tats," she told me as she rubbed scar-fading cream onto her skin. "Too hard to get rid of."

Like I said, she never explained the whole plan to me, but once as she was getting ready to go out for the evening, she said to the mirror, "I can please a rich man just as easy as a poor one."

Mom started reading the newspaper, but not the front pages. She looked at the local section to see who went to charity events. On the Internet she researched the single men in Remus County who might have money. She was interested in what hobbies they liked, what causes they gave their cash to, and what family ties they had. She didn't make the mistake of signing up for a dating site. She said that was too obvious. Instead, when some big event came that local businessmen might go to, she put on her new clothes and went: charity fundraisers, wild game dinners, even a pro-am golf tournament. I'd watch her get ready to go, changing from her waitress uniform to her Cinderella outfits and putting on the perfume she sold my iPod to buy. She toned down the sexy, but she never turned it off.

Sometimes she told me about it the next day. "I sit off by myself," she'd say, practicing correct grammar and enunciation as she talked and watching the mirror to be sure it looked exactly the way she wanted it to. "I act like I'm perfectly comfortable to be alone. I refuse the first few offers of a drink or a dance, but all the time, I'm watching."

Some of the men who approached were married. Some were looking for a one-night stand. Some had family who'd stand in the way of their dating someone like Mom, no matter how good she looked. "That's why I did my homework," she told me. "I know when to say no thanks and when to agree with just the right amount of nonchalance."

I had to look that word up. It means "casual indifference," and I imagined my mother smiling into the eyes of some guy who can't believe this beautiful stranger has agreed to sit next to him. Mom didn't care how old he was or what he looked like or what he thought of politics or religion or crime in the streets. All that mattered was that he had money. She said she'd know when the right one came along.

The right man, at least in my mother's opinion, was Dickweed. He had plenty of money. He'd been divorced for ten years. He had no close family ties. He was fifteen years older than her, but Mom guessed he was ready to get married again. Dickweed, a.k.a. Richard Hopgood III, wanted a wife he could show off to his friends and expect to be home when he came back from doing what he wanted to do. Mom was willing to be that woman if Rich was willing to pay the bills.

I don't know how much Dickweed knew about Mom's background. He didn't seem to care, even when she admitted she was broke when he finally popped the question. She told me with a little smile that she'd chosen exactly the right moment, when he was unlikely to back out of his offer.

I know she sounds like a gold-digger, but once they were married, Mom did everything she could to be a good wife. She never got bossy, and she didn't redecorate his house or complain about how much he was gone. What she thought he wanted in a wife, she tried to be.

I was part of the package, but nobody paid much attention to me. I kept my mouth shut, as ordered, but I paid attention. I noticed that Rich seldom talked to my mother, and when he did, it was only to give orders or relay information. He never patted her or kissed her neck the way a lot of her boyfriends used to do. I'd been kind of excited when I saw the nice house and all, but I never warmed up to Rich. When I saw how hard Mom tried and how little she got in return, I started calling him *Dickweed* in my head. Everywhere else I didn't talk about him at all.

As time went on, Mom became different. She seldom laughed, and she never stomped through the house in her *Flashdance* routine the way she used to. When Rich was at home she showed no emotion at all, and the only time I got a glimpse of the old Mom was when she was with her friend Marie. She never complained though. "We both got what we wanted, Rich and me," I heard her tell Marie once. Marie nodded like she knew exactly what Mom meant.

As far as I could tell, what Dickweed wanted wasn't a real live woman. He wanted a good cook, a beautiful lady on his arm when he went out in public, and a warm—make that hot—body in his bed, no matter how late he came home at night.

CHAPTER FIVE

LOSER

Mabel arrived a week later, the ambulance, without siren and lights, winding its way up the hill and turning into my driveway with the creeping caution of those who aren't sure they're in the right place. I stood on the porch, trying to look welcoming and hoping I hadn't destroyed the peace I'd found here. I told myself I wasn't as crazy as I'd once been. Maybe Mabel too could behave normally under the right circumstances. Or more normally.

The attendants seemed a little stressed, but they made sure my guest was comfortably installed in Marta's bedroom. Mabel helped out with advice—lots of it. They'd brought along equipment she'd need, a wheelchair, a walker, and shopping bags full of medical supplies. I'd been relieved to learn there were visiting nurses in Beulah, and I'd arranged for daily visits from them and the aides who assisted with home care. Meals and Mabel's constant conversation I could handle. Blood, not so much.

I got a dozen discharge sheets that outlined all aspects of Mabel's condition. There were suggestions for what she should eat, when she should take medications, how much she should do (on a gradually increasing schedule) and what her mental state was upon leaving the hospital. "Mabel is a cheerful woman with a colorful style of speaking and an unshakable belief she has many improbable ailments," wrote the hospital social worker.

I couldn't have said it better. Mabel had, at one time or another, informed me she had pneumonia, liver failure, elephantiasis, cancer, and several heart attacks of varying degrees of severity. I'd learned not to let her get started on the workings of her digestive system unless I was willing to lose my appetite for the rest of the day.

When the ambulance and the visiting nurse were gone, Mabel and I settled down to talk. Well, she talked, I listened. First, I heard the details of her accident, the ride to the hospital, the handsome E.R. doctor, the surgery, and her recuperation. The unknown writer of discharge papers was right; Mabel's story was compelling if you didn't count hyperbole and grammatical errors against her.

When she'd exhausted her story, Mabel turned to recent changes in my situation. Looking around the room and out the door into the living room, she said, "This is a nice place, Loser. Is it yours?" I nodded. "I looked out the windows some in the amb'lance. We came a long, long way, and uphill a lot too."

I nodded again. "West Virginia."

"Huh." I might have chosen Cambodia or Antarctica. Anything outside Richmond was alien to her. "We gonna live here now?"

I was taken aback by her simple acceptance of a completely new situation. Mabel had months of rehabilitation before her. She was miles from anywhere she knew, in a town full of strangers, staying with a woman with a severely limited ability to function. And she was fine with that.

EDDIE'S SECRET BLOG, AUGUST 30

So I come home from the store with a jug of milk and some Cap'n Crunch to find Mom sitting on the couch, crying. It's happened a few times since we left Romulus. She's sad because all her plans blew up and she doesn't know what to do next. I sit beside her.

"It'll be okay," I say.

She sniffs, and I stretch out to reach a box of tissues sitting on the end table behind me. "I was a good wife to him, wasn't I?"

"The best," I tell her. "Whatever happened, it wasn't your fault. He's a—"

"Let's not talk about it." She wipes at the corners of her eyes with a tissue. "We'll be okay." But she glances out the window as she says it, like something outside might make a liar out of her.

"Don't be so paranoid, Mom!" To make her laugh, I add, "You make me jumpy. Just now, this black Hummer like Dave used to drive went by, and I ducked into an alley and stepped in some dog crap. I had to I remind myself no one knows—"

She grabs my arm, her nails digging in till I yelp in pain. "A black Hummer? Where?

"Where was it?"

"Mom, there are lots of Hummers around, and black's the color everyone wants."

"Where?" She shakes me like she used to do when I was little and acting like a brat.

"At the party store. Well, not *at* the store. It was parked across the street, kitty-corner. But it—"

She's out the door before I can finish. In no time, she's back, eyes jumping everywhere. "Pack your things. We've got to get out of here."

"Mom—"

"Eddie! Do as you're told!"

Shaking my head, I obey, wondering what the next rat hole she drags me to is going to smell like. I guess I should just be grateful if nobody's cooking meth next door.

LOSER

As the weeks progressed, Mabel and I settled into a routine. She appeared not to notice that I slept on the porch. I'd decided to stay close in case she needed me, but only once did she call out. Her hip was hurting, and I gave her one of the pain pills the doctor had sent along.

She looked at it thoughtfully before swallowing. "A lot of 'em back home would hit me or you or even both of us over the head for this."

I nodded. One reason we'd bonded was that neither of us was interested in drugs. I'd always resisted the idea of dampening my pain, because pain was, for a long time, the only thing that made me feel the least bit human. On the street, I'd have defended Mabel and me from addicts and users if necessary, but it was usually best to let Mabel talk them into submission.

For many sun-drenched days, we did as we pleased. Although hampered by her healing hip, Mabel had lived rough too long to be delicate. She cleaned the vegetables I found at stands in Beulah. She ate whatever I made from them and praised it to the skies. She talked a lot but didn't mind that I didn't answer or even pay attention at times. She watched a lot of television, and I often heard her laughing. "Did you see this?" she asked me once, pointing to the screen where some reality show played. "People doin' stupid stuff, even when they know there's cameras running. And they call us crazy."

When the sun began to sink over the hills, I would help Mabel onto the porch, so we could watch it go. We drank tea; sometimes we had pie. Along with making pretty good meals, I'd reclaimed my ability to bake. Everything in the way of equipment I'd found in Marta's kitchen, and I bought flour and spices and other ingredients at the grocery. The apples I picked myself. I found it distinctly satisfying to peel, core, and slice fruit from trees I'd climbed as an adolescent, often with a saltshaker in my pocket. My pies came out golden and perfect. Again, Mabel approved.

When the sun had set I'd help Mabel into bed, where she watched a second TV I'd bought for her until she was tired enough to go to sleep. At first I thought she'd be lonely with only me for company, but she seemed content. Gradually, what I suspected was the original Mabel began to emerge. She still talked almost nonstop, but there was less medical emergency and more reminiscence. I learned she'd had brothers and a sister, that her father had been a night watchman, and that she'd once wanted badly to be a ballerina. "They got to be tall, though," she said, "Or at least not all squashy-short like me."

Mabel seemed happy, which made me feel I'd been right to bring her here. The pain of her injury she accepted as part of life. "It hurts," I heard her tell the nurse, "but it's better than bein' dead, ain't it?"

One night I left her watching *NCIS* and took my bedroll onto the porch. I liked a spot along the east wall that allowed a view of the driveway but had enough angle so the security light near the back door didn't shine in my eyes. When Mabel finally shut the TV off the night went silent, and I listened to my own breathing. Country nights aren't really silent, but compared to city nights, they are. Mabel often commented on the stillness. I didn't have a problem with it.

I did have a problem with the sound I heard a few minutes later. A car was coming up the road, but there were no lights. It traveled slowly up the driveway and purred softly toward the house.

I lay unmoving, hoping Mabel was asleep. She might call out if she heard a noise, and I preferred we remained unnoticed. The people in the car were probably teenagers looking for a place to have a little alone time. A house at the end of a dead-end road was no doubt an ideal place for romance.

There were other possibilities: someone curious about the new arrivals, vandals looking to do some damage to an empty house, or even thieves eager to see if there was anything worth stealing. I told myself that discretion was the better part of valor, no matter what the visitors' purpose.

The car sat in the drive for at least three minutes before I heard the click of a door opening. The dome light came on, and the door was pulled shut, though not latched. When it opened again, there was no light. Someone had unscrewed the bulb.

The figure who exited the car was a woman. She stood looking at the house for a few seconds before squaring her shoulders and making for the door. I was up and moving in a flash, and by the time she raised a hand to knock, I stepped into the spill of light at the corner of the house.

She jumped back, covering her mouth to muffle a scream. I stepped toward her, arms at my sides. This close, I could see her pretty clearly. She was beautiful, with a face that might have graced a magazine cover. She was also more frightened than the presence of one undersized woman should have made her. Though she made an attempt to pull herself together, the whites of her eyes showed large, and I saw her lick her lips before she spoke.

"Who are you?"

"Beth."

That didn't help. "Where's Marta?"

"Dead."

"No." She swayed a little, and I realized she was near collapse.

Taking stock, I came to some simple conclusions. The woman wasn't a threat, despite her approach without headlights. She was scared, but she'd come to the door intending to knock. She'd expected Marta and was rattled further to learn of her death. I took a guess.

"You a foster?"

Her head turned toward me, and the muscles of her jaw relaxed a little. "Yeah. You?"

I nodded. Turning the knob, I pushed the door open, indicating with a hand that she should enter.

A light came on, and Mabel stood in the bedroom doorway, leaning on her walker and blinking at us. "Thought I heard somebody," she said. "Didn't figure Loser was talking to herself."

When the woman looked uncertainly from Mabel to me, Mabel chuckled. "You ain't gonna get no explanation from her," she told the newcomer. "Go ahead. Have a chair."

Hobbling into the open kitchen, Mabel approached the stove and turned on the burner where the teapot sat. Taking a teabag from a canister, she readied a cup and turned the walker around, sitting down on the padded seat. Rather dazedly, our visitor came to the table, touching Marta's rocker lightly as she passed. We both sat; she faced the ancient buffet that held Marta's good china. It had a mirror, and she saw her reflection and frowned. She smoothed her long, dark hair absently. I thought she was a woman used to looking perfect. She dropped her hand, unable to focus at the moment.

The kettle whistled, and I rose to pour hot water over the teabag and set it in front of her.

"Thanks," she said, sipping at the liquid that had hardly had time to become tea yet. "Marta's dead?"

I glanced at Mabel, and she answered. "Marta's the lady who used to live here, right? I saw her name on stuff in the desk." Confessing to snooping didn't seem to bother Mabel in the least. "She died a year or so ago, but she left her house to Loser here." Mabel gestured toward me to clarify any confusion, though there was no one else there. "Her name's Beth, but she likes Loser better. We used to live—" I twitched slightly and Mabel got the hint. "—in Richmond. We was neighbors. When I had surgery, Loser asked me up here to recuperate at her new place." She grinned, proud of how normal she'd made us both sound.

I expected an account of Mabel's medical trials next, but our visitor asked, "How'd she die?"

Mabel didn't have an answer to that one, so I said, "Heart attack."

She nodded. "I know she had a family history."

I hadn't known that. Had Marta kept it from me because she'd been experiencing symptoms? Was that why I'd been her last foster child?

Mabel apparently figured she and I had done our share of explaining. "So who are you?"

In answer, the woman rose, went to the wall, and pointed to one of the pictures. "That's me. Foster child number eleven. The agency called me Rose, but Marta let me rename myself. I chose Nadine."

The picture she indicated showed by far the prettiest of Marta's foster children. As a teenager Rose/Nadine had already been beautiful, though her eyes stared back at the camera with ungracious challenge. I knew that face and recalled Marta's look of sadness when I'd asked where the pretty girl went after high school. "She ran away," she'd said sadly. "The only child I ever lost."

Returning to the table, Nadine sipped noisily at the hot tea, which seemed to revive her a little. Her spine straightened, and she glanced again in the mirror, smoothing her hair again and fluffing it away from her ears so it fell in loose waves. "The people from the state thought this place would be perfect for me, but I hated it from day one." She grimaced. "I thought I hated Marta too. Later, I realized how good she was to me." Sipping again, she added, "And for me."

That was Marta: good to her kids and good for them. She'd found something each of us could excel at and then fed that something. I'd loved growing things in her garden, liked to hoe and plant and reap. Without realizing it, I'd carried that to Richmond, where I'd put flowers everywhere around my house. Marta had seen the enjoyment gardening brought me and encouraged it, knowing such pastimes bring comfort in good times and bad.

"Manure and mountains aren't for me," Nadine said, wrinkling her nose. "Marta had two other kids at that time. The girl loved the chickens—chickens, for god's sake! And the boy, Arnold—or Andrew, maybe—was so glad to have a home, he wouldn't have cared if Marta lived in the middle of the Gobi Desert." Nadine glanced again at Marta's rocker. "I ran away after six months. I moved to...a big city."

I recalled the kids at school telling the story of a girl at Marta's who'd stolen the neighbor's truck and was never heard from again. I was looking at her now. She was regarding herself in the mirror again, this time straightening the collar of her blouse, making sure it lay just so.

"I looked older than fifteen," Nadine said, "and I knew how the world worked. I made it."

Mabel is a little simple and maybe a little crazy, but she went for the right question. "But now something bad happened?"

Nadine sighed deeply. "Yeah. Something bad." She turned to me. "I need a place to stay for a while." When I didn't answer right away, she added, "I've got money. I can pay."

I shook my head. That wasn't the issue. What I needed to know was what kind of trouble Nadine was bringing. Had she committed a crime? Was she running from something? Was she going to bring media attention, police cars, or an angry husband?

She must have read my thought. "No one knows where I am. There's no way they can know. I never told a soul about Marta, and I've used the name Nadine Forsythe ever since I left. If we hide my car in the barn, I could—" She looked down at her hands for a few seconds. "Marta didn't deserve the worry I put her through. I never even let her know I was okay." She passed her fingers over her lips as if sealing emotion back inside. "I was so angry back then, you know? And later, I was ashamed."

I glanced again at the picture on the wall. A typical school-picture pose, but the girl within those four corners had refused to smile at the camera. Comments Marta had made over the years about people who couldn't be reached returned to me. She'd had many successes, but this failure had haunted her.

"Okay," I told Nadine. And because this day was almost done and I had words left over, I added, "I'll help with your car."

She looked relieved. "Thank you," she said, rising again. "There's just one more thing."

"One more thing" was a teenage boy. I followed Nadine outside, carrying a flashlight. The boy was hunched down in the back seat of the mid-sized Ford, but he sat up when Nadine said, "Eddie, it's okay." He looked rumpled and shaggy, but the smile he gave me was sweet and honest. He didn't say anything, but I thought he looked exhausted.

We both got into the car, which smelled like dirty laundry and old French fries. Nadine started it up, this time turning on the lights. "I remembered that nosy couple down the road," she said. "If they saw a car go by after dark, it would be all over Beulah in no time." After my own experience upon arrival, I didn't have to wonder if she was correct.

Nadine drove to the barn, where I got out and opened the doors so she could park in the largely empty space. Shutting the car off, she got out, and I heard the trunk pop open with a metallic clunk. The kid got out, hurried to the back, and retrieved a suitcase and a battered gym bag. Slinging the bag over one shoulder, he hefted the suitcase easily in one hand. Nadine took a tote bag and an expensive purse from the back seat, closed the car doors and the trunk, and followed Eddie to where I waited.

I closed the barn doors, noting the lubricant I'd applied recently had quieted the squeaking hinges, and slid the wooden bolt home. Focusing the flashlight on our path until we reached the spill of the security light near the back door, I led the way to the house. Mabel still sat in the kitchen, and she looked the boy over warily. Teenagers, boys in particular, can be tough on unlovely people like Mabel. On the streets, she'd usually shuffled away when harassed, unlike some who went on the offensive, shouting obscenities and acting scary in order to be left alone.

Mabel had often suffered casual cruelty. Even if her clothes had not been grimy and ill-matched and her cheap tennis shoes cut at the sides to relieve her bunions, Mabel's face would have gotten attention. One side of it went cockeyed, the result of a childhood accident. The cheek was drawn back, pulling her mouth up and exposing a saliva gland that never stopped running. The eye was pulled downward, giving her a perpetual squint. I was used to it, but I'd seen kids stare at her, some laughing while others turned away in disgust or scuttled away in fear.

Facing Mabel across the room, Eddie set down his burdens, smiled the same sweet smile he'd given me, and said, "Hello, there."

Nadine put an arm around his shoulders. "Mabel, Loser, this is my son, Eddie." Turning to the boy, she said, "Eddie, these people are going to let us stay here for a while, until we figure things out."

"That's great," Eddie said, glancing at Nadine. "Mom's been pretty worried."

"About what?" Mabel asked boldly.

I stepped between Mabel and our visitors. Curious as I was about Nadine's predicament, I knew how hard it is to talk about things you don't want to talk about when you're over-stressed. "Tomorrow."

Nadine gave me a quick smile of thanks. "Where do you want us?"

In answer, I led the way upstairs and waved a hand to indicate they could have their choices from the four bedrooms there. "I guess I'll take my old room," she said, switching on the light of the first room on the left. She peered inside. "Pretty much the same stuff, just moved around." Eddie set the suitcase inside the doorway as she moved down the hallway and turned on the switch in the next room. "Here, babe. You can sleep in here."

Eddie started for the door, his bag still on his shoulder, but she changed her mind.

"Wait. That's a girl's room." Moving down the hall, she peered into the last room. "This one's better."

He looked at her, then at me, and shrugged, giving me that sweet smile again. "Okay, Mom." He kissed her cheek, and she put her arms around him briefly with a fierceness that seemed to surprise him. To me, he said, "Goodnight, Mrs.-um, goodnight. And thanks. We'll try not to be any trouble."

I walked Nadine back to her room. She turned, one hand on the frame. "He's a good kid, and he means it. We won't be any trouble."

I gave her a goodnight wave. Nadine went inside for some much-needed rest, and I went back downstairs to shoo Mabel to bed and take up my spot on the porch again. I didn't sleep for a long time, but there was no more trouble that night.

EDDIE'S SECRET BLOG, AUGUST 31

We're at this house on top of a mountain with two weird ladies. I guess it's where Mom lived as a kid, but the woman who took her in is dead now. The old lady is crippled and kinda scary-looking. The other one is pretty, not like Mom, but sorta normal. She doesn't talk much though. Neither of them will give me any trouble. I gave them Smile #2 (the Good Boy), and they were dazzled.

This place is sure different from other places we've been. I think the last Taco Bell I saw was like fifty miles back. The town doesn't look like much, though I saw a pizza place that looked okay. While we were climbing the twisty road up here, I tried again to get Mom to tell me why we keep running. I got a little mad, cuz she keeps saying it has to be this way. I almost told her about seeing her bloody shoes and that I know something bad happened back at home, but I chickened out.

Now that we're so far away from about everybody on Earth, she should start to feel safe. Tomorrow, I'll take her for a walk, and when we're alone, I'll make her tell me who she killed. Whoever it was, whether it was Dickweed or somebody else, they must have deserved it.

CHAPTER SIX

LOSER

The trouble Nadine promised wouldn't happen came in the morning. I woke early, having slept pretty well once I got used to the idea of having company. The kid seemed nice enough, and I guessed Nadine was escaping an abusive husband or boyfriend. If he'd never known her real name, he'd be unable to trace her. Ignoring my reservations, I told myself they'd move on in a day or so.

I decided to make a hearty breakfast. With a good night's sleep and some scrambled eggs, Nadine might be ready to say exactly what she wanted from me.

Except Nadine was gone. When I rapped on her bedroom door, there was no answer. I waited, rapped again, and finally looked in. The bed was still made, though there were indentations where she'd rested, waiting for us to fall asleep. The window over the porch roof was open. Her suitcase was gone.

Racing down the stairs, I ran out the back door and headed for the barn. The doors hung open. Nadine's car was not inside.

I turned, surveying the landscape as if the car might be hiding behind a tree. How had I not heard her leave?

The barn sat against the hillside, and the driveway sloped down to meet the road. She must have coasted, giving the car a push to get it rolling. No lights, no engine sounds. Nothing but downhill from here to Beulah. For a girl who'd lived here for six months, a girl Marta had considered her biggest failure, escape had been no problem at all.

I returned to the house more slowly than I'd left. Would I find the place ransacked? Marta had had nothing worth stealing. So why had those two shown up last night? What was their game?

Things got a whole lot clearer when I got inside. Coming down the stairs was Eddie, his hair more rumpled and his shirt more wrinkled than before. "Hi," he said. "Where's my mom?"

"Car's gone," I said. "Suitcase too."

He was at first incredulous, then angry, then terrified. "No!" he kept saying. "She can't be gone!"

Mabel hobbled out of her room, remote in hand. When she learned what had happened, she suggested alternatives. "Maybe she went to the store," she told Eddie soothingly. "Or maybe she had an appointment somewhere."

I shook my head, and she lapsed into silence. A person doesn't sneak out in the middle of the night with her suitcase to get her hair done.

Eddie insisted we should not notify the police, and honestly, I couldn't see how it would help if we did. Nadine had left of her own volition, stealing away in the night from my home and her own child. If we called the authorities, Eddie would be taken into foster care. I doubted their willingness to spend resources chasing down a parent who'd abandoned a teenager. Having been part of the system, my first instinct was to delay turning Eddie over to it, however good the intentions of those who worked there might be. If there was a chance Nadine was coming back for him, he was better off here, with Mabel and me, than he could possibly be in the system.

The kid was devastated. Mabel tried to tell him his mother would be back, but it was a hard sell. It was obvious Nadine's plan all along had been to leave him behind. Finding that Marta was dead had been a setback, but she'd simply adjusted, leaving Eddie with Mabel and me though she had no idea what kind of people we were. Some mother.

Going out into a golden morning he had no eye for, Eddie searched the outbuildings on the wild assumption that Nadine had gone inside and been knocked unconscious somehow. While he rattled through each shed in a panic, I went into the room she had briefly occupied, looking for a clue to her reason for stealing off in the night. There was a faint smell of expensive perfume on the bed, and under her pillow I found a strip of dry, crackly wallpaper she'd torn from a corner. On the back she'd scribbled with a bad ink pen, "Please take care of him."

When Eddie finally stopped his useless, manic search, he sank into anger, throwing himself into a chair on the front porch and glaring at the mountains. I left him there for a while before going out to let him rant and vent and ask the questions none of us could answer.

In profile I saw a resemblance to Nadine that wasn't obvious face to face. Eddie had a masculine version of his mother's forehead and chin. His hair was dark, like hers, but cropped close on the sides of his head and left longer on top. His pant legs and one shoulder were covered with cobwebs and grime from his fruitless search of the outbuildings.

When I sat down in the Adirondack chair beside him, his anger had turned to despair.

"Why'd she do this, Loser?"

I showed him the note. As he read it, his lips quivered, but he maintained his man-voice after a little throat clearing. "She'll come back." His eyes dropped as he said it. He didn't believe his own words.

I moved my chair toward his with a scrape of wood against wood. "Tell me."

"She took me out of school one day. We've been moving around ever since."

The story that followed was disjointed and full of holes. They'd left a city he refused to name. Nadine had insisted their lives were in danger.

"You were followed?" I asked.

He shook his head. "I didn't think so. She'd started talking about getting a job. Then I came home from the store and mentioned seeing this one truck, and she freaked. That's when we came here."

I must have seemed concerned, because Eddie added, "She was real careful. We drove around for a long time, and she'd pull off the freeway without signaling or go through an alley to see if it was clear."

"Worried," I said.

He sighed. "Yeah."

"Why?"

His mouth turned down. "She said it was better if I didn't know."

I'm not good at reading teenagers, but I didn't think I was getting the whole truth. Eddie's hands gestured vaguely, as if his subconscious wanted to say more. I didn't think he was lying, but there was more he could have told me. And I noticed his wording: he'd reported what Nadine said about the situation, not what he knew.

I'm good at letting other people talk, so I waited. Eddie's hands moved again, but then he shook his head. "She didn't tell me anything." He turned toward the door. "We gotta go after her."

A knock interrupted our talk, and Eddie sprang up and hurried through the house to open the door, his face hopeful. I followed him and found Danielle, the aide who visited Mabel each afternoon. The sight of her made me realize that Cheri, the morning aide, hadn't visited. Mabel came from her room and made brief introductions, telling Danielle that Eddie was the son of an old friend of mine who'd come to stay for a while. Eddie managed a smile, and I wondered if the kid was used to hiding his true emotions behind a pleasant expression.

"Where was Cheri today?" Mabel asked.

"She broke her ankle this morning," Danielle reported, setting her clipboard on the kitchen table with a clatter that betrayed fatigue. "Looks like we'll be short-handed for a few days."

Mabel turned to Eddie and said, not as tactfully as I'd have liked, "Now you got to stay. It's what your momma wanted you to do, or she wouldna brought you here. Loser's got work to do gettin' this place in shape, and I need help gettin' around." She put one hand on her chest.

71

"I need you, boy. I'm pretty sure I'm coming down with them shingles they been tellin' about on the teevee."

Eddie looked at me doubtfully. I rubbed my forehead, unable to decide what was best. Maybe Nadine would return once she'd resolved the situation that had forced her to leave home. Still, I was uneasy, having seen the fear in her eyes. I was almost sure the kid knew more than he'd admitted. Despite her betrayal, he was determined to protect his mother.

What if I'd misread Nadine? She'd seemed pretty self-absorbed. Had she dumped her son on me to rid herself of an encumbrance so that she could party on? It was hard to choose a course of action with so little to go on. In the end, I went back to scraping old paint off one of the sheds, making the kind of decision I prefer, which is none. Time would work things out, the way it always does.

EDDIE'S SECRET BLOG, SEPTEMBER 1

I can't believe she left me here like a pair of shoes she didn't want anymore! I never begged for stuff or complained about her dickweed husband or whined when she didn't come to a single one of my track meets or parent-teacher conferences. I loved her, and I told myself she loved me, but it isn't true. When things got bad, she left me with two retarded strangers and went on with her life. She's not just a murderer. She's a terrible mom too.

So I've got to figure things out for myself and not trust anybody. I can't go back to Romulus, but no way will I get put in the foster care system. I probably can make it on my own, but I think I should stay around here for a while, until I work out a plan. Once I think it through, I'll head out.

Mabel's not as scary as she looks or as dumb as she acts. Once I realized my mom was really gone, I started working on getting Mabel to like me. I stayed in the house with her all afternoon, in case she needed something, I said, but it was really an excuse to look the place over. Mabel doesn't move around much, and a guy never knows what he'll find that might help when he's on the road.

Mabel's pretty un-mobile but real verbal, and she talked to me the whole time, even from the smallest room in the house. At first, it was weird, cuz she said she had cancer and MS and something wrong with her pancreas. After a while I figured out those were things she dreamed up. What she does have is a bunch of pins in her hip from a car accident. That I believe, cuz she showed me the X-rays.

When she's around, the look on Loser's face helps me decide if Mabel's disease is real or imaginary. Arthritis? Loser nods. Later, I found pills for that (I looked through Mabel's things while she talked from the bathroom). Restless leg syndrome? Loser's little grin let me know that one's imaginary. "I can't keep my good leg still," Mabel told us at lunch. "Jumps just like a frog in a fryin' pan."

Anyway, Mabel likes me. I listen to her and I smile, and for somebody like her, that's all it takes. I'm pretty sure I can get Loser on my side, cuz she's a softie. When Mabel said about her leg being jumpy, Loser had her sit in the big easy chair in the living room while she massaged it for a few minutes. I bet Loser knew Mabel wanted some attention, and she didn't mind giving it. I'll get her to like me too.

Aside from talking a lot, Mabel's okay. Some of what she says is actually interesting. For instance, she remembers her dad building a bomb shelter in their backyard when everybody was afraid the Russians were going to attack us. "I hated it," she told me. "Even as a little kid, I didn't want to live through no nuculer war. Best to just blow up first thing."

It was Mabel's idea that we should clean the photographs on the living room wall. "They're so dusty you can't see who's who," she said, pointing at them with a crooked finger. "House sat empty too long." I guess she was trying to take my mind off Mom leaving me here, but I said that would be good. If you're willing to give people their way on little things, they start to trust you. I need these women to think of me as a guy they can trust, at least until I figure out what I'm going to do.

We worked out a system where Mabel sat at the table with a pan of water with dish soap and vinegar in it, some newspaper, and a couple of dishtowels. I brought her the photographs, a few at a time, and she wiped the dust off the frames and washed the glass, drying it with newspaper, which she said cleans glass better than anything else. When she finished, I put them back together and hung them up again, each one where it was before. It seemed important to get that right.

As she worked, Mabel told me about living on the streets. I said it sounded kind of cool, but she set a frame in her lap and pointed at me. "It's bad-bad, Eddie. On the street, you're nobody. Only people has any time for you is people as bad off as you, and some of them is dangerous."

"Was Loser on the street too?" I asked. "Is that how you two met?"

"She was, but she didn't belong there." Mabel's good eye went to the picture on the wall that was Loser at eighteen. "She had a terrible-terrible spell and didn't know who she was for a while. She had to forget, cuz what happened to her was bad-bad." Mabel touched the heavy oak table like she needed to prove to herself it was real. "Loser brought me here cuz we're friends. I helped her out when she was in trouble, and now she's helpin' me."

"She likes helping people?"

"She does," Mabel replied, handing me a squeaky-clean frame to rehang. "She just can't figure out how to help herself."

LOSER

The next few days were odd. Eddie was restless, missing his mother and asking himself repeatedly why she'd left him in a place where there was nothing to do. We could see he was hurting. He never blamed Mabel or me for his situation. In fact, he helped Mabel with whatever little chore she took on each morning. When he wasn't helping, he spent hours on the porch, looking down at the treetops below us. The third afternoon, the house seemed to become too small for him. He roamed from room to room, sticking his head into closets and corners, and went outside. I saw him circle the yard a few times, looking down at the ground and kicking at things I couldn't see. Finally, he entered the woods behind the barn cautiously, as if herds of wild beasts were waiting just out of sight to devour him. For a while he hung around the edges, looking back at me from time to time as if to assure I was nearby if danger threatened. After a while, I heard him crashing his way through the undergrowth, and he emerged a few minutes later covered with burrs, grinning triumphantly, as if he'd slain a dragon.

The next day he went into the woods again, this time for over an hour. I spent a few minutes worrying, because that's what I do, but I told myself he couldn't get lost. It was a mountain. If he went up, he had to return on the downslope, and vice versa.

After that, Eddie wandered Marta's forty-acre plot as if it were undiscovered territory, which for him it was. I gathered from his comments at the dinner table that he'd lived in several different cities but never in a rural area. When Mabel asked where home was, he didn't say the name of the town but told her it was south of Beulah. "We lived in the same house for the last three years, and I went to the same school all that time," he added. It sounded like that was an accomplishment unequaled in the rest of his life. I wondered again what forced Nadine to leave, to cut her son off from all contact with the people he'd come to know.

Eddie was a good houseguest, taking on chores like loading and unloading the dishwasher and vacuuming without being asked. He was a polite kid, listening to Mabel's endless chatter with no sign of irritation. I heard her as I came and went, telling the boy whatever came into her mind. He even asked questions sometimes, but then, what else

75

did he have to do? Other than Eddie, Mabel's diversions were therapy, visiting nurses, and *Law & Order* reruns, which were all new to her.

I continued the work I'd been doing, getting the house and outbuildings into shape. I spent mornings, when it was relatively cool, painting, scraping, nailing, and cleaning. Afternoons, I sat in some shady spot, reading from Marta's bookshelf. I started at random and moved through the books from left to right without prejudice. I'd never been a reader before, but those long afternoons brought contentment in discovering the lives of others: Marjorie Morningstar, Ari ben Canaan, and Bertie Wooster.

Eddie continued to explore, ranging a little farther each day. He returned with sweaty armpits and coltsfoot fluff and various insects stuck to his clothes. Before he entered the house I examined him for ticks and such and swept the grass seed off him with an old whisk broom I'd found in a closet. He stood obediently, talking about things he'd discovered that I'd almost forgotten. He brought things for me to identify: leaves, bark, even sap rolled between his fingers into a perfect ball. He mentioned deer glimpsed briefly before they disappeared into the hills and curious noises that turned out to be ground birds or rabbits or squirrels. I thought it was good for him to play Thoreau a little. It's true that in the woods we're able to find the good in the world again.

Despite his sorrow at his mother's abandonment, Eddie seemed content to stay with Mabel and me.

At the end of the first week, he returned from a trek through the woods with his t-shirt filled (and stained) with blackberries. When Mabel praised him and suggested I make a pie with them for the next day's dessert, it was like a ray of light shone on the kid for a moment. The next day, he went out again, and this time, he came back with a head of cabbage. Mabel gave me a wry look, but neither of us asked where he'd gotten it. I thanked him solemnly and made slaw with a sweet-vinegar sauce.

The next day, when Eddie came home with a medley of fresh fruits and vegetables stuffed in his pockets and almost overflowing his arms, I gently suggested he shouldn't go around raiding people's gardens. At first, he insisted someone had given him the vegetables, but Mabel snickered, and I gave him a look that let him know I didn't believe it.

Giving us that sweet smile of his, he bit off a chunk of carrot with a sharp snap. "I took a few things from a bunch of different gardens," he said with a shrug. "There's lots left for everybody else."

I recalled days on the street when I'd helped myself to a peach or a carrot from a bin when the grocer wasn't looking. When the world treats you badly, it's easy to feel you're owed something, no matter how small that something might be. Still, I didn't want the kid to think stealing was okay. I took a ten-dollar bill from my pocket and handed it to him. "Buy, don't steal."

He smiled again as he pocketed the bill. "Sure, Loser. If you say so."

The next morning I came in from the porch to find Eddie at Marta's old secretary desk. He was bent over the old drop-front, where a ring binder I remembered from my teen years lay open. Stepping up behind him, I put a hand on his shoulder. He turned, smiling up at me with no visible embarrassment. "I was just looking at this old stuff."

The bottom drawer of the desk gaped open, though I was sure it had been locked. I'd tried it once, looked around for a key, and given up. The smell of old paper and wood, unexposed to air for years, hung in the air. I wondered how Eddie had gotten the drawer open, but I didn't ask.

The binder he'd taken from the drawer was one Marta had used to keep the paperwork for us kids organized and accessible. She'd kept the drawer locked, claiming we didn't need to know each other's business.

Eddie had come to the information about me. There were copies of court documents, school records, and immunization lists, all slid into plastic covers threaded onto the metal rings. I'd seen some of it, but new things had been added. A newspaper clipping with the headline

Candidates Graduate Police Academy was accompanied by my picture in uniform, neatly cut out and slid in with the article.

"You were a cop?" Eddie asked.

I nodded once. From her bedroom doorway, Mabel spoke. "Loser's a hero." I waved a hand in warning, but Mabel does as she likes. "Saved a kid from killers back in Richmond."

Eddie turned to me. "Really?"

I shrugged, moving to his side and turning the pages until I found Nadine. I pointed at the picture, and he bent closer. "That's my mom."

I nodded, and he returned to the documents. "Rose? Her name is Rose?"

Another shrug. Rose might be the name she was given at birth. It might be the name someone at an adoption agency gave to a foundling or the name some foster parent chose for her. If she preferred Nadine, she should be called that.

Together we read what there was on her. Orphaned at two (mother, drugs; father, robbing a pharmacy), Nadine had been in the system all her life. She'd been in fourteen different foster homes by the time she came to Marta. I guessed by then she'd seen the worst of life. She'd done well, considering her early troubles, to end up with a nice car, a loving son, and, despite the anxiety she'd shown when we met, signs of good living. Though her appearance had been somewhat neglected of late, I'd noticed that Nadine's hair had been expensively cut and highlighted; her body was toned and bronzed as only those with gym memberships attain, and her eyes had been clear: no drugs or alcohol abuse as far as I was able to tell. She'd lived well until recently, when things fell apart.

Eddie read and reread the information. When he finished, I closed the book and put it back into the bottom drawer. "Key?"

He handed it over. I locked the drawer and put the key into my pocket with deliberation. "Locked," I said. Eddie said nothing, but I did get another smile.

When he'd gone outside, I got the book out again and opened it to my section. This time, I took the sheets out of their plastic holders and turned them over. I'd seen most of it before, since Marta had believed in being honest with us. Added after I left Beulah were traces of Beth Lousiere's life: a wedding invitation, a baby shower notice. There were a couple of birthday cards I'd sent her from Richmond, one funny, one more serious and decorated with flowers and ribbon.

Shuffling through the papers, I looked at bits of my life, recalling them as if they'd happened to someone else. Marta had been good to all of us, but she'd never been blind to our weaknesses. On the back of my freshman year's grade report, she'd written a note to herself: *Build confidence*. She'd seen, way back then, the fragility of my sense of self.

I'd gone to the police academy with the idea I'd protect others. At the same time, I now realized, I'd been trying to overcome the fear that I wasn't strong enough to survive in the world.

Marta had seen my insecurity. She'd known I was a loser.

Putting the stuff about me back, I turned to Nadine's section, curious to see what Marta had seen as her weakness. There were fewer sheets; Nadine's stay had been brief. There was, however, a letter folded and slid between the other sheets. In it, her former foster parents complained that Rose was "manipulative and dishonest." On the back of the letter Marta had written, *Trust issues.*

79

CHAPTER SEVEN

I know some things now. My mother's from Wheeling, but no city of birth was mentioned for my father. She wasn't much of a student, but her test scores were pretty good, so she could have gotten good grades if she wanted to. I didn't get to read the whole report from the social worker, but she had some bad experiences in foster homes.

I guess that helps me understand her a little. Maybe her marrying Dickweed was meant to give me something better than she had. I mean, she wanted it too. I know that. Dickweed gave us security, and we sure weren't starving to death. I wonder what he did that made her kill him, and I hope she didn't go back to confess. If Mom killed Dickweed, he for sure did something to deserve it.

LOSER

That afternoon Jen, my teacher turned real estate agent, stopped by in what had become her weekly visit. She claimed to be checking that we were all right, but there was always a hint—sometimes an outright statement—that she'd love to list the property if I wasn't going to stay. "Nothing sells up here in the winter time," she'd say, "but if we list by October, we could get you a nice check by Christmas."

I tried to be patient. I'd liked Jen as a teacher, and she was just aggressively going after a commission. But nothing says, "We can live without you in Beulah" like constant pressure to sell your property. She'd seemed so glad when I moved back to town, but now that I'd shown no interest in joining—well, anything, she was determined to make some money on the deal. I shook my head and tried to smile. Jen smiled back, but there was a light in her eyes that told me she'd be back next week.

Eddie was gone for a long time that day. I was starting to worry when he returned, ambling up the steep incline to the veranda in a nonchalant manner, a stalk of grass between his teeth. I smiled at his rube-like appearance. The city boy was adapting to country life in a big way.

Mabel was in the kitchen, cutting up vegetables for stew. She was getting around well, at least for short periods, and had taken an interest in helping with meal preparation. "Always liked cooking," she said from her seat on the walker, where she peeled potatoes with careless ease. Her voice changed as she added, "Then, there wasn't nobody who cared anymore."

Eddie came around to the back door, where we did our de-bugging and de-seeding routine. He entered the house, sliding out of his shoes and kicking them into a corner. He'd stolen no food today, for which I was grateful. Sitting down opposite Mabel, he snatched a piece of carrot from the pile she'd made and crunched it between his straight, white teeth. "I've been reading about you," he said, giving me an innocent look.

Mabel started on an onion, holding her head back to avoid the tear-inducing spray. "You been to the library. That's quite a hike, ain't it?"

"Not if you go straight downhill," Eddie replied. "There's a path."

I knew that path and knew the trip back up the steep hillside was somewhat arduous. His teenage legs probably hadn't noticed, as mine hadn't when I was his age. "They've got a whole two computers that connect to the Net, so I had to wait forever, but I finally got my hour." He turned to me. "You're Beth Lousiere, the Homeless Hero."

I sighed, telling myself it was inevitable. Kids his age were bound to be curious, especially after being left with two strangers in a remote, unfamiliar place. Still, if Eddie had found my name in the Richmond papers, he knew I'd left the police force two years ago under a cloud of suspicion. Had he concluded, as the majority of my colleagues on the force had, that I was a crazed murderer?

81

Mabel shot me a sympathetic look. "Loser don't like to talk about it."

"Loser doesn't like to talk, period," he observed. "But that's okay. I appreciate you letting me stay here till my mom comes back."

Again I caught a look from Mabel. Obeying her silent request to keep my disbelief to myself, I simply nodded and turned to browning the beef for dinner.

EDDIE'S SECRET BLOG, SEPTEMBER 4

I sure surprised Loser with what I found out. She didn't say much, but when does she ever? I think it's cool she's got secrets. Maybe she'll understand why I don't tell everything I know.

The Richmond newspapers from June were full of stories about Loser, aka Beth, because she saved some little kid from killers. Before that, the stuff was even more interesting. Until a couple years ago, Loser was a cop married to a guy named Darrin Lousiere. They had a baby girl, and one night, somebody stabbed the husband and smothered the kid. Beth claimed she was on a stakeout, but nobody else knew she was supposed to be on one. The cops couldn't prove Beth was the killer, but it's pretty clear they thought she was. She left the police force, and a while after, Loser showed up on the streets. She didn't talk, at least not much. Nobody knew she was "the killer cop" for a long time. I guess she did odd jobs, and that's how she met this guy Nick who got accused of murder. Loser liked Nick's little girl, so she tried to prove the dad was innocent. She almost got killed herself, but in the end, she found the real killers, which is how she became the Homeless Hero.

So what's she doing up in the mountains of West Virginia? I think she came here to get sane again, like R&R from a war zone or something. As far as killing her family goes, I don't think Loser did it. I mean, she was a cop, so she's probably drilled a few bad guys, but that was in the line of duty. From what I've seen, she isn't the type to murder someone in cold blood.

Then again, I'd have sworn my mom was no killer either. I guess sometimes people do stuff you don't expect them to do. It's kind of hard to figure it out.

LOSER

The next afternoon Eddie took off again. I guessed he'd spend another hour on the Net at the library. I hadn't been down there since he arrived on my doorstep, but I promised myself I'd go soon and send Bert an email to let him know I was doing okay.

That reminded me of the phone Alex Bronson had brought. Where was it? Looking around, I found it right where I'd left it, on a shelf by the door, wrapped in its power cord. Thinking Eddie might like it, I decided to charge the thing. Finding an empty outlet (no small feat in an old house like mine), I connected the cord's two ends and heard the beep that let me know I'd done it correctly. Wow. What a techie I was becoming!

Supper that night was chicken breasts on a rice pilaf. I was proud of the fact that I could recall many of the recipes I used to make for Darrin and me. Sometimes I had to look up amounts in Marta's cookbooks or check out what they suggested for spices, but mostly I cooked by instinct, letting my taste buds tell me when I got it right. "Smells like something that needs eating," Mabel said as I opened the oven.

When the meal was ready, Eddie wasn't back. Seeing me glance out the window toward the trail, Mabel said, "Kids come and go on their own time. Better get used to it."

A little frustrated with him, I dished up the meal anyway. Eddie would have to learn we wouldn't delay meals on his account. Mabel kept looking at the door, but she did justice to the chicken anyway.

When we'd finished he still wasn't back, and worry began to prickle in my mind. Despite his newfound love of Nature, Eddie was a city kid. He might have fallen and hurt himself. He might have met some critter and panicked, running wildly through the woods until he lost his way. Pointing to an old bell Marta had kept as a souvenir when they tore down the crumbling schoolhouse she'd attended, I told Mabel, "Ring that if he comes." She nodded, and I set off down the hill.

The day was getting old, and I took along a flashlight that would soon be necessary. As I descended, I watched for places Eddie might have left the trail but saw none. Tennis shoe prints showed he'd headed straight down the dusty little path. Overgrown at first, the path became clearer, better traveled farther on, where people from other houses joined it, heading for town. Just as I got to the flat spot that constituted most of Beulah, the streetlights came on. I decided the library was a good starting point. There were evening hours on Wednesdays, and Eddie was probably caught up in reading about my shocking past. I hoped he hadn't shared it with anyone else.

The library was cramped and a little musty-smelling, like some of the books had been wet at some point. The librarian on duty had been on the job when I was in school, but I hadn't seen her since my return, having made my visits early in the day. "Beth!" she said, looking up from her computer. "I heard you were back home. It's good to see you."

"Hello." I put a smile with it to detract from the skimpiness f the greeting.

"It's good to have our young people return," she went on, setting her reading glasses aside. "We're getting to be a town of senior citizens." She leaned toward me. "I retire from here in six months."

It was obviously big news, so I tried to look impressed. "Congratulations."

She gave a little nod. "Thank you. I'm anxious to do some traveling, and I plan to spend some time with my grandbabies. They're in Houston.

Rick—you might remember Rick from school—works for BP. He travels a lot, but he wanted his kids to have a home base, so he bought a house out there."

Rick's name brought the slightest of jingles in my memory. Serious guy, maybe four years older than I. It seemed like he'd married someone I knew.

"And you'll remember Angie. She's teaching out there. Kindergarten." As she named and described their three children, I couldn't keep my eyes from searching the building, and she finally asked, "What are you looking for, dear?"

"A boy."

"You mean Eddie?" She chuckled at my surprised expression. "A nice young man. So polite! Continuing in Marta's footsteps, are you?" She waved toward the computer terminals. "Last I saw he was over there, but that was a while ago. I didn't see him leave, but—"

She looked around helplessly. In the end, we searched the library, checking the carrels and the corners and even the upper story, where dusty maps and ancient books on county government were kept. Here, the smell was stronger; the roof leaked somewhere.

Other than that I learned nothing. Eddie had left the building.

When the girl sitting at the computer Eddie had been using left, I slipped into the still warm chair and called up the history. She'd been writing a report on Charles Dickens, so the top four listings related to her research. Under that was the *Romulus Reporter*, which seemed an unlikely source for information on the Boz. I clicked the link and got the masthead of the newspaper. A sidebar claimed the paper served Romulus, West Virginia, a town of 146,000 citizens. A headline in the local news section revealed that one of them, Nadine Hopgood, had died the night before in a tragic accident on a rural road in a blinding rainstorm.

EDDIE'S SECRET BLOG, SEPTEMBER 7
I had it all wrong.

Dickweed's alive. Mom is dead.

She's dead.

She's dead.

LOSER
Using the flash to light my way home, I clambered up the hill to find Eddie in my backyard, sitting under an apple tree heavy with fruit. Beside him lay a small electronic device, maybe an iPod. It was a few feet away, as if he'd tossed it half-heartedly, unsure if he wanted it or not. I didn't ask why he'd left us to worry, knowing too well the selfishness of grief. Instead I stopped at the tree's drip line, where apples in various stages of decay dotted the ground and scented the air. "Eddie."

He looked up, and his lips began trembling. He pressed them together, wrinkling his chin. For once, I took the lead in the conversation. "I'm sorry." I almost reached out to him, but I didn't think he wanted me to. He was focused on holding himself together, unwilling to cry in front of a relative stranger.

He took refuge in anger. "She was nothing to you."

I don't do words well, but words were what he needed. "She was your mother."

He passed a palm over his cheekbone, mopping away a traitorous tear. "He killed her."

I opened my mouth to say it had been an accident. That's what the newspaper said; that's what the police said. Then I recalled how grief shuts out well-meant words of comfort and explanation. Nothing makes it better; nothing makes death all right or understandable or believable.

"I don't have a home now," Eddie said as if tasting each word's truth. "I don't have anyone."

Since the smile he usually shared so freely had deserted him, I gave him a small one of mine. "You've got me," I said. "And Mabel."

His tears overflowed, but he wiped them away on his shirtsleeve. "I have to go back there. I need to know what happened."

I might have argued that a fifteen-year-old was too young to investigate a death. I could have explained that Eddie was too grief-stricken to think logically. I should perhaps have reminded him that he'd told me himself the place was dangerous. None of that would have done any good, even if I'd had the words.

Eddie licked his lips and laid out his argument. "The road where they say it happened? It leads to my stepdad's hunting camp. Mom went there one time, and she hated it. She told Rich she couldn't take the altitude, but the truth was, she hated that rustic crap. When he wasn't around, she called it BFE Camp."

A small animal moved somewhere nearby, and I tensed, not wanting to encounter a skunk in the dark. Eddie didn't appear to notice as he went on to his next point. "The paper says she was drunk, but Mom doesn't drink, ever. She says drunk people look stupid."

I thought of Nadine's obsessive concern for her looks, noticeable even on short acquaintance. If an insecure foster kid based her self-worth on her looks, she might never want to appear stupid, as drunks usually do. On the other hand, a parent might lie to her kid about such things as how much she drinks, and people visit places they don't like if the reason is compelling enough. Nadine might have gone to the hunting lodge to speak with her husband, despite her dislike of the place. Still, I'd seen for myself that she was terrified of something, and now she was dead.

That's what the police are for, I told myself. *They'll investigate Nadine's death. If there are questions, they'll find the answers. Things will resolve, and Eddie will go home.*

He sensed my doubt. "Something happened in Romulus back in June. Mom wouldn't tell me what it was, but I know it was bad. She had blood on her shoes and her blouse, and there was a lot of cash in one of those make up carryall things. We were always moving, and she was real spooky all the time. She'd just started to be a little better when I mentioned the Hummer, and she freaked again."

At the questioning sound I made, Eddie raised his hands in a gesture of frustration. "I told you. I saw this black Hummer that looked like one that Dave, my stepfather's game manager, drives. That's what made her freak out all over again, and that's when we came here. She thought they were looking for us."

I'd been marshalling arguments against his murder theory. Instead, I felt my jaw tense. I'd seen that Hummer here. In Beulah.

I couldn't let myself get caught up in a teenage boy's dramatics. Nadine's husband might have sent someone looking for her, but that didn't mean he killed her. Eddie was grieving, and he didn't want his mother's death to be an accident. He'd invented a conspiracy, as some do when they've lost a loved one and feel somehow responsible.

"It's messed up, Loser." Eddie wiped his nose and both eyes with the tail of his t-shirt. "She was all I had, and somebody killed her."

There were probably a hundred things I could have, should have said, but my mental word calculator was sounding its warning. I'd used up most of today's words and had only five left. What could I say to help this boy cope with the biggest sorrow he'd yet encountered in life?

Before she became Loser, Beth would have put an arm around a grieving boy. She'd have said, "Your mother's in a better place," or "No one can hurt her now." She might have tried to make Eddie see a point of hope for his own future. "Someday, we'll understand why these things happen," or "Only God knows why, but He gives us the strength to keep going."

But Loser lost track of God when He lost track of her, somewhere on the streets of Richmond. And words are deceptive. You have to watch every one. "Come inside," I told Eddie. "Your supper's cold."

The house still smelled like chicken paprika, and a single lamp lit Mabel's anxious face. When Eddie brushed past her without a word and hurried up the stairs, she knew enough to wait. I handed her the newspaper article I'd printed out at the library.

Mabel doesn't read unless she has to, and it takes her a while, but finally she said, "Lord!" She glanced up the stairs, assuring that Eddie was out of hearing, and asked, "What we gonna do with him now?"

I shrugged helplessly. It wasn't any of my business. Eddie's custodial parent was dead, but he had a stepfather he'd never bothered to mention. According to the article, the guy was a more-than-prosperous car salesman with a string of dealerships. The boy was his responsibility now, legally and morally. There was nothing I could do for Eddie that his stepdad couldn't do better.

"You're gonna send him back home." Mabel's tone was faintly accusatory. "What if the stepfather is what Nadine was running away from?"

I shook my head, running a hand over my hair and turning away to avoid the stern judgment in Mabel's eyes, at least the one that looked my way. My words were gone for the day, and I had no argument to make anyway. Eddie was not my kid. I had no right to him. All I could do was drive him to Romulus in the morning and let him tell the authorities his story. If his stepfather was abusive or crazy or whatever, Eddie had to say so.

"Maybe they'd let him stay here for a while," Mabel said, but she didn't sound optimistic. I could offer him a home, at least temporarily, but would the court give custody of an unhappy boy to two formerly crazy women living in a house at the outer edges of civilization? I shuddered at the thought of trying to explain to a judge why he should. The words that would require!

Without another word to Mabel (I had no more to give), I left the house. Even the porch seemed confining tonight, so I ended up bedding down in the orchard. I lay there thinking for a long time, interrupted at irregular intervals by the soft plop of ripe apples falling to the ground. Thoughts of Eddie's situation plagued me, but each piece of falling fruit served as a distraction. How my friends in Richmond would have loved those apples! There were far too many of them for us to eat. We picked what we wanted and let the rest lie on the earth, rotting into brown, mushy lumps. The deer came in at night and ate their fill, but there were still plenty.

Another example of the unfairness of the world. Nature provides wasteful bounty in some places and scant comfort in others. Or was it that mankind shut Nature out, allowing hunger to move into the empty spaces? I wanted to scoop up all the apples, drive to Richmond, and hand them out to Lewis, to Bubba, even to Aisha. But would it help? They needed more than apples to smooth out their crooked lives. Still, I'd feel a little less like just another oxygen thief in the world.

Sometime in the night I fell into a deep sleep. I know that because I didn't hear Eddie exit the house and pull the door shut behind him. I didn't hear his shoes crunch on the gravel when he reached the road. Like his mother before him, Eddie was able to outwit Loser. When morning came, he was gone.

CHAPTER EIGHT

I thought Mom and Dickweed had a fight and she killed him, but he's alive and she's dead. I know he killed her, but how can I prove it so they'll put him in jail forever?

Mom left Romulus because of him, something he did. According to the newspaper article, Dickweed's been searching everywhere for us, making appeals on TV and everything. They said he's been "distraught" because his wife and her son were missing and now he's "devastated" that she's dead. Bull.

Maybe it's a mistake. Maybe Mom faked her own death so he won't look for us anymore. She was so scared! I keep remembering how she grabbed me when I told her about seeing the Hummer that day. I could feel the panic in how hard she squeezed my arms. We should've kept going, maybe to California or something.

Why'd she go back to Romulus? She said one time that Rich owed her. Did she go back to get money from him? Why didn't she tell me what was going on? And why'd she leave me with Loser?

I could ask Loser to take me to Romulus. I can usually get people to do what I want with my nice-boy routine and a smile or two. I could tell her everything. I mean, Loser used to be a cop, and the police might pay attention if she told them they needed to investigate Mom's death better. Loser's weird for sure, but kind of in a good way. It's almost like you're having a whole conversation with her when she hardly says anything at all. Would it help if she went with me?

No. Loser doesn't act like a cop anymore. I guess what happened to her family messed her up a lot. Besides, she'd probably take me straight to Dickweed, which I don't want.

I have to figure it out by myself. I'm going to find out what really happened to my mom, and then I'll leave Romulus and live on my own, maybe in Florida or Texas. I bet Mom was going to come back for me after she got the money. I'm gonna find out how she ended up dead.

LOSER

After my night in the orchard, I entered the house to hear Mabel calling, "Can I get some help?" Her most difficult task was getting out of bed at the beginning of the day. Because of her arthritis, the surgery, and eight hours without a pain pill, she sometimes needed assistance to get from lying to standing. Once she was upright, she managed pretty well with the walker. I went in, served as fulcrum, and she headed for the bathroom. I went upstairs to see how Eddie was doing.

I found the door open and his bed neatly made—neatly for a teenage boy, at least. His bag was missing. I went back downstairs, where Mabel was guiding her walker across the hardwood floor to the kitchen, grunting softly with each step. "Eddie's gone."

Her eyes went wide. "Oh, that poor child. What you gonna do, Loser?"

My first reaction to his absence, I'm ashamed to say, was relief. I didn't have to tell him to go back. I didn't have to listen to his arguments and be the bad guy. He'd chosen his way and done as he wanted.

Hard as I tried, I couldn't absolve myself of responsibility. A grieving kid makes decisions based on pure emotion, and they're likely to be wrong. Eddie had the idea in his head that his stepfather had killed his mother. No doubt he intended to ride into town like an avenging superhero and punish the evildoer. It wasn't likely to end well.

Could his version of the story be correct? Something caused Nadine to run. After months of ducking from place to place, she'd left him with me and gone back to Romulus, where she'd ended up dead. I didn't understand, didn't know enough to understand, but I sensed Eddie knew more than he'd told me.

What awaited Eddie in Romulus? An abusive stepfather who'd driven his wife away and perhaps murdered her when she returned? Even if Nadine wasn't innocent in whatever caused the split, the guy was not Eddie's dad. Would he turn the kid over to the juvenile system? And what if Eddie didn't make it to Romulus? What if he got picked up on the road, hit by a drunk driver, or lost in the middle of nowhere?

I considered a text message to the police, who could intercept Eddie. I knew he'd hate it, but a kid who runs off in the night should expect unhappy results.

But would they listen to him—really listen?

It was the worst of combinations: Loser's fears and Beth's maternal instincts joining forces. I bit my bottom lip, overwhelmed by choices I didn't want to make. *Take care of him*, Nadine's note had begged.

Mabel repeated her question. "What you gonna do?"

I said the only thing I could say. "Go after him."

Despite the simplicity of that statement, I couldn't just get in the car and go, leaving Mabel alone. I floundered for a few minutes, unsure where my duty lay. She'd been thinking though, and she unplugged the phone Bert had provided and handed it to me. "I don't know how to text," she said, "but you can tell my nurse we need to change the schedule. If they'll come a little earlier and help me get going in the morning, I'll be fine while you're gone."

I opened my mouth to object, but she added, "That man that cuts the grass will help if I need him. He's pretty nice, and he likes your apple bread." Mabel had been sharing apple bread with Calvin? My cop's observational skills must have deteriorated badly.

I did as she asked, requesting one early-morning and one evening visit for the next few days. Cheri had returned to work on a walking cast and stumped efficiently around our house the last two mornings, so I figured they could manage. While I was at it, I asked them to set up delivery of Mabel's dinners for a few days with a local restaurant. She could handle her own breakfast and lunch, but one meal she didn't have to prepare each day would be a treat.

I wished I'd installed a house phone so Mabel had a way to communicate if she needed to. With sudden inspiration, I texted Bronson, asking him to overnight a second, simpler phone for Mabel's use. Once she got it, she could not only call for help if necessary, she could let me know if Eddie gave up his misguided quest and returned.

Only a few minutes later my phone beeped, and after a few missteps, I found and read the return text. Danielle would deliver the meal each day and let Mabel choose from the menu what she wanted the next night. I showed the text to Mabel, who said, "Won't be as good as your cookin', but you'n me learned a long time ago not to be picky!" She thought that was funny, but it reminded me of hungry days I preferred to forget. The echo of children's voices jeering, "Dumpster Diver!" as I emerged from an alley with a half-edible tomato would probably never leave me.

Once I'd provided for Mabel, I dug through the desk, found a map of West Virginia, and began planning the route I'd take. Romulus was southeast of us, off the freeway about twenty miles. I figured I'd be there by noon. It was ironic, I thought, that Loser the loser, who'd once had only herself to worry about, couldn't stay out of the lives of others. Despite being a loner for so long, I felt responsible for a teenage boy who was probably in trouble and an elderly, slightly dotty woman who looked more each day like a permanent houseguest.

I packed a small bag in case I had to stay in Romulus for a few days. As I folded my unimpressive clothes and added a few toiletries, I hoped Eddie had misinterpreted his mother's motives. I hoped the stepfather was an okay guy who really wanted Eddie back. If I could find Eddie, take him home, and see that things were all right, I'd feel a lot better. I could return with a quiet mind to the piney woods and the house that was bringing the feeling of home back to me.

On the other hand, if Eddie was right and Nadine's death was something other than an accident, I had to make sure he was safe. I had a sobering thought as I tossed the small suitcase found in Marta's closet into the back seat of my car. It would be pathetic if Loser the loser was all the kid had to see that order was restored in his world.

EDDIE

I left the house with just what I could carry in my pockets. My recorder stayed behind, stuffed under the mattress, which meant the end of my secret blog. It's over now, but the rest of this is what happened from the time I left Loser's place. I guess that lets anyone reading this know I lived through it—barely—but I'm still trying to answer the question I started with: When someone you like a lot kills someone you didn't like much, what are you supposed to do about it?

My escape started out good. I got away from the house without Loser hearing me and followed the road down the mountain. The path would have been quicker, but it was too dark for that, and I was a little scared of what I might meet in the woods at night. When I passed through Beulah there was only one car on Main Street, parked and empty. It was so quiet, I could hear the streetlights overhead buzzing, all six of them. I didn't just take off like a crazy person. I had a plan. At the library, I'd overheard two women talking about the newspapers they got every day. They wondered how much longer it would go on with publishers going out of business right and left. One of the women was married to the delivery guy.

"His route starts in Parkersburg," she said, talking way too loud for a library. "I don't know what we'll do if the *News* folds, cuz with his bad back and the diabetes, he ain't good for much else but deliverin' papers." She sighed. "I get tired of hauling him out of bed at four in the morning though."

"He has to get up that early?" the librarian asked, stacking books into piles as they talked.

"Well, yeah. He leaves at four-thirty, drives to the city for the papers, and delivers them all over before most people are out of bed. The good thing is he's done by nine, so he watches the kids while I work."

"You got a job?"

"Stocking shelves at the grocery store. It doesn't pay a lot, but it's only a block from home. Larry can have the truck when he needs it."

That conversation inspired my plan. If I could find the delivery guy's pickup before he left, I could ride along. It shouldn't be hard to hear a vehicle a block from the grocery store start up in the early-morning quiet. All I had to do was get there before he drove away. At Parkersburg, I could get a ride south and then angle east to Romulus. It should be pretty easy.

I could have been a mile away and still heard that truck start. I headed toward the sound and, rounding a corner, saw back-up lights come on a few houses down. Fifteen feet away from me was a stop sign. I backed into the shadows and hoped the guy at least slowed for the sign. A full stop might be too much to ask for.

Luckily, he braked to let a sorry-looking mongrel cross at the corner. The street lamp shone on the guy in the cab, a mug of coffee in one hand and a cigarette in the other. As he peered left, I came from the right, opened the hatch, and climbed in, centering my weight so the truck didn't tip and give me away.

The guy was clueless. He made the corner and headed out of Beulah, turning the radio on once he was gone from town. Soon, I was treated to a duet featuring Travis Tritt and my hillbilly chauffeur, who sang a little behind and a lot off the key Travis was using. It was okay, though. I was on my way.

Isn't it Murdock's Law or something like that that says if something can go wrong, it will? Well, that's what happened to me. As I rode along in the back of the truck, I realized I hadn't thought about how I'd get out. I couldn't wait till the driver stopped to get his papers, because he'd see me. I'd have to get out at a stoplight somewhere before he reached his destination, but I had no way of knowing where I'd be. It wouldn't be good to climb out of the back of a truck in the middle of traffic, either.

It was hard to see ahead or behind, because the camper windows were filthy. Headlights came and went behind us, not many at first but more as daylight neared and we reached busier roads. When the truck passed more and more neon, I figured we were on the outskirts of the city. I wanted the freeway ramp, but I'd have to take what I could get. At a red light where no cars were behind us, I exited the truck, backing away reluctantly as it went on, leaving a cloud of exhaust. I was on my own.

I had money. After my mom left, I'd found a couple of hundred-dollar bills at the bottom of my duffel bag. I'd sat on the bed, looking at them and trying to figure out how I felt about her. She'd dumped me, but she'd found a safe place for me to stay, and she hadn't left me broke. Bad mother or just pathetic?

I knew better than to walk into a restaurant and pay for breakfast with a hundred-dollar bill. A guy might as well wear a sign that says, *Remember me!* I started walking, passing strip malls and fast-food places, trying to look like I belonged. A half mile or so down the road was a Wal-Mart that was open twenty-four hours. I went in, bought a bag of cookies and a soda, and went to one of the self-check lanes. Machines don't notice who's feeding big denominations into them; they just spit out the change.

The store wasn't very busy at six a.m., and the woman who was supposed to be monitoring the self-check lanes was sweeping the area with a battered broom. While her back was turned, I set the bag of cookies on a magazine rack, approached the checkout, paid for the soda with one of my hundreds, and received my change. The coins I dropped into the big pocket of my shorts. Two twenties I stuck in that little inside pocket at the waistband, figuring that would be my spending money for the day. The rest I put into a bag with the soda. Once I got outside, I'd hide it under the liners of my shoes.

Making sure the woman was still paying attention to her sweeping, I set the bag at the end of the shelf, off the scale, and backed away a few steps. Retrieving the package of cookies from between *People* and *Prevention*, I approached the lane a second time. The clerk, who had now swept the litter into a dustpan, turned. I gave her Smile #7, (Nice but Disinterested), and touched *Start* on the screen, going through the process again and paying for the cookies with the other hundred-dollar bill. I collected four twenties, a ten, a five, and some change, and put that and my cookies into the bag with the soda. The mechanical cashier ordered me to take my receipt, which I did.

As I left the store, a girl with a baby stood off to one side of the entryway. Her clothes were cheap and kind of gaudy; her hair was limp and colorless. Sores on her face signaled possible meth use. The kid looked messed up too, like it had brain damage. Seeing me looking, the mother smiled in that vague way strangers do. I smiled back, trying to act like they were both okay.

Outside, I opened the cookies and the soda and started on breakfast. As I ate, I went around the side of the building, looking for a spot where I could transfer the money from the bag to my shoes.

"Hey."

I turned, and there she was, behind me. It was kinda dark in the shadow of the building, but I could see her outline, the kid a silhouette against her light-colored shirt. Something moved behind her, and a taller figure appeared at her side. "We need that money, man."

Shit! How stupid could I be? She'd seen me stash the bills and signaled to her boyfriend. And I'd made it easy for them by separating myself from help. I was up against a wall with nowhere to run.

As my eyes adjusted to the available light, I saw that the guy was scary-looking. Big, but with that starved look druggies get and eyes that didn't quite focus. He held a two-foot piece of pipe in one hand. I shivered as his hand rasped along it, caressing the metal. "I said, we need the money you got in that bag."

I had no doubt he would smack me if I offered the least bit of resistance. Grinding my teeth, I dug the bills out and handed them over. The guy gave the money to the woman, who quickly counted it and then stuffed it into her bra. The man wasn't quite done with me. "You got any more?"

If I said no he might search my pockets, and if he found the two twenties, he wouldn't be happy with me. But if I gave them up, I'd be completely broke.

"No."

"What's in your pocket?"

I almost freaked, but he pointed at the other side, where the track phone Mom had bought made a lump on my thigh. I'd brought it for emergencies, but I hadn't foreseen this one. "Just my phone."

The guy's head turned slightly toward the girl. "We can use that." Avoiding looking me in the eye, she stepped forward, put her hand in my pocket, and took the phone. "You got anything else?"

I tried for an accusing tone, but it sounded more like whining. "You cleaned me out."

His grin was both goofy and frightening. "I hear you, man. Now stay here for a few minutes and keep your mouth shut." Speaking to the girl without looking at her, he ordered, "Come on."

They were gone in an instant, turning away like I wasn't there. As they moved to the lighted parking lot, the baby looked over his mother's shoulder at me, his lips slack and his eyes expressionless. Soon, I heard two car doors slam and a wheezy engine start up. In a few seconds, it was gone.

Leaning against the building, I sank to the concrete, legs shaking. It took a long time before I could stand again, and longer still before I pulled together the courage to go on.

CHAPTER NINE

LOSER

Romulus straddled the Maricoo River. The mountains around it gave the water lots of push, which provided electrical power to the area and great fishing as well, at least that's what the signs promised. I arrived around eleven a.m., tired and anxious. There'd been no sign of Eddie on the way, and I told myself I'd been foolish to think I might find him on the road.

I'd programmed the GPS for a home address I found by going through the things Eddie left behind. The fact that he hadn't mentioned a stepfather until news of his mother's death came indicated their relationship wasn't the best. That didn't mean the guy was evil incarnate. In fact, the newspaper article I'd copied made him sound like the exact opposite.

I'd been surprised to learn that Eddie had told Mabel a little about home. "His name's Richard Hopgood," she told me as I packed to leave, "but Eddie called him Rich." The name had slipped out one day as they talked, and under questioning, Eddie admitted Nadine married a wealthy car dealer around the time the kid was eleven.

"He's got money but no personality," Mabel said. "Eddie says he just walks around with his chest stuck out, showing everybody what a big deal he is." She hadn't pressed the kid for details. "You got to let people have their secrets," she opined, and life on the streets had certainly taught us that. "One day, Eddie seen some deer in the orchard, and he told me about his stepdad's hunting lodge. He never got invited up there, but he said that was okay, cuz he never wanted to kill anything for fun."

When I'd looked at Mabel questioningly, she gave her assessment. "I don't think the man abused the kid, but Eddie always knew he didn't want him for a son." She clicked her tongue in sympathy. "He tried real hard to act like it didn't matter, but I'm pretty sure it did."

Thanks to Mabel, I had three possible places to look for Rich Hopgood. On the premise that a grieving widower would be at his house, not at work or his hunting lodge, I went there first. Eddie's former home was an impressive structure of the faux-Southern-mansion type, though the Tudor home on one side and the Edwardian one on the other dulled its historical impact. The development was typical of such places: winding streets with cul-de-sacs every few blocks, a fake pond with benches no one ever sat on, short driveways, and teensy, over-green patches fed by visitors in trucks that said things like *Reallawn.*

I pulled into the driveway of a house with a *For Sale* sign in front and watched Hopgood's place for a while. It looked deserted, and when I walked by, holding my arms bent like a serious exercise enthusiast, I saw through the garage window that the inside was empty. The next stop, then, was Hopgood Motors' main office. Maybe Nadine's husband was avoiding grief by burying himself in work.

GPS led me there in less than twenty minutes. I went inside, marveling at the lengths these places go to impress prospective clients. The building was huge, with an open-to-the-sky showroom complete with a fountain, a comfortably furnished lounge, and semi-private offices tucked into corners. A sign at the back with arrows directed me to showers, and exercise room or restrooms. I didn't care to know about showers at a car dealership.

When I entered the air-conditioned, musically accompanied main area, a woman about my age approached with a professional smile. I guessed I'd been vetted somehow in the distance between the parking lot and the door and pigeonholed as a buyer who'd respond best to a female of my own generation. This one looked like she wouldn't know a camshaft from a steering wheel.

"Hi, can I help you with something?"

"Waiting." I told her vaguely. She retreated with a command to let her know if I needed anything. I went to the coffeepot and helped myself to a cup. Free is free, and on the street, a girl learns to take what's offered. It wasn't bad coffee either. Picking up a magazine, I sat down on one of the couches located at the back of the room, near the door to a maintenance area that might have done double duty as an operating room. Everything I saw through the windowed wall was pristine, white, and efficient. A young woman put paper covers on the floors of each car that came in as well as a drape over the driver's seat. Apparently, no human contact was allowed in modern car repair.

The woman who'd approached me watched for a while, but I kept my attention focused on the magazine, and she finally turned to other tasks. Nothing much was happening, but I was in no hurry. As I watched from under my eyelashes, employees came and went, each appearing to be busy, though there weren't a lot of customers present. Finally, I heard heels clicking on the metal stairs and glanced up to see the man I'd come looking for. His picture in the paper hadn't done him justice, and I understood what Nadine had seen in him.

Handsome, confident, and impressively dressed, Richard Hopgood's entire being said money, which for Nadine had meant security. He came down winding metal stairs at one side of the showroom from what was presumably his office on the second floor. He carried an accordion folder in one hand, braced against his body as he lightly touched the stair rail with the other. Behind him came a forty-ish woman with a tablet computer in hand, poking at the keypad as she descended. Beside him a smaller man explained something, waving his hands as he hurried to keep up with the longer-legged Hopgood. "—can't get here tomorrow, Rich," he was saying. "He says he can come on Thursday."

Hopgood stopped at the base of the stairs. "All right. Tell the Monsignor we'll go with that." He turned to the woman, who'd stopped on the last step, still typing. "Can you handle that, Ann?"

Ann's eyes lit with hero worship. "Of course, Mr. Hopgood. I'll call the funeral home and set it up."

"We'll close all the dealerships for the day, but please let the staff know they're not required to attend the funeral. I don't want anyone to feel obligated." He stopped, bit his bottom lip, and stared out the front window, which was also the front wall. "They don't have to—"

"Of course they'll want to come," the man said, and Ann made a little hum of agreement. "Mrs. Hopgood was a lovely woman, and they'll want to pay their respects."

"She *was* lovely, inside and out," Hopgood said. "I wish I knew what happened, why she—" He paused, gulping audibly. "I'm sorry. It was a mistake to come to work today. I—I'll call you later." Turning quickly, he walked away. His companions watched as he disappeared out a door marked *Employee Exit Only.*

"He's so broken up about this," the man said. "To not know why your wife left you—"

"And that poor boy," Ann said. "I wonder if he even knows his mother is dead."

"Sad."

"Yes," she agreed. "Very sad."

EDDIE

I spent a miserable hour wandering Petersburg under a sun so hot, I felt like a slice of bacon, curling up in some places and turning crispy in others. After asking a couple of times for directions, I located the freeway and took a stand at the entrance ramp, trying to look like a college student hitching home. It worked once; I got a ride about twenty miles with some real college kids who asked way too many questions. I invented a small school across the border in Ohio, a bunch of classes, and names for the parents who were too cheap to send me bus fare to get home.

When they left the freeway I got out at a gas station near the exit. I hung around there for a while, looking for another ride. It seemed like a miracle when I saw a van pull up at the pump that said, *Michelle's Custom Draperies, Romulus, WV.*

The question was whether to ask for a ride or steal one. When the driver and a passenger went inside, I chose the not-asking option. A single person might offer a ride for company, but with a witness, I guessed the chance of that happening lessened. Besides, there wasn't room for anyone else up front. The cargo area was separated with one of those mesh things, so I moved a bunch of fabric over and settled in.

I'd been miserable walking in the hot sun, but it was worse in the back of that van, where the A/C didn't reach and fabric dust choked me. After a while, I started breathing through my T-shirt for fear I'd have a coughing fit and get thrown out onto the road. The couple up front talked a lot, but it was just a low hum. When we stopped again two hours later, I faced the same problem I'd had with the newspaper guy: how to get out of the vehicle without being seen. The engine shut down, and I heard a door open. The warning bell sounded briefly, and the other door opened. I heard the man say, "Do you have to go too?"

"Don't I always?" the woman answered. Two slams followed, and there was silence except for some birds chirping. I made a guess at where we were and figured it was time to go. Easing the cargo doors open, I saw I was in the parking lot of a rest area. People moved toward the building and back to their cars, most of them focused on where they were going, not the other vehicles. I stepped out of the van, closed the doors softly, and took a seat at a nearby picnic table like I was waiting for someone to do their business. Soon the couple returned, got into the van, and left. I smiled to thank them for the ride, and the woman smiled back, clueless.

They hadn't done me any favors, it turned out. After I used the facilities myself, I checked the map, and the *You are Here* section hit me like a train. Michelle wasn't heading home with her draperies. We'd gone east, not south, and now, at almost noon, I was outside Clarksburg, West Virginia, and no closer to Romulus than I'd been at five o'clock that morning.

LOSER

I stayed at the dealership for a while, observing. I'd come thinking in a certain way about Richard Hopgood, since Nadine's flight seemed to indicate trouble with a significant other. When I'd seen her husband at work just two days after her car was found wrapped around a tree, I'd been ready to condemn him as a fat-cat wife abuser with no love for anyone but himself. Now I reconsidered. Hopgood seemed truly stricken by the loss of his wife. And the world does not stop for death, no matter how much we grieve. There'd be things that had to be handled by the boss, even in the midst of tragedy. As for Eddie's view, I reminded myself that stepsons are often notoriously difficult to get close to. A guy standing between a boy and his mother is in a bad position.

That left a new question. If Hopgood didn't know why Nadine had taken off, what sent her running? I turned my interest to Hopgood's employees, looking for a likely source of information. When a pale-faced salesman who'd been drumming his fingers on a desktop for the last half hour finally slid from his chair and headed out the back, I rose and followed him.

Behind the dealership were the less-pretty places every operating business has to have: piles of boxes waiting to be broken down, a barrel that smelled like used motor oil, and a shed that probably held tools and such. The man I was following disappeared behind the metal building, and I guessed we were headed to the smokers' patch, a place familiar to a small but regular group. West Virginia was finally, like the rest of the country, banning smoking in public places. Though some businesses resisted the idea of clean air, apparently Hopgood Motors was on board.

The guy I'd targeted had moved from person to person in the showroom for the last hour, chatting up a storm. He liked to talk. He had to smoke. Perfect for my purposes.

"Willing to share?" I asked as I stopped a few feet from where he was lighting up. He was surprised, but he was also a Southern male, born and bred. What women ask for, they get, unless it's the truth about how long that special-order car will take. He shook out a cigarette for me and flicked his lighter again. I tried to appear competent, not having smoked since eighth grade. "Thanks."

"Long wait for your repairs?" he asked. He wore a white dress shirt with a tie that had the Carolina Panthers' logo imprinted on it. His black suit pants were pleated in front from sitting. The jacket probably hung over the back of his chair inside. He had that scrambled-egg hairdo guys were sporting, gelled into place, or non-place, I guess, with shiny stuff that made the black strands kind of gold around the edges. He sucked on the cigarette as if it contained the only oxygen available to him. I nodded and tried to remember to puff once in a while.

"Day off Thursday?" I asked.

He blinked as he figured out what I meant. "Oh, yeah. The boss's wife died in a car crash." I put a hand to my mouth as if speechless with shock, and that was all it took. I'd chosen well. "Didn't you read about it in the papers?" he asked. I shook my head, and the guy launched into the story with relish. "Mrs. Hopgood went missing, oh, maybe three months ago, her and her kid. Rich had no idea where they went or why they left. They just disappeared. Yesterday they found her car smashed against a tree. She was killed instantly. Nobody knows where the kid is."

Well, somebody does, I thought.

"He broken up?"

Jutting his bottom jaw outward to blow smoke toward the sky, he nodded. "Big time." He lit a new cigarette off the old one and crushed the butt into the sandy ground. It joined lots of others, a little cigarette

107

graveyard. "He keeps saying it's his fault, but you can't do that to yourself. Things happen. There's no way a guy can foresee it."

My own guilt caused me to empathize with Rich Hopgood. I hadn't murdered my husband and child, but I felt the guilt of their deaths every day. If I'd been there, it wouldn't have happened. Or maybe I'd have died with them, which would have been okay too. I knew what Rich felt: he'd missed something, a clue that would have prevented disaster.

"Why the guilt?"

"He'd gone up to his lodge, to get away from the stress of her being missing, you know? When she came home and saw he was gone, she must have guessed that's where he was and started up there. Nothing he could have done, though. Kalcutt Road is always treacherous, but with the rain and—everything, she didn't make it." He tactfully didn't mention the "alcohol was a factor" part the news had reported, probably out of loyalty to his boss.

"He good to work for?"

"Sure. He's got his quirks, like any boss." I gave him my interested look, and he shrugged, flicking ash to the ground with his thumb. "We gotta send thank-you notes every single time a customer talks to us. We have to keep pictures of our kids on the desk—makes us more like real people. Nobody can open the mail or check in new vehicles except Rich. We all have to—" Recalling that he spoke to a stranger, he stopped himself. "Just normal stuff."

He went to staring at his knuckles, and I guessed that was all the information I'd get from a Hopgood Motors employee without creating suspicion. Gesturing at his tie, I said, "Carolina, huh?"

EDDIE

I was ready for desperate measures, but looking around the rest area, I had no idea what those measures were going to be. People came and went, but I sat there at my picnic table, waiting for an idea. In front of me was the parking lot and beyond it, the restroom building. Behind me, I heard the rumbles and hisses of semis starting up, shutting down, or idling while their drivers used the facilities. Finally, I turned to look at the larger lot where they sat. Trucks. Truckers.

I took a minute to come up with a story. Then I crossed the grassy strip that separated the two lots. The first truck's door said it came from New Jersey. The one beside it came from Jackson, Mississippi. Several vehicles down, I found one that said, *Wheeling West Virginia*. I waited until the driver, a stocky man in jeans and a plaid shirt, returned from the rest room. He had curly, gray sideburns and thinning, salt-and-pepper hair. When he saw me standing by his truck, he slowed for a second before continuing.

"Any chance you're headed toward Romulus?" I asked.

He looked at me with an expression that said he'd heard it all. "Where you from, boy?"

I'd anticipated that question. Pulling my learner's permit from my pocket, I held it out to him. "Romulus." I gave him #8 (the Rueful Bad Boy). "I left last week, but now I'm wanting to go home."

He rubbed his chin, and I knew I had him hooked. Who wouldn't help a mixed-up kid who's trying to make his life right again?

Of course it couldn't be that easy. "Walt's my name, Edward," he said, handing the license back to me. "I'd take you back to your parents, but I'm headed a different direction." Turning, he considered the semis lined up like dominoes along the lot. "Come along here."

We went down a few trucks, where a black man smoked with one hand and rubbed his back with the other as he paced the length of his vehicle. The truck was battered, its paint faded, but the lettering said, *Bringing the Best of West Virginia to Your Local Store*.

"Where you bound for, friend?" Walt asked.

"Down to Charleston, then over to Beckley," the man replied, using the cigarette to point east. My new friend explained the situation while

I locked Smile #2 in place. "I can take him halfway," the man said, glancing at me to see if I had any objections. "I could get on the radio, see somebody's heading east from there."

"There you go, son," Walt said. "Will that do?"

"I appreciate it," I told him. I guess watching Dickweed taught me something over the last few years, because I knew enough to shake the man's hand before climbing into the old truck's passenger seat.

CHAPTER TEN

LOSER

Leaving the dealership, I pressed the GPS command that led me back to Hopgood's house. Sure enough, the garage door was open and there was a snazzy little sports car parked inside. On the way over, I'd made a stop, despite the car's "Route recalculation!" objection. In the back seat was a vase filled with lightly scented seasonal blooms and greenery, topped with a card that said, "With sincere condolences, Bill." I figure everyone has at least one Bill among their acquaintances.

I rang the bell, waited, and rang it again. While it was understandable that he might not answer the door, I didn't intend to leave without meeting Eddie's stepfather. I went to the side of the house, where a tastefully carved board fence and gate hid the backyard from view. The gate wasn't locked, and I had flowers as an excuse to trespass. I entered, closing the gate softly behind me.

Hopgood was sitting at a glass-topped table beside a good-sized swimming pool. His back was to me, his elbow planted on the tabletop as he spoke into the phone. "We're not going to share that with the police," he was saying. If I'd been a dog, I'd have turned my ears to hear better. As it was I held my breath, waiting. "Oh, they do." He sounded defeated. "All right. If they know, they know. I'll deal with it. I'll come up there after the funeral and we'll talk then." He ended the call, resting his head in the palm of his hand for a few seconds.

When I thought he'd had time to collect himself, I coughed discreetly and he turned, surprised. He rose, as a gentleman must, but it seemed to take a lot of effort. He'd changed to khakis and a green, collared shirt with a tailored look and a discreet logo.

"Oh," he said, glancing at my burden. "Another one."

I nodded, saving my words for more important things.

Hopgood gestured at a sliding door behind me. "Come in," he invited. "I'll find a place for it." I followed him into the house, through a gracious family room, down a wide hallway, and into a large, open living area sunlit by a huge, irregularly shaped window over the door. There were floral arrangements on every single surface. Hopgood moved a tall vase filled with yellow roses closer to a squatty one with daisies and lilies and set the flowers I'd brought next to them on the highly polished end table. It would have looked more esthetically pleasing between the other two, but he didn't look like he cared. In fact, he never even looked to see who'd sent it. I guessed Ann or someone like her would make a list and fill out thank-you cards for him to sign after the service.

Stacked on a table by the front door were several small, cream-colored envelopes. Sorting through until he found the one he wanted, he handed it to me. On the front a feminine hand had written, "Floral delivery." I guessed the cash inside would be a proper, even generous, tip according to decorative industry standards.

Having no reason to stay, I made one up. "I met your wife once."

He stopped seeing me as a nameless nobody for a second, and his eyes focused. "When was that?"

I shrugged. "April?"

His shoulders drooped. "Oh. I was hoping you meant recently."

The doorbell sounded directly above my head, and I jumped. Standing aside, I let Hopgood answer. On the doorstep stood a tall man in uniform. "Sheriff Garms."

"Mr. Hopgood." The man gave me a curious look. "Miss."

"Flowers," I said by way of explanation. Officers of the law were supposed to be observant; I hoped this one didn't find delivery people interesting.

"Would you like to come out by the pool, Sheriff?" Hopgood asked. "I have some cold—" He glanced at me. "—drinks out there." I got the hint. Giving them both a nod, I stepped outside and closed the door, leaving them to their private matters.

I started down the sidewalk and past the Remus County Sheriff's Department car parked in the driveway. (Romulus was in Remus County. The classics are big in the South.) Hopgood had been unhappy about the police knowing something, and I really wanted to know what that was.

Stopping on the sidewalk as if to retie my tennis shoe, I looked around. No one in sight, no tell-tale bends in neighbors' curtains to reveal peepers. I'd gone through the gate once without Hopgood noticing. Why not do it again?

Sliding the gate open far enough to slip through, I made my way along the side of the house. At the back corner, I heard the men's voices, the scrape of chairs being pulled away from the table, and the sound of an ice chest opening and closing again. Crouching down, I peered through the branches of an azalea bush. They were seated at the wrought-iron patio set, each with a beer, and they popped them open at almost the same moment.

"It'll be ruled accidental," the sheriff told Hopgood, his voice gentle. "We did what we could to keep the blood alcohol level quiet, but it is public information."

"I can't believe she was drinking." Hopgood's head drooped. "I've never seen her abuse alcohol. Ever."

The sheriff's tone turned even gentler. "Did her running off have to do with the boy?"

Hopgood sighed. "You know about the money."

"We heard."

"He isn't a bad kid, Sheriff. He got confused, like boys do at that age. He wanted a car, and he thought I should give him one." Hopgood took a long pull on his beer, but the sheriff held onto his, waiting. "It's hard for a kid to understand that with all those cars at my lots, I wouldn't just hand one over. I tried to tell him we have to work for the things we get, but…"

After a space, the sheriff finished for him. "You found money missing from your desk."

A sigh. "Yeah. I reacted all wrong. All wrong. I threatened to have him arrested, but Nadine knew I'd never do that to her son." Another quiet space and Hopgood added, "I thought she knew." He set his beer down as if it no longer held any appeal to him. "I should have been more of a father to the kid."

"You gave him everything," the sheriff said. "He should be grateful."

Hopgood appeared not to have heard. "When I married his mother, Eddie was hostile. He was used to having her to himself, you know, and nothing I did pleased him. We settled in eventually, but we never got to be close. Eddie wasn't—" He wiped his face with one hand. "I should have tried harder. These last few years have been brutal on the business, and I—I let things go here at home. When the money came up missing, it all bubbled to the surface."

"And that's why your wife left?"

"I suppose so." Hopgood cleared his throat. "I know I should have told you, but I thought if I could get them back, we'd start over. The money didn't matter; it really didn't. What's a measly thousand dollars if you've got a wife like—" His voice broke. "Like she was."

The sheriff rose, put a hand on Hopgood's shoulder, and said, "We'll find Eddie. Don't worry." Hopgood didn't look up to see his visitor's face, but I saw that where Eddie was concerned, the sheriff wasn't nearly as forgiving as Hopgood.

"Is there anything else you know that might help us find the boy?" he asked.

A long pause. "Nothing more." Hopgood sat hunched in his chair, his voice choked with tears he was fighting not to shed. "I'm sorry I didn't tell you everything from the start."

The sheriff nodded noncommittally and rose, leaving the almost full can of beer sweating on the tabletop. He was probably used to being lied to, but it didn't look like he was happy about it.

I backed into the corner behind the gate, letting the sheriff leave before I made my own exit. His feet tapped down the sidewalk, and I heard his car door open and close. When he'd backed out of the driveway and driven off, I left my hiding place. I couldn't resist one more look into Hopgood's backyard. He sat perfectly still, one elbow resting on the table while his other hand cradled the beer. He was staring into the water in the pool as if it might roil and turn and show him a vision of the future. It winked calmly in the sunlight, telling him nothing.

Suddenly I felt like exactly what I was, an interloper intruding on a man's private tragedy. Hopgood had a lot to think about. I slunk toward the front of the house, assured no one was looking my way, and left.

Eddie

My new friend Jared was a man who didn't talk much. He drove with both hands on the steering wheel and his cap slid back so that the bill slanted almost straight up. When he did speak, he called me "Mr. Edward," like I was the Massa's oldest son. Maybe he meant It to make me feel grown up, but it just made me feel stupid. Not "Mister" anything, I was feeling like a dumb kid who'd gone off on his own and screwed up big time. Murdock's Law was still operating. About thirty miles down the road, a man in an SUV passed, pointing toward the rear of the truck. "Hellfire," Jared said, glancing in the side mirror. His tone was more resigned than upset. Downshifting, he steered to the side of the road and stopped, at the same time letting out a string of curse words that covered pretty much all the possibilities with no repeats.

"Stay here," he ordered and got out to look.

In a few minutes he was back, but I was the last thing on his mind. Grabbing a cell phone from the dashboard, he punched a couple of keys.

"Yeah, Etta, I got a problem out here on 22. Something went with the electrical and pretty much fried everything. I put out the fire, but it ain't good."

I didn't understand all of what followed, but I could smell smoke and got that the truck couldn't go on until something was fixed. Plans were made, and when he hung up the phone, Jared turned to me. "Boy, you can't be here when they come. I'll lose my job." He pointed to a fence lining the road. "Down a mile or so, you'll find a little town. Stay off the highway, now. I'm real sorry."

He wasn't that sorry. His eyes turned to watch for the help that was on its way, and I was pretty sure he'd forgotten me before I waded through the damp weeds that clogged the ditch.

Loser

I left Hopgood's house almost certain he didn't know where Eddie was. The man was in the throes of grief, struggling with the whys of his wife's disappearance and subsequent death. He seemed genuinely concerned about Eddie too, and I was pretty sure the kid had misjudged him. Stepparents often aren't high on a kid's list of people to like.

As for Eddie's current whereabouts, I had no idea. I put my impressions of him with what I'd learned today from his stepfather, trying to make a coherent picture. Eddie was likeable, but I'd seen signs of rebellion. He'd snooped in my things, gone off on his own, and lied to Mabel and me, or at least not told the whole truth. According to Hopgood, he'd stolen money from him. Had Nadine left Romulus to protect her son from prosecution? Had she come back to beg Hopgood to forgive him? I wondered what the real Eddie was like, the one behind that beautiful smile.

My mind prickled with guilt. I should tell the police what I knew. If Eddie was dishonest, he needed to be held to account for it. And if he

116

was on the road somewhere, alone and possibly in danger, what right did I have to withhold what I knew from his legal guardian?

Part of me argued that we're not always guilty of what people think we've done. I liked the kid, and he was grieving for his mother. Who knew better than I that people need time to adjust to a tragedy? If Eddie's actions seemed selfish, it was because there are times when we can only think of our own sorrow. He hadn't meant to worry Mable and me; he was acting on instinct.

Though I shuddered to think what might have happened to him on the way here, I had to operate on the assumption that Eddie had made it to Romulus. He hadn't let his stepfather know he was back, so where was he? He might be staying at a friend's house, waiting to see what the verdict was on his mother's death. I hoped Mabel's stories of life on the street hadn't inspired in him the idea that he could survive in the city alone.

No matter where he was, Eddie wouldn't thank me for alerting the police to his presence in Romulus. My own wish to avoid contact with authority might have contributed to my decision, but I told myself I'd give him a few more hours.

Deciding what I would not do about Eddie left the question of what I would do. I didn't know his friends, didn't know what school he'd attended, didn't even know what grade he'd been in. As I sat there trying to decide my next move, a pickup truck outfitted with those noisy-on-purpose pipes roared by, and I noticed a gun rack in the back window. The gun brought to mind the stepdad's hunting lodge in the mountains. Eddie would know he'd find food and shelter from the elements up there. It seemed like something the kid might do, hide in a place no one would expect, at his stepfather's expense.

The idea of checking out the lodge interested me for another reason. Nadine's accident had happened on the road to the lodge. I'd done some work at accident scenes when my captain heard I was a decent photographer. I'd learned to read the story left behind, to make conclusions about how such things came about.

Eddie insisted his mother would not have gone to Rich's hunting lodge by choice. So why had she been on that road, alone and apparently drunk? Seeing the scene of the crash and the lodge where Hopgood spent his free time might help me make a decision about involving the police. If I could find out where the place was.

EDDIE

The town Jared the trucker sent me to was Calliope, and it was big enough to have both McDonalds and Burger King. The smell of fry grease set my stomach growling. I'd shared the last of my cookies with Jared as we traveled south, and I was starving. I figured I was about twenty-five miles from the turnoff, but there was no freeway, only a series of two-lane roads that widened to four a few miles out of the city and then shrank again on the other side. You don't just happen to find Romulus. You have to want to end up there.

So I had fifty miles to go. Sick of traveling in the wrong direction, I made a sign that said *Romulus* from an old cardboard box, using a marker I borrowed from the girl who served me my Whopper. Within an hour, I was invited into the car of a pharmaceutical rep who, I learned right away, wanted someone to talk to between stops. That was okay, because his last stop for the day would be Romulus. I was finally headed in the right direction.

LOSER

With the newspaper's mention of Kalcutt Road as a starting point, I began my search for Rich Hopgood's hunting lodge at the public library. Romulus had a nice new one with spacious rooms and specialty areas for children, teens, local history, and more. According to the plat book I consulted, Kalcutt was about thirty miles west of Romulus, up in the Yew

Mountains. I got into my car, told the GPS to find the nearest town, which was a tiny dot on the map called Cranville, and followed the directions I was given.

Cranville turned out to be a crossroads with a gas station, a hair salon, and, oddly enough, a scrapbooking shop. I pulled up to a pump, filled the tank, and went in to pay for my gas. Inside, I also bought what turned out to be a surprisingly good hot dog, a bag of chips, and a soda. Behind the counter was a pleasant-faced woman of about thirty. Leaning against the counter on my side, in no hurry to get anywhere, was a man a decade older whose shirt said, *Markham's Varmint Control.* From the condition of the shirt, I guessed Markham's was a one-man operation. No boss would have tolerated those stains.

As I paid, I asked, "Anyone finding berries?"

"A few," the woman replied. "Maybe ten quarts. Not like last year."

"I picked thirty quarts so far," the man said around a chaw of tobacco. I guessed he'd have claimed fifty if she'd said twenty. That kind always has to do better.

"Off Kalcutt?"

"Haven't been up there," the woman said.

"Lots," Mr. Big Mouth agreed. "But ya have to know where to look."

I gave him my interested expression and he continued, pleased to have an audience. "Take the first side road and go till the branches reach right out and scratch your car." He glanced out the window at the Buick. "Maybe you don't want to take a nice car like that up there."

I shrugged as if I couldn't care less about vehicle damage.

"Be careful," the woman warned. "A lady went off that road a few days ago, right, Markham?"

He waved a dismissive hand. "It was rainin', and she was drunk." To me, he said, "You can't go all the way to the top. That's Hopgood's place, and he don't like trespassers."

"Hopgood?"

"He's a businessman with a lodge up there," the woman explained. "Hunts about every animal there is, I guess, and he's got some big bucks up there. His land is all fenced, and his men patrol to keep violators out and people from wandering in and getting shot."

Unwilling to be upstaged, Markham removed his grubby cap, scratched at the ring it had made on his head, and gave us both a history lesson. "That lodge was his daddy's place way back when, and Rich got it when the old man died. He bought up the land after the timbering companies were done with it, addin' on till he owns the whole mountaintop. Calls it GoodRich Lodge now."

"It's a big place," the woman said, and I made a sound to show I was impressed. "A few years back he brought in crews to renovate it. I hear it's real nice."

Markham gave a little huff of resentment. "Nobody around here gets asked up there. My brother-in-law Jerry's a contractor, and he'da been glad for the work, but Hopgood brought in his own people. Guess us locals ain't good enough."

"He takes wounded vets up there sometimes and lets them stay for a while," the woman said, apparently trying to deflect a rant she'd heard before. "To say thanks to them for their service. And there's been some celebrities too. They come in quiet so the reporters don't know where they are, and they can get in a few days of hunting."

"But he don't like uninvited guests," Markham added. "If you step foot on his property, somebody's liable to show up and ask your business."

He looked like a violator if ever I'd seen one, and I guessed he'd been chased away a time or two.

"Thanks," I told them, setting the ice-cold can in the crook of my arm and taking the chips and hot dog in one hand.

"Watch for bears," Markham said as I left. I waved to acknowledge the warning.

CHAPTER ELEVEN

Kalcutt was a narrow gravel road snaking up the mountain a mile outside town. I saw it from some distance away, a pale ribbon among green trees that disappeared and then reappeared sharply to the right or left. Turning off the pavement, I followed its sinuous path, driving slowly. The gravel center had dried, but the edges were still damp from the rain that had caused the accident Eddie insisted was something else.

I was afraid I'd miss the crash site, but that would have been difficult. On a sharp curve, several small trees were broken off at headlight level, the ground was torn to shreds where a tow-truck had pulled the car back onto the narrow road, and bits of metal and glass shone in the grassy shoulder.

Pulling off the road a few yards back, I approached the scene on foot. In addition to the trees that had broken off, several others had been damaged by the impact, the bark scraped off and streaks of paint left in its place. Due to the traumatized trees, the smell of pine was stronger than usual. In the flattened grass, I could see where the car had come to rest, its side against two sturdy pines that had lost some lower branches but held firm. From what I could discern, Nadine had been coming down the hill at some speed when she lost control of her car.

After treading carefully along the tire tracks, I turned full circle to study the scene. The road itself showed no sign of disturbance. I looked for some sign Nadine had braked, but if she had, the rain had obscured the skid marks. If she'd been drunk, she probably wouldn't have realized she'd left the road.

Next to a scarred tree, I found a pile of broken glass intermixed with various coins that must have been on or near the dashboard at impact. My street instincts kicked in, and I almost stooped to take the coins and pocket them. I reminded myself that I was Beth, who didn't need to pick up loose change in order to survive. Loser argued that it wasn't a bad idea, just in case. I kicked at the pile with my foot, turning up nickels, dimes, and pennies. For a second something different winked at me and crouching, I sorted gingerly through the broken glass until I located it again: a woman's ring. It was flashy, and if the stones were real, valuable. Taking it to my car, I put it in that little box in the console that no one knows the reason for. At best, the ring would be a memento for Eddie. If I guessed correctly and it commemorated Nadine's engagement to the man he disliked, Eddie could sell it to buy a car or something.

Once I'd satisfied myself that I would remember the details of the spot where Nadine died, I returned to my car and continued up the road. When it split a half mile up, I did the natural thing, bearing right. The fork I chose wound around the mountain and came to a dead end at an old logging site. Here the bushes closed around me, and I saw the berries the guy at the gas station had predicted. I turned the car around, went back to the fork, and took the other road. This one meandered too, but at least there were a few cabins along the way. From what I could tell, they were either completely abandoned or only used to celebrate centennials.

When the road forked a second time, a gate closed off the option directly before me. Above it was a sign: *GoodRich Lodge—Invited Guests Only*. I got out of the car and approached the fence, stopping at the side of the gate where old pine needles had collected, softening the ground underfoot. Up a sandy driveway, I could see the lodge, not exactly the spruced-up version the guy at the gas station had led me to expect. It wasn't falling down or anything, but it was definitely old. Hopgood must have spent his resources on the inside, modernizing and upgrading the living space and leaving the outside in its original form.

I thought about climbing the gate, but I was in plain view of the lodge. If Eddie was hiding in there and didn't want to be found, he'd see me coming and slip out the back and into the woods. In addition to that, there was an old pickup truck parked at one end of the building. If someone other than Eddie were in there, how would I explain my trespassing?

Deciding to do some reconnoitering before I approached head on, I got back in my car and turned to the left, following what was more of a two-track than an actual road. I soon faced another dead end at an open spot in the trees. Along the woods at my right was the fence that protected Hopgood's property. Signs posted every few yards advised against trespassing.

Parking the car off to one side I got out, trying to imagine my location on the map I'd studied. Everything above me was the top of a mountain set apart from its brothers by two rivers I'd observed on the way, wide but shallow and rocky. The forest growth around me was fairly recent; most of the trees were less than fifteen feet tall. There was a lot of laurel, thick-clustering shrubs a foot or so over my head that had taken over when the larger trees were removed. I figured the area had been heavily timbered twenty or thirty years ago and the land sold off afterward. It had probably been a thrill for Hopgood to expand his father's hunting camp until he owned a huge spread with a 360-degree view of the Yew Mountains that only he and his invited guests could share.

What if I went up, knocked at the lodge door, and asked whoever was in there if I could pick berries on their property? They'd most likely say no, but it would give me a look at the lodge, and if there wasn't anyone there, I could explore the place a little and see if there was any sign Eddie had been up here. Gnawing at the problem and my bottom lip as well, I traced the fence line back toward the main gate.

Following a practice I'd developed on the street, I found a spot some distance back from the wooden gate and watched my target to see if anyone was around. The lodge sat silent; the old pickup waited beside it. For a full half hour, nothing happened. Once I'd decided there was no one around I rose, crossed the road, and climbed the fence, sliding over boards rough with age without picking up a single splinter. Once safely on the other side, I proceeded cautiously toward the building.

Situated to take advantage of a flat spot on the mountainside, the lodge was constructed of logs, with cedar shake shingles and a long porch supported by rough-hewn posts. Each post had been carved with fanciful figures: dancing sprites, frowning elves, and animals with human faces, grinning, laughing, and crying. They'd been there a long time, and weather had taken some of the liveliness out of them.

The place had been built in the forties, judging from the CCC-like architecture. Long and low, it was well maintained, but not what anyone would call modern. Recalling Eddie's statement that Rich spent lots of time up here, I decided he must like roughing it. There were no electrical wires overhead, although a metal housing at the far end of the building looked like it might contain a generator.

Approaching a blank wooden door, I knocked. The sound was hollow, and no one came to see what I wanted. I circled the lodge slowly, but there wasn't much to see. The windows were shuttered, the doors firmly latched. The porch showed a few muddy footprints the most recent rain hadn't washed away, but they were boot prints, so they weren't Eddie's or Nadine's. That was the only sign of recent human habitation.

To my right were a couple of unlocked outbuildings, and I wandered over to see what was inside. One held tools for yard work; the other was stacked with old lodge furniture. Dealers in antiques would undoubtedly have drooled over mission-style oak chairs and heavy wood tables. I imagined Hopgood, unconcerned about patinas and such, banishing them in favor of comfy microfiber recliners.

At the back of the lodge was a clearing with targets set up at the far end. Near where I stood were sawhorse-type structures that I guessed served as gun rests. Though not up to the standards of the police academy range, they were adequate for practice shooting. Hopgood and his guests no doubt sighted in their rifles here before setting out to hunt the creatures that roamed these woods.

Along one side of the shooting area was a road that disappeared into the woods. It looked well-traveled, and I guessed the hunters drove to their chosen spots in some kind of all-terrain vehicles.

Turning in a half circle, I listened to the quiet around me. I'd seen the lodge, at least the outside of it. I hadn't found Eddie or any sign of him, and I'd exhausted my options.

It was time to tell the police what I knew and let them start a search. The kid wouldn't like it, but it was in his best interest. The fact that visiting a police station made the muscles of my neck tense had to be ignored. I wanted to help Eddie, despite the objections both of us had to the process.

I glanced around, wondering why Nadine would have come here. Eddie said she'd hated the place, and I understood why she would: rustic setting, antiquated facilities, and masculine, woodsy décor that no doubt included lots of antlers. It wasn't most women's idea of fun, but I knew that for a lot of men, a place like this was perfect. Ignoring society's conventions, wearing the same socks for days, belching as the need arose, some males needed brief periods of anarchy and release from being in charge and under control. I could have told them that living on the street provides the same results without property taxes, but I doubted Hopgood and friends would go for that.

Why had Nadine driven up here on a rainy night when the road was treacherous? To have it out with Rich over whatever it was that sent her running? To ask him for money? To beg him not to have Eddie arrested? Eddie said she didn't drink, and Hopgood had confirmed that. If alcohol had been Nadine's way to get up the courage to face her husband, she'd paid for it with her life.

126

I'd been standing still, caught up in my thoughts, my hand on the rough wooden wall of the shed. In the quiet woods, an alien sound caught my attention. It was very faint, and I probably noticed only because it didn't fit. I couldn't place it at first, but I tuned in, turning until it became a little clearer. It was Indian music—as in Mumbai, not the pow-wow kind.

Curious, I started toward the sound, which came from beyond the wooden gate. Skirting the practice range, I followed the two-track road around a curve. The music came from below me, wafting upward in tinny waves. Cautiously I followed the road and the sound, stopping to peer ahead before rounding each curve. The road bore marks of frequent travel. My path descended, but the face of the mountain rose again ahead of me. It seemed impossible until I realized I was entering a natural valley folded into the crown of the mountain, a pine-scented bowl. Though I'd never been in one before, I knew such features were called *hollows*, or for some, *hollers*.

The trees around me changed. Unlike the re-growth on the outer edge of Hopgood's property, these were huge specimens with trunks angling toward the sharply rising slopes as they clung to the mountain and reached for the sky. No timber men had been allowed to harvest this land. I traveled half a mile, maybe a little more, feeling the descent in my legs. The ground was still wet from the recent rain, and fallen branches and tree trunks littered the ground like black punctuation marks on the forest floor.

The road made an *S,* curving back on itself to make the slope more gradual and accessible to vehicles. Trees blocked my view of what was below, but I discerned the roughly oval shape of the hollow from the encircling land. From the air, it would look like a giant finger had poked a hole in the mountainside. A stream cutting its way downhill was the more likely, though less imaginative, cause.

As I drew closer, my original impression was confirmed. The sound I heard was the tinkle-y, sitar-generated music I associated with *Slumdog Millionaire*. Someone in the area was into Sufi music. The road curved again, and the music stopped, right in the middle of a phrase, as if someone had unplugged the player. The woods went quiet, and I heard nothing for a while. Peering around a substantial pine tree, I saw that the way ahead was blocked by a barrier much more substantial than the board fence I'd climbed to get onto the property.

The fence before me was ten feet high and all metal. Tight cyclone links supported by two-inch galvanized-metal posts were topped with barbed wire extensions that leaned outward to make entering the area more difficult. There was a camera mounted above a sturdy metal gate, a touchpad at one side for entering the code that would open it, and a sign in the middle warning against trespassing.

The barbed wire bothered me. I knew people put up high fences to keep deer inside an area, but this one was designed more to keep people out than to keep animals in. Was Hopgood that paranoid about violators? After seeing the slightly crummy lodge, the high-tech setup here felt out of place. I sat down with my back against a tree, opened my can of soda, and tried to decide what might be going on behind that fence.

The answer, at least a partial one, came strolling along a few minutes later. Hearing a twig crack, I'd scrambled into the foliage and watched as two men passed in front of me, patrolling the fence line. Their bearing suggested military training, though they were dressed casually in jeans and long-sleeved shirts, no doubt chosen for protection as they traversed the woods. In each man's belt, a pistol protruded from a shiny, well-maintained holster. One held binoculars, the strap draped loosely around his neck, and he stopped once to survey the area on my side of the fence through the lenses.

A soft voice called out from behind them. "Don?"

One of the men looked at the other with faint disgust on his face. The second man raised his brows and grinned apologetically.

"Man," the first guy said, "you're gonna get us into trouble."

The other—Don—shrugged. "Can I help it if she's lonely and I'm irresistible?"

"You shouldn't be messing with the clients."

"Just finish the round and wait for me at the last stop. I'll catch up with you."

The first man went on, waving a dismissive hand as if to indicate that he'd done his best. As soon as he was out of sight, Don whistled softly, and out from the trees stepped a figure I couldn't have predicted, though the music should have given me a clue. A girl of about nineteen approached in a manner half shy and half expectant. I pictured the romantic scene she'd set somewhere nearby: a blanket, food and drink, and music to set the mood.

A girl meeting a man in the forest is an old story, but this girl wore a sari in patterns of gold and green, which you don't see often in West Virginia. The man raised his arms with an inviting smile, and she stepped into his embrace. The two of them turned and went deeper into the woods, heads bent toward each other as they talked in low tones.

I did some quick figuring and decided I had at least an hour before time for another patrol. If I wanted to see where the Indian girl and the armed security guards came from—and I did—now was the time.

I was aware of my crimes. I could blame it on my time on the streets, when breaking society's laws is, at times, necessary for survival. I might explain that I'd gotten pretty good at ignoring the legal rights of people who bar others from their property simply because they can. I'd have to admit, however, that my main reason for climbing the fence was curiosity. I kept telling myself Eddie might be in there, or at least what was inside the fence would help me figure out where he was.

EDDIE

My return to Romulus wasn't as fast as I'd have liked. Dale, the sales rep, had stops to make at small medical clinics along the way. Most didn't take that long, but when we finally got to Romulus, office hours were over. He was okay with that. "I'll hit 'em in the morning," he told me, "when people are still in a good mood." He dropped a friendly hand on my shoulder and squeezed. "I can take you right to your front door."

I'd used the prodigal son story with him, and I could tell he wanted to see how my return played out. I imagined him adding my story to his string of monologues, and believe me, he had a million of them. On the drive over, I'd learned that the pharmaceutical industry was misunderstood by the general population, misrepresented by the media, and mistreated by the regulatory agencies of our government. I'd also learned that waitresses respond (wink, wink, nudge, nudge) to a man with a love patch, hotels screw you by charging extra for Wi-Fi and movies, cops target and ticket single drivers in nice cars and nice suits, and picking up hitchhikers wasn't as dangerous as movies make it seem.

"I've been giving people rides for thirteen years," Dale told me. "Only once did I make a mistake." He looked over at me, which he did a lot, though I'd have preferred he watched the road. "I saw this girl hitching and felt sorry for her, you know? So I stop. When I ask where she's headed, she says—" He tapped my arm— "I swear this is true. She says, 'I need to get to Narnia. Aslan sent for me.' True story!"

As he went on about his nutty passenger and how he dumped her at a rest area by pretending to go inside and taking off without her, I could almost hear my story as he'd tell it in days to come: "Once I picked up this kid who'd run away from home. He was looking pretty rough, and I could see he'd been through a lot, so I took him right up to his front door." A great ending would require that Dale see for himself whether the reunion ended in warm hugs or a family fight.

No way did I want him to take me home. "It's across town. I can take the bus from here."

He was going to play good guy whether I wanted him to or not. "It's no big deal, son. I just feel like I should drive you."

To solve the problem, I directed him to the house of a kid I knew from school. It was in a bad neighborhood, and I knew there wouldn't be anyone at home. Both Jerry and his mom worked at a movie theater, where their shift started at four and ended at midnight. Jerry's mom did the scheduling, and she set it up that way so he didn't miss school and they could ride together. Jerry was always tired and had a rough time getting to his first-period class on time, but he got to see all the new movies for free, so it was worth it.

Jerry's house wasn't impressive like Dickweed Mansion. Dale might wonder why I'd left the house on James Madison Circle, but any kid might run from a ratty, green-coated house like Jerry's.

It was tricky getting him to leave me there. He waited out front, craning his neck to see who came to the door. I couldn't just walk into someone else's house, and there was no one to answer if I knocked. I solved the problem by going around to the back, waiting a few seconds, and then returning to give an "It's okay!" salute. Dale hesitated, but I moved out of sight like I was going inside. Soon, I heard the engine clunk into drive and pull away. *Aaaaah. Alone at last.*

Chapter Twelve

LOSER

I walked along GoodRich Lodge's inner fence, looking for a tree with at least one branch that was close to the ground and others higher up that extended over the fence. In Richmond, we'd found a certain live oak next to the walled back garden of an expensive restaurant. More than once, I'd climbed the tree after midnight and let its overhanging branches set me down inside the wall, where I'd passed whatever edibles I could find to my friends and then let myself out the gate. I'd been popular those nights, being light and limber enough to accomplish a feat that benefited the whole group.

About fifty yards down the fence line I located a tree suitable for my purpose, a big, old pine whose lowest branch was just within reach. I had to jump several times before I got a handhold, but once I got a grip on the rough surface, I pulled my body up, clamped my feet around it, and twisted myself to a sitting position.

Pines aren't fun to climb. They're sticky, they have lots of little pointy places, and their branches are close together, making it hard to maneuver upward. I managed to get to a point where I was about six feet above the top of the fence. The branch felt sturdy, but it was nerve-racking to sidle away from the trunk, listening for a crack that signaled it was about to break under me. I scanned the ground constantly, worried about the patrols. It would be hard to explain to them what I was doing up there in broad daylight.

The branch wobbled under my feet, but it was springy, not brittle. Using the branches above me to take some of my weight, I continued with tiny, crab-like side steps. After what seemed like hours, I was past the barbed wire extensions, and the fence itself was directly below me. The branch under my feet bent to almost touching the metal, and the branches I held onto had thinned to little more than twigs. The tree wouldn't hold me much longer.

Letting go of the upper branches in an abrupt movement, I crouched and grabbed the lower branch with both hands. The jolt caused my feet to slip, but that was part of the plan. The branch swept downward under my full weight, and I caught myself with my arms, hanging suspended long enough to prevent a headlong tumble to the ground. My shoulders protested at the sudden wrench, but other than that, I landed safely, bending my knees and catching myself with my hands.

I hurried away from there, fearful that at any moment the guard's tête-à-tête with his lady friend would end and he'd hurry by to catch up with his partner. Angling toward the gate, I looked for the road I'd seen on the other side. It had to lead to something, and without direction, I might wander around in circles all afternoon. When I saw the road ahead I moved parallel to it, listening for sounds of human activity. Half an hour ago, I'd thought I was exploring a deserted hunting lodge. This was something else.

The road continued to descend, but the slope became gentler. Trees rising on all sides muted sound and outlined the hollow. From what I could tell, I had entered an elongated bowl with steep sides and a relatively flat bottom.

Lost in imagining the topography, I came around a bend and almost blundered into a large open space. Scrambling into cover, I maneuvered sideways through the trees, cringing at each snapped twig and crushed leaf underfoot. Leaving only a few bits of myself on the bushes as I passed I cut through, trying to see into the open area without being seen. Through the branches I caught glimpses of something that was part Holiday Inn and part maximum-security prison, except it was hidden in the middle of nowhere.

Another ring of cyclone fencing, this time fifteen feet high, enclosed a space the size of a football field. The metal uprights were at least thirty feet high, and on each, about halfway up, a surveillance camera pointed down and outward. In addition to fencing and cameras, the posts supported a huge canopy of netting covered with greenery. From above the place would appear to be unbroken line of treetops, and the presence of the hollow would remain a secret. Another sturdy metal gate closed off the only visible entrance, which had a little guardhouse just inside it. From my hiding spot I could see the top half of a beefy young man whose head was bent almost to his chest as he fiddled with an electronic device that wasn't doing what he wanted it to do. He jabbed at it with a finger, jabbed again, shook it, and finally slapped it in frustration. The scene might have been funny, but the AK-47 slung over his shoulder took all the fun out of it.

I surveyed the woods behind me, wondering if I'd unwittingly passed a camera. It was a bad feeling, the sense that I might already be caught on tape. Still, the guy in the guardhouse didn't seem the least bit concerned with what might be outside the fence.

Forcing myself to remain where I was, I considered the possibilities. I didn't know a lot about the technology of spying on people, but my former partner on the police force, Jake, had done some moonlighting for a company called MaXXimum Security. I tried to recall what he'd told me about surveillance.

"It looks easy in the movies," Jake had said. "And there's all this equipment out there that really can do cool stuff. However, it isn't exactly cheap, and it can be tricky to maintain outdoors. Most people make do with some basic pieces." He'd explained that security cameras require constant monitoring. Motion detectors sound their alarm at any movement, whether it's a man or a dog that passes by. Wind, rain, or temperature extremes can corrode or damage equipment. "People are the best option for security," Jake maintained. "They go out and investigate, where a machine just tells you something's happening." Scratching his head, he'd added, "Of course, people also lose interest, fall asleep, or stay inside because they're lazy. Your best bet for securing property is a combination of the two." Having seen the cameras and the men on patrol, I hugged a scaly tree trunk and hoped Hopgood's men had gotten lazy and he hadn't gone too high tech with equipment.

Exactly what combination of man and machine had Hopgood chosen? The fact that I'd gotten past two gates without being caught suggested electronic surveillance was concentrated on the inner compound. Purchasing and maintenance costs would dictate that he protect the smallest area possible with the highest-tech equipment.

The girl I'd seen earlier hadn't acted like a prisoner, and the other guard had referred to her as a client. That indicated the people inside the compound paid to be there, to be guarded and kept secret from the locals. I recalled the woman at the gas station mentioning celebrities seeking privacy. This place was certainly private, but armed guards gave me the feeling its purpose was more than privacy and probably less than legal. The setting was lovely, at least if you discounted the fences and the guys with guns.

The canopy provided a shield but also cooling shelter from the sun. Random bits of sunlight penetrated the green, lighting spots on the ground with dappling exactly as it did through real foliage. The building inside the fence was downright luxurious compared to the old lodge out front. It resembled a Frank Lloyd Wright library, with flat roofs on two levels and decorative flourishes on the corners.

As I watched, two men and a woman exited the building with the air of people with things to do. They were dressed casually, but they seemed faintly military with straight backs, crisp movements, and alert eyes. At one side of the compound was a raised wooden tower that allowed a view of the whole area, both inside the fence and out. A man and a woman stood inside, AK-s slung across their backs. Using binoculars, they periodically swept the area with slow deliberation. When they turned to where I was concealed, I had a hard time staying put. I thought I was invisible behind what might have been elderberry bushes, but my muscles tensed of their own accord, ready, even anxious, to run.

Once the binoculars had moved on, I got another surprise. The door of the main lodge opened, and out stepped two women. Like the girl I'd seen earlier, they wore saris, one a brilliant orange and the other with colors from red to purple. One was young, maybe seventeen, and the other was older. They leaned together, arms around each other's waists, and the girl said something to the woman as one of the men passed. The reply seemed faintly admonishing, and the girl giggled self-consciously. The man paid them no attention whatsoever. *More clients?*

Sauntering idly, the women crossed the yard and sat down in some lawn chairs set at a table. Lighting a cigarette, the girl smoked and talked, casting glances at each man who came within view. The older woman seemed disapproving, waving the smoke away from her face repeatedly and even coughing in a theatrical manner. Still, conversation flowed back and forth between them. A mother whose daughters were beyond her control? One smoked in front of her while the other carried on in the woods with one of the men assigned to protect them.

Eventually the women returned inside, and after that, nothing of interest happened. People moved in and out of the building, but their activities weren't sinister. They spoke to each other; they carried things from here to there. I didn't see any surface-to-air missiles or large numbers of armed soldiers drilling in the yard. I counted twenty people in total, including the two in saris and a couple of women with a linen cart who were probably maids. It was the secrecy of the place itself that felt wrong. I had no idea what to make of it.

As my knees started to ache from supporting my weight in a locked position, it occurred to me for the first time that I should be afraid. Beth's cop mind had brought me here, but having seen the place, Loser's fears began to undermine curiosity. No matter what the purpose of the compound was, I wasn't supposed to be there. The longer I stayed, the more chance I would be discovered. I'd come to find Eddie but saw no sign of him. I wanted to go, and the feeling of *needing* to go grew stronger by the second. I began to retreat, moving slowly to avoid drawing attention.

By the time I was away from the compound, Loser was imagining men with guns behind every tree. It had been a mistake to come here, a mistake to stay so long. There would be another patrol by now. I would step directly into their path, being Loser the loser. For the first time in months, the voices in my head took over.

Loser! What did you think you were doing?

They'll find you and arrest you! How will you like spending the next six months locked up? How will you sleep in a cell, Loser?

I began to run, cutting through the trees on an angle I vaguely hoped would bring me back to the place where I'd come in. It would have been better to go slowly, but fear wouldn't let me. I wanted out. I ran and ran, ignoring the branches that swept across my face and tugged at my clothes. Nothing mattered but getting out, regaining freedom, reclaiming my anonymous existence.

When I came to the fence, I climbed it in a burst of desperation, using my hands, feet, and momentum to carry me to the top of one of the uprights. Grabbing the cap, I hauled myself onto the fence, sitting painfully on the uneven surface with my legs hanging down. Slowly I pulled one leg up, twisted my body, and set it onto the metal rod supporting the barbed wire extension. Once it was in place, I moved the hand on that side over my leg and grabbed the fence top, which allowed me to bring the other foot up and onto the rail. With both feet on the rod, I pulled one hand forward and grasped the wire strand between barbs. Getting the other hand over was trickier, since I had to shift my weight forward and push myself onto my feet using only arm strength. Crouched like a big turkey vulture, I found new respect for the birds' their sense of balance. It isn't easy to remain on a pole two feet long and an inch in diameter. Once I was fairly stable, I looked down. The ground, ten feet below, seemed both inviting and threatening. Reminding myself that a guard might come along at any second, I shifted my hands and fell forward, doing a clumsy somersault. I smacked the fence with my back as the wire sagged and squealed, but I managed to hang on. Kicking my feet, I pushed myself outward and dropped, rolling like a parachute jumper as I landed to cushion my fall. After a few seconds to recover, I was running again, heading at an angle through the woods, in the direction I was pretty sure the old lodge would be.

The woods opened suddenly, sending me stumbling as the resistance of tree branches across my path disappeared. I'd returned to the road. It rose to my right, indicating that was the correct direction. Having a clear path and a sure destination, I ran with renewed energy, with the long strides my long-ago softball coach had advised. The vague dread that I might meet someone coming in was easily superseded by the fear of someone with a gun coming out. There was one advantage to panic: my breath pounded so hard in my ears that I couldn't hear the voices anymore.

When I reached the shooting range, I stopped, hands resting on my knees as I sucked air in noisily. It was still quiet there. The old pickup rested in the sun, ticking as the heat expanded its surfaces. The building still looked deserted and faintly sad, but I knew now that it was a set piece, hiding the reality beyond it. I jogged across the yard, hopped the fence in one quick movement, and landed on the outside with a sigh of relief. No one could arrest me for trespassing anymore. I was simply a curious visitor on the correct side of the fence.

I staggered to my car and sat for a few moments, exhausted by my adventure. Finally I fumbled with the key, started the engine, turned around, and headed down the mountain. I must have looked in the rearview mirror a hundred times as I navigated the turns and twists that led back to the highway. There was nothing.

At least, there was nothing behind me. At the spot where the road's last fork came back together, a truck blocked the road and a man stood beside it, looking relaxed. I had no choice but to stop. Rolling down the car window I leaned out, one hand on the frame and the other tense on the gearshift. "Problem?"

He smiled apologetically and pointed into the woods. "I saw a couple of deer and got out to take a closer look."

I didn't recognize him at first. The truck was a dark green Ford with lots of chrome and a faint coating of dust. I waited, but he didn't get in and move out of my way. Instead, he set one foot on the running board and studied me with a fair amount of interest.

He was about forty, with blond hair dulled by a few gray streaks. His blue eyes crinkled when he smiled, but they didn't convey any warmth. He wore jeans and a black T-shirt that showed off a flat stomach and well-muscled arms.

It was his boots that triggered my memory. I recalled seeing them before, remembered the sound they'd made on my porch in Beulah. It had been at a distance and several months ago, but this man had come looking for Marta, claiming he knew one of her foster children.

Nadine. I glanced at the road ahead, wondering if I could take the narrow shoulder and maneuver my car around him. If he was up to something, I didn't want to stick around and find out what.

"Excuse me for askin', but are you lost?" He spoke softly, smiling as if to indicate he was no threat. I wondered how terrified I looked. Probably near the top of the chart.

I gave him my pre-fabricated excuse. "Berrying."

He nodded as if I'd said something very wise. "They're good this year. Have any luck?"

This was probably the part where the proud berry-picker was expected to display a bucket full of fruit. Not only did I not have any berries, I didn't even have a bucket. "Got scared off. Bear, I think."

Another nod. "Yeah, they like berries as much as people do."

I met his eyes directly, hoping he'd get that I was waiting for him to let me pass. He seemed unaffected, surveying the greenery around us in a leisurely fashion. "You from the city?"

I shook my head. "Florida." Tourists from Florida are everywhere these days.

He still didn't move. I watched him, my gut tense. Behind him I noticed the logo on the truck door: *Goodrich Lodge*.

It was my turn to ask a question. "You live up here?"

He glanced up the road I'd just traveled. "I manage a hunting lodge for a local businessman." He pointed at the truck door. "Did you see it up there?"

I kept my face blank as I shook my head. "Didn't go up too far."

His left eyebrow shifted slightly, and I knew I should have admitted I'd gone by the place. He'd see my tire tracks and know I lied. I'd be gone by then though, one way or another.

I glanced ahead again. I thought I could get around the truck, and he'd have to turn around before he could come after me.

He slid his foot off the running board with an abrupt scrape, surprising me so that I jumped a little. "I'm holding you up with my daydreaming." He got into the truck, started the engine, and pulled forward, opening the way for me. As I passed, he called out teasingly, "Watch out for bears!"

It seemed to be a form of entertainment for the locals, warning tourists about the dangers of wildlife.

I waved and went on, keeping my speed down until the next turn. Glancing in the rearview mirror, I saw him start up the mountain. After only a few yards, he hit the brakes and turned sharply left. I wondered briefly if he was going to turn around and follow me, but after a few seconds, he straightened his wheels and continued upward.

After I made a turn that hid me from view, I drove as fast as I dared down to the main highway. The encounter didn't feel right, but I was free to return to Romulus. Whatever the secret of GoodRich Lodge was, apparently, no one thought I was a threat to it.

Chapter Thirteen

EDDIE

I took Jerry's bike, figuring I'd get it back before he knew it was gone. He's not the kind of guy who'd call the cops or anything anyway.

Wheeling through the side streets, I realized I had a problem. What came next? You can say you're going to go somewhere and do something, but lots of times when you get there, the doing part is harder than it seems.

When I got to the house, Dickweed's car was in the garage. In the driveway behind it was the black Hummer. I ditched the bike in a hedge along the front of what used to be Purple Pants' house. I never knew the guy's name, but he'd worked in his yard all the time wearing the same disgusting pants. One day he was gone, and the house was up for sale. That was a lucky thing for me, cuz I could watch Dickweed from behind the sweet-smelling cedars Purple Pants had spent so much time tending.

Nothing happened that was worth watching. After a while, a guy came out of the house that I recognized as one of the guys from the lodge. He might have been in a little bit of a hurry, but not much. He got into the Hummer and backed out of the driveway, not mad or upset or particularly evil looking, just on his way to do something. Following his master's orders.

No more action, and I found myself wishing I'd stopped on the way over and got some take-out. What was I doing here, anyway? Spying on Dickweed, yeah, but why?

I called myself all kinds of names. Had I expected him to stand on the front porch, drooling and babbling, "I did it! I killed her!"

It got dark. I thought about creeping up to look in the windows and see what he was doing, but the lights downstairs went off, and the chance passed. I sat there, feeling the grass go cool under my rear and trying to make a plan. What if I called and told him I knew he'd killed my mother? That would scare him, and maybe he'd do something stupid.

I'd have to call from a pay phone, though, since mine had been stolen. The only one I knew of nearby was the dinosaur at the back of Minelli's Deli, which was closed by now. I'd have to wait until morning.

In the meantime, I was stuck there on Purple Pants' overgrown lawn. I stretched out on the grass, thinking that Loser must have done this lots of times. It was a first for me, sleeping outside, having nobody know or care where I was. It wasn't a great feeling. I kind of missed Loser, who seemed to understand a lot though she didn't say much. I even missed Mabel, who said a lot, but—who knew how much Mabel understood?

LOSER

I registered at the local Quality Inn, counting out in twenties the extra deposit required of those who pay with cash. Once I'd tossed my duffle bag on the bed I went off to look for dinner, since my hot dog from the gas station was long gone. I had a choice among three cheap chains and one almost upscale one. I went for the latter and was escorted to my seat by a hostess who rattled off the specials of the day like they were her children's birthdays.

Less than a minute later, a woman informed me that her name was Bobbi and she'd be taking care of me this evening. My caregiver provided a glass of water to start me off and later brought my order, a chicken breast smothered in cheese and some kind of crispy noodles. It was pretty good, though not as good as what I'd have made at home. Of course, the manager wandered by to ask how my meal tasted. I resisted the urge to tell her I'd eaten far worse in my days on the street.

Returning to the motel, I watched a few innings of baseball without much caring who won. The most interesting thing I saw was a commercial spot for Hopgood Motors. There on the screen was Richard Hopgood in full camo, shouting about hunting down the best deals. He looked like a maniac, quite different from the man I'd observed today.

Somebody had to believe such craziness sold cars, but I'd never met anyone who did until today. It was hard to reconcile the grinning buffoon on the ads with the stunned husband who'd begged the sheriff to find his stepson. Maybe other car dealers acted like normal people off camera too.

When night descended, I began preparing to leave. Yes, I'd rented a motel room, but no, I didn't plan to sleep inside. I rumpled the bed, used the toilet, took one of my four pillows, and got the extra blanket from the overhead shelf in the closet. After peering out to make sure I didn't run into a member of the motel staff, I slipped out the back door with my borrowed items.

I'd parked my car in a far corner of the lot, next to the odiferous trash bin, a spot few people choose. I'd never tried sleeping in a car, which is kind of inside, kind of not, but I figured if I couldn't doze off in the back seat, I could use the Buick for cover and sleep next to the trash bin. Like old times.

Right away, my plan encountered a problem. On the trash bin side of my car, a man lay on his back, reaching under the fender with one hand as if he was trying to locate something.

"Hey!" My shout caused him to jerk in surprise, and he swore as his head bumped against the rocker panel. With no more than a glance in my direction he jumped to his feet, pushed off the car with one hand, and lurched into some spindly trees that separated one parking lot from the next. By the time I recovered and followed him through, he had disappeared. I didn't even get a good look at him, just a guy in khakis and a light shirt.

I scanned the area, wondering what he'd been doing to my car. I'd heard of people losing catalytic converters to thieves, but that guy hadn't had any tools. I guessed the incident was linked to my recent visit to GoodRich Lodge, though I didn't understand it.

How had they found me? The road from Cranville to Romulus was fairly open, and I'd have seen anyone following.

Lying down in the same place the man had been when I spotted him, I felt the underside of the fender. Sure enough, there was an alien lump at the rear. I couldn't see it in the dark, but my fingers recognized the feel of duct tape. I pulled the lump away and found a cell phone, the no-frills kind, wrapped in the tape. I guessed it was untraceable, but cell phones have GPS. That was how they'd located me.

I thought back to my encounter with the guy in the pickup. He'd been stalling, I realized, to allow time for someone, probably the guy I'd chased off, to sneak up and tape the phone to my car. The braking I'd seen as I drove away was the driver stopping to pick up his passenger. Mission accomplished.

Crouched between the car and the trash, I tried to gauge how much trouble I was in. The people at GoodRich Lodge suspected I'd been on their land; that was obvious. I hoped they didn't know I'd made it to the compound, but I was pretty sure I'd avoided the surveillance cameras.

No matter what was going on up there, they couldn't simply kill everyone who drove up the mountain road to the property. I might have been the clueless, innocent berry-picker I'd pretended to be, and they probably wouldn't have minded if I'd sneaked in, explored the old lodge, and left. However, the compound in the hollow, guarded by guns and cameras, was meant to be a secret. They'd want to know if I'd seen it, and if I had, they'd want to stop me before I told anyone about it. What would they have done once they'd retrieved the phone? Kill me? Threaten me? Watch to see what I did next? It must have been frustrating for them, not knowing who I was and what I was after.

I was beginning to think Nadine's flight had less to do with her feelings for Rich and more to do with what she knew about him and his secret place.

My neck began to prickle with the feeling that someone was watching, and I turned to see if anyone was looking my way. As I did, a glint inside the car caught my eye. The ring I'd picked up at the accident scene caught and reflected the security light's beam, which added to my dread. If they'd seen Nadine's ring in my car, the berry-picker scenario was much less believable. I looked around again. Finding the phone they'd planted didn't mean I was safe. If Nadine had died because she found out about the compound, and if I was connected to Nadine, the people at the lodge would see me as a threat. If they'd already killed once, they had nothing to lose in killing me.

After wiping away my finger prints, I attached the phone to the metal side of the trash bin with the still-sticky tape, got into my car and drove away, watching behind me for a green pickup or a black Hummer.

I saw neither as I zigzagged through the streets of Romulus, checking the rearview mirror and turning at the last second to watch for anyone doing the same. No one was following. They probably hadn't expected me to find the bug. A normal person would have gone back inside the motel and reported the incident. Little did they know.

Satisfied that I was once again anonymous, I pulled into an all-night drugstore parking lot to think. I would not leave town without knowing that Eddie was all right. If Hopgood was crooked, as I now believed he was, it was possible he'd killed his wife. If Nadine's knowledge of her husband's crimes was the reason he'd desperately searched for her all summer, it was also why he was now desperately searching for Eddie. If he'd murdered Nadine to keep her from telling what she knew, he'd assume that Eddie was a threat as well. Recalling what he'd told the sheriff, I wondered if he'd invented stories of Eddie's dishonesty to discredit anything the kid might tell the police.

My mind made it worse. If Eddie had reached Romulus and gone to his former home to confront his stepfather, he might already be dead.

The thought made my gut wrench. Another person I'd been charged with caring for, another failure on my part.

I forced my mind away from the sort of hopeless thinking that could only lead back to self-destructive behavior. Eddie might still be alive. He might be in the city somewhere or still making his way south. Even if Hopgood had caught him, which was likely given the kid's inexperience, could he murder his stepson so soon after his wife's death?

Wouldn't he need to show the boy alive at least once in order to stop the three-month police search and answer the questions in the minds of the public?

Hopgood, a man used to manipulating people, might try to convince Eddie to accept his mother's death as an accident, maybe with logic, maybe with bribes. That was a slightly happier thought to concentrate on. If Hopgood had Eddie, and if he was alive, a secret compound in the woods was the perfect place for brainwashing. If Eddie was up there, I had to convince the police to free him.

Around midnight I returned to the business strip, passed the Quality Inn where I'd rented the room, and pulled in at the Super8 next door. My pursuers didn't know my name, and one silver car looks a lot like another. When no police arrived, I hoped they'd conclude I'd gotten scared and left Romulus. That way, they'd return to whatever no good they were up to on the mountain.

As I filled out a second motel registration form, using my old Richmond address and giving fake license numbers, I told myself I didn't need to stay. I could contact the police anonymously. They could ride to Eddie's rescue while I headed north to Beulah and forgot the whole thing. It didn't work though. I wanted to be close, wanted to assure myself that the cops followed through on the information I'd provided.

Of course I didn't sleep in my second hotel room. Heading out the back door, I stole to my car, where the blanket and pillow from motel #1 awaited me. Stretching out on the back seat, I tried to organize what

147

I knew. Nadine returned to Romulus and ended up dead. Hopgood, who seemed broken up about it, had things going on at his hunting lodge that were probably illegal. If Nadine had tried to blackmail her husband, she'd badly misjudged his capabilities. I couldn't make the same mistake.

The car seat made a cool and comfortable bed. My spinning thoughts quieted, and I slept. I guess the inside of a car isn't really inside. Or maybe at that point, it didn't matter anymore.

EDDIE

I woke up cold and stiff, understanding for the first time in my life what old people mean when they say it takes a while to get going in the morning. I knew right away where I was, and all the crap from yesterday and the plans I'd made spun around in my head. I wondered what time it was and spent a few seconds cussing out the guy who'd taken my phone and my money.

Standing up, I checked the street. The houses were all quiet, though there were a few lights on. I saw cars in some of the driveways and a Beemer parked on the street a block away. Our garage door was closed, but there were lights on in the kitchen. Dickweed was up but hadn't left home yet.

It was too early for Minelli's Deli to be open. I thought about asking a neighbor to let me use their phone, but people here knew I'd been missing for three months. The first thing they'd do was call the cops. Mom's friend Marie might listen to me, but if her husband came to the door, I'd be in a cop car before I said two words. I needed to get away from the place where everyone knew me.

I turned to pick up Jerry's bike, but as I bent to grab the handlebars, I felt a hand grip my shoulder. A man's voice spoke, and I knew I was in trouble. "We need to talk, son."

LOSER

The next morning I returned to my original motel, slipping in at a quarter to six when the clerk on duty was busy setting up the deluxe continental breakfast. I went up to the room I'd rented, showered, put on the other outfit I'd brought along, packed my things, and went back downstairs. I checked the lobby. No one there but the clerk and an older woman who'd served herself and was watching CNN. Breakfast was a nice surprise: the fruit was fresh, there was yogurt, and the coffee didn't taste like battery acid.

The hotel had a computer desk set up in the lobby for guests' use. Before I had breakfast, I went online, found the "Contact Us" section for the local sheriff's department, and typed in this message: *You should investigate the GoodRich Lodge. Weird stuff goes on up there.* After a moment, I added, *Don't stop at the old building. There's more behind it.* I considered signing it, "A Friend," but that sounded tacky. I left it unsigned.

I ate my bagel and had a second cup of coffee and some orange juice. When I'd finished, I checked out, crossed two parking lots, and entered the Super8 again. I could have had a second breakfast, but instead I went upstairs and stashed my things in my room. On the way out I extended my stay for a second night, which seemed to make the desk clerk happy.

I approached my car cautiously, but no one lurked behind it. I looked across the parking lot at the entrance to the other motel. If the guys who'd tracked me here came back, they had no way of knowing I'd simply moved next door. I hoped they'd found their phone on the trash bin and concluded I'd left town.

As I worked to convince myself I'd outwitted the bad guys, a patrol car pulled up at the inn. Two officers got out, hiked their heavy belts into place, and headed inside as if they meant business. Chances were good that the local police had traced my message about GoodRich Lodge to the motel's computer. Eager to know what their reaction would be, I told myself it was safe to eavesdrop. The cops couldn't know who'd sent the message, and the clerk would assume I was waiting for a taxi. I sauntered in, picked up a brochure, and pretended to be absorbed in the wonders of Tamarack.

The two men in uniform stood at the desk, talking to a clerk who was not the one I'd seen at breakfast. One cop was young, skinny, and freckled; the other was paunchy and tired-looking. He was the spokesman. The kid stood back a step, hands on his hips.

"I can't help you," the clerk was saying. "The computer is out of sight when we're setting up the breakfast room." There was a hint of objection to that duty in her tone.

"So you don't know who used the computer this morning?"

"I didn't come on till eight. Duane was here. He might have seen someone."

"Have you got a phone number for him?"

The woman turned aside, and I heard plastic sheets flip as she looked up her colleague's information. "Did somebody send pornography to the White House or something?"

"Nothing like that." The cop's tone hinted she should abandon her questions.

Getting the idea, the woman wrote the information on a slip of paper and handed it over. "You should call right away. He'll be going to sleep soon, and he'll probably shut the phone off. I would."

"Thanks." This time the tone was disapproving. He didn't like being told what to do.

It looked like they were leaving, so I slipped out the door and took a seat on a bench at the front. Again I studied the pamphlet, learning that Tamarack was an economic development site for craftspeople of the state, where artists and artisans could sell their work in a beautiful, welcoming setting. Mabel might like to see that. Maybe we could drive over there one day this fall.

When the cops came outside, they stopped to reconnoiter, as I'd hoped they would. "We gonna call the guy?" Skinny asked Paunchy.

"Yeah, but I ain't holding my breath we're gonna track this messenger down."

"Don't sound like they pay attention to who uses the PC," Skinny said. "We could dust it for prints."

"How many people you think have touched that thing since six o'clock this morning? And whoever it was wiped the keyboard if he has a brain in his head, anyway."

I do and I did, I told them silently.

"I don't get why somebody's trying to get Mr. Hopgood in trouble," Skinny said. "The guy's got enough goin' on right now without having cops running all over his property."

"Ain't gonna be any cops up there," Paunchy told him. "I seen the place. Ain't nothing bad goin' on."

"How'd you get in there? It's private."

"Hopgood lets anybody on the force do target shooting up there a couple times a year." Paunchy wheezed what might have been a chuckle. "He's real proud of the place, but I hafta say, it ain't much. A few bales of hay and some sawhorses to stand behind. What's nice is the spread he puts on when we go up there, a big ol' picnic. Anything you want to eat and lots to drink too."

"Really?" Skinny went around the car and got in the driver's seat, which I hadn't expected. Maybe his partner was too lazy to drive. "You think I can go next time?"

"Sure." Paunchy got into the car, letting out a grunt as he landed. "Hopgood did two tours in Iraq, and he's a good guy. We're s'posed to check out the anonymous complaint, which we did. It's just so much bull—"

That was all I heard, because he shut the car door, but I got it. They'd done their duty, investigated the message, and closed the case.

I rose and watched the car pull away. Hopgood was smart, using free food and booze to build camaraderie with local cops. I'd never get them to investigate with email messages, and it was unlikely I'd convince them in person, being a stranger to the area and unable to provide a complete explanation. I might try a bigger, more objective organization, like the FBI or Homeland Security, but I doubted my ability to convince them either. They're used to dealing with crackpots and conspiracy theorists, and I was likely to be dismissed as one of those, especially if they looked up my background. All I would achieve was a delay in my own efforts to find Eddie.

The next step was up to me, but I struggled against the idea of playing the part of rescuer. I was better at running and hiding from life than I was at taking on evil. If Eddie had appeared beside me, I'd have loaded him in the car, driven straight home, and pretended Rich Hopgood never existed. That's what the Homeless Hero wanted to do: run.

That wasn't an option. I needed to find out what Hopgood was doing that he didn't want the world to know about. I had to get some sort of proof that would force the police to investigate and rescue Eddie if that was still possible. I had to go back up there. My legs shook a little as I made the decision, and I sank back down on the hard plastic bench, letting myself get used to the idea. I was scared, but I was also angry and even curious. I rose and started for my car, holding my legs steady with firm command by reminding myself that a loser has nothing to lose. If criminals caught and killed me, who would honestly care? And if they didn't, I'd find Eddie and take him somewhere safe.

Scanning the parking lot, I saw no one watching my car or paying particular attention to me. I'd lost the guys who'd trailed me to Romulus, and I figured I was safe for today. There wasn't much chance they'd think to look for me at the local library.

CHAPTER FOURTEEN

Seated in the same quiet corner I'd occupied the day before, with a bag of peanut M&M's in my pocket for sustenance, I read everything I could find in the local papers about Rich Hopgood, Nadine Forsythe Hopgood, and Eddie Forsythe. Eddie, a better than average relay runner, was mentioned for his participation in a couple of track meets. Nadine got no press until she started seeing the wealthy Richard Hopgood. At first columnists seemed faintly disapproving, but things changed once Hopgood married her. Suddenly, she was "the lovely Mrs. Rich" and "stunning Nadine Hopgood." Pictures showed a couple who apparently had it all: money, looks, and charm. Nadine, incorrigible foster child and truck thief, had come a long way from where she began.

Hopgood was a local boy who'd inherited his father's good business and made it into a string of excellent businesses. The papers loved everything he did, probably due to the charitable donations he made to just about every organization in Romulus. In all the pictures I found of him, he was smiling. Shaking hands, raising a glass, or handing over a check, Rich smiled as if there was nowhere else on Earth he'd rather be. Not one reporter had the nerve to make fun of his tacky advertisements. Instead they were deemed "inventive" and "original." Maybe Rich donated to the Newspapermen's Orphan Fund along with all his other good works.

The morning wore away as I pored over library records. It felt good to sit there, as I'd often done in Richmond, and let the outside world fade away for a while. I'd started visiting libraries to escape rain, heat, or cold, but they turned into comfort zones for me. The hushed footsteps, the low voices, and slaps of book cover on book cover were restful. I might even have napped, waiting for the day to pass. There's no better way to wait, in my humble opinion, than a light snooze in a quiet library.

EDDIE

When the man grabbed me, my first thought was to slip out of his grasp and take off, but three things stopped me. First, he had a pretty strong grip. Second, he didn't look like one of Dickweed's outdoor he-man types. Third, there wasn't anywhere to run to.

What he said was, "Do you want to go get some breakfast?"

That was easy. I was pretty close to starving to death. But *want* isn't the same as *will*. He seemed to know I was undercover. Pointing at the Beemer down the block, he said, "I'll pull into this driveway like I'm turning around. You can get in and stay down till we get out of the circle."

Now I'm not totally stupid. I know how men get kids into their cars and what happens afterward. "I don't think so, pervert."

He actually grinned. "It's totally up to you, but Mabel says you like pancakes, and I saw an IHOP a few blocks from here."

His name was Alex Bronson, and he worked for some lawyer in Richmond. On the way to the restaurant, he said he'd gone to Beulah to see Loser—he called her Beth—and Mabel told him everything. I shuddered a little to think what the old lady might have added for color commentary, but he seemed to have the basics right. "You want to know what happened to your mother. Beth wants to know that you're okay. I'd like to help you both out, if I can."

Bronson saved his questions till after we'd entered the IHOP, got our seats, and ordered. I eyed the bargain menu, remembering my low budget, but he said, "This is my treat. I want to see how much a guy like you can put away." I appreciated that he didn't say "a growing boy."

As the waitress wrote my order down, my stomach growled real loud in anticipation of Belgian waffles, bacon, and a side of fries. "And a Coke." Bronson frowned a little. "Please," I added, and the frown went away.

After she left to put our orders in, Bronson explained why he'd come. "You probably know Beth has trouble communicating," he said, adding with a grin, "I don't. Romulus isn't that far out of my way back to Richmond, so I figured I'd stop and talk with your stepfather." I'd got a glimpse of his phone when he checked his messages, and it was awesome. I bet he found Dickweed's address with it. In fact, he could've found the combination to Fort Knox on that thing. "I'd just pulled up outside your house when I saw you peeking through the hedge across the street."

Guess I wasn't as careful as I'd thought. "Mabel described you pretty well," Bronson said. "I thought I'd be helping Beth find you, but it worked out the other way around." He stirred a packet of sugar into his coffee. "Any idea where she might be?"

I had none, but it felt good to know she'd come looking for me. Maybe I wasn't as alone as I'd thought.

The waitress brought our food, and we spent some time getting it ready, me adding salt to everything and Bronson buttering the toast that came with his omelet. As we ate, he asked about my mom's decision to leave Romulus. It was kind of a relief to tell somebody the whole thing, so I started with her pulling me out of school and ended with her leaving me with Loser and Mabel.

Bronson asked why she might have gone back to Rich.

"I think she got mad," I said. "At first, she was scared, but later, she talked about how it wasn't fair that some people get away with stuff all the time."

"You think she came here to confront your stepfather."

"Yeah." I guessed she'd wanted money, but I didn't try to explain that to Bronson. It made her sound greedy, but I understood. She'd spent four years of her life with that arrogant poser, and she ended up with nothing. "He must have asked her to meet him at the lodge." I shook my head. "She didn't realize what he was capable of."

Bronson's expression was kind of blank, and I wondered if I'd lost him. It's one thing to say your stepfather is a jerk. It's something else to convince people he's a murderer. Instead of commenting he went back to the reason we left Romulus. "You don't know what she saw?"

"No. But there was blood." I told him about Mom's shoes and blouse.

Bronson digested that, taking a few bites of his omelet. "Why didn't she go to the police, I wonder?"

"That's why I thought—" I stopped to think about what I was about to say. It couldn't hurt her now, what I'd thought at first, and I'd been wrong anyway. "I thought she'd, um, hurt Di—Rich. Now, I think she saw something he did to someone else, and she was afraid to tell anyone."

"Why?"

I shrugged. "He's pretty tight with the local cops. She probably thought they wouldn't believe her."

Bronson leaned against the wall of the booth. "Maybe he threatened to hurt you if she told."

It felt like the truth, though I hadn't thought of it myself. Mom had been so paranoid about getting me away from Romulus. For a long time she hadn't let me out of her sight. She'd kept hugging me too, which wasn't like her. Rich could have hinted he'd do something to me if she told, and the threat made her want to get me away from him forever.

If Bronson was right, my mother had given up the life she'd planned and schemed for to protect me. I felt tears coming, and they weren't the kind you can blink away. They felt fat, even on the inside.

Bronson rose abruptly. "I'm going to go pay the bill. You can wait for me outside."

Stumbling half-blind out the door, I hurried to the back of the building and stood among empty boxes, leaning against the brick wall as I sobbed like a baby. For a while, I wasn't aware of anything but the fact that my home, my friends, and my mother were all gone. Three months of tension and pain turned me to jelly, and it all came out at once.

When I finally felt myself calming down a little, I looked around. It was cool. No one had seen me. I wiped my eyes and nose on the inside of my t-shirt, licked my lips, and went to where Bronson had parked the BMW. He didn't come out for a while longer, which allowed my red eyes and swollen face to get a little better. I might not have looked totally like myself when he finally strolled out, a toothpick at one corner of his mouth, but I was close.

LOSER

When I left the library, my car's interior was hot enough to bake biscuits, so I opened both front doors to let the heat dissipate. As I stood there, fanning one door to speed the process, I noticed a second-hand store across the street. I rolled the car windows down halfway and went shopping at Betty's Consignment.

My plan for tonight required an outfit of a certain color but no particular style. However, as I'd read in the library, a second plan had formed in my mind. Nadine Hopgood had often appeared at local events with a woman named Marie Chevrolet. I'd looked up Ms. Chevrolet's address, and in order to meet her, I needed clothes of no particular color but with a certain style.

I stuck with classic clothing, having little idea what passed for current fashion among the wealthy. A linen shift in pale green hung on a mannequin in the front window, and I asked the clerk to take it down. After choosing a pair of leather flats and a real bra, I tried the outfit on, coming out of the stuffy little dressing room to check my look in the full-length mirror. I stared at the sight before me: it was Beth. Only a haunted look around my eyes betrayed that Loser was still inside, waiting for failure to strike.

"This would set it off nicely," a voice said behind me. The clerk held out an airy scarf that was indeed perfect for the dress, blending greens and blues in a riot of color. I hesitated, unsure what to do with it. "They're tying them like this right now," the woman said, putting the scarf around my neck and deftly twisting it into a knot I could never have achieved.

"Thanks." I went to the jewelry counter and located the only pair of clip-on earrings they had, small hoops that were real gold and only a little bent out of shape. The holes in my earlobes had long since closed. Maybe I should get them pierced again. Gazing at the woman in the mirror, I realized Beth was doing a lot of the thinking. Could she keep it up?

Piling those things on the counter, I began shopping for another outfit, one suited to night work. A few minutes later I paid for my purchases, the stylish ensemble along with black cotton pants, a long-sleeved black turtleneck, black shoes and socks, and a black cap to cover my hair. I wasn't able to find greasepaint or even dark makeup, but I figured dirt would do to darken my face. With my new-to-me treasures I drove back to the motel, where I put on the dress and fiddled with my hair more than I'd done in a very long time. I'd left the scarf tied, so I only had to slip it over my head again. The woman in the mirror looked a little tense but quite respectable. I added some of the motel's complimentary ginger lotion on my hands and neck for scent, and I was ready to meet Ms. Chevrolet.

The house was a few blocks from Hopgood's. Edwardian in style and ringed by a wrought-iron fence that was meant more for looks than security, it looked solid and a little staid, even antiseptic. Ms. Chevrolet was working in her yard, planting bulbs of some sort, and I took a deep breath before leaving my car. I'd saved words like mad all day, nodding and bobbing like an idiot to avoid speaking aloud. I had twenty-four words remaining with which to question this woman and eliminate the possibility that Eddie was safe with his mother's friend. It wasn't much.

"Hi. Did you know Nadine Hopgood?" *Eighteen.*

Rising from her knees, she came forward and put her hand on the metal *fleur de lis* between us. "Who are you?"

"Her foster sister." *Fifteen.*

"Really." She didn't sound convinced. "So you know her well?"

Something in her voice made me answer honestly. "No." *Fourteen.*

Although somewhere over fifty, Marie Chevrolet was a beautiful woman. A head taller than I, she was what magazines like to call "willowy," with even features, delicate hands, and hair straight out of a shampoo commercial. She wore jeans and a polo shirt better than most women wear an evening gown, and she looked as fresh as leaf lettuce, even on a scorching afternoon. I guessed she was one of those women who don't know the female body is capable of producing sweat. Looking me over, she made a decision.

"Come inside. I just made iced tea."

Without waiting for a response, she turned toward the house. Skirting the fence I went through the open gateway, hurrying up the sidewalk to where she held the front door open for me. Soon I was seated in a room with orange sherbet-colored walls and silver accents. I chose the chair nearest the window, wishing we'd stayed outside. Despite the air-conditioned cool, the place made me nervous, all fragile elegance. I took the glass of tea Marie offered with both hands, holding it in front of me like a tinkling talisman that might ward off all forms of trouble, like spilling the brew on the ecru rug or being thrown out of the house as an imposter.

Marie sat down across from me. "Forgive me if this seems rude, but what's Nadine's real name?" It was a test, one I'd unknowingly prepared for by reading Marta's notes. "Rose." *Thirteen words.*

She nodded. "And how did her father die?"

I had to think about that one. Would Nadine have told the truth? If she hadn't, I had no way of knowing what her lie would have been. The truth was my best chance. "Shot." *Twelve.*

Marie sat back a little, and I guessed I'd passed the test. "Nadine and I were very close," she said, and her lashes lowered briefly in deference to the dead. "I was afraid you were a reporter looking for dirt on her, but if you really are from Beulah, I'm pleased to meet you."

"Tell me about her." *Eight words left. Can I do this, or will I have to run away in mid-sentence?*

"Nadine and I recognized our similarities from the start," Marie said. "We both married for, shall we say, practical reasons. I was plain old Mary Conklin until Terrance Chevrolet met me twenty years ago. He needed a wife willing to ignore his peccadilloes, and I wanted a better lifestyle than what I was accustomed to." Her eyes met mine, challenging me to judge her, but I learned long ago not to judge. I'd bet Marie had never awakened in the middle of a street with a city bus horn honking in her ears.

Seeing nothing in my expression that was objectionable, she went on. "Nadine and Rich had a similar arrangement, although she was, of course, much younger than I. Their reasons were different from Terry's and mine, but both marriages were based on the classic alliance model rather than the modern ideal of love." She added with a chuckle, "However warped that might be."

We lapsed into silence, Marie apparently reminiscing and me hoping I wouldn't have to say something to get her started again. I was really low on words, and I sipped the cool, perfect tea to give her time, hardly able to swallow for the constriction in my throat.

Finally she spoke again, eyes focused on the floor. "It was nice to have someone to really talk to. I can chat golf with the sporty women and do the 'Can't-find-good-help' discussion with the homebodies. I can discuss the merits of Botox and dermal abrasion, but Nadine and I talked about what matters. We'd been through tough times, and we'd both done things it isn't wise to tell to the Ladies Who Lunch." She stopped suddenly, her eyes meeting mine. "Did you ever know Nadine to drink?"

I shook my head, and her chin jutted belligerently. "I told the police I never saw her take alcohol, ever. She'd suffered abuse from alcoholic foster parents as a kid and been smacked around by drunken boyfriends as an adult. She hated booze. I don't believe she got drunk and drove off the road!"

"How, then?" *Six.*

Marie shook her head sadly. "I don't understand any of it. I would never have believed she'd leave without a word to me. I didn't know she was back in Romulus until I heard she was dead."

"Hopgood?" *Five.*

Marie sighed. "She never gave any indication he was violent. Arrogant, yes, but Nadine knew what she'd signed on for." She rose and went to the window, looking toward Hopgood's house as if unable to keep still with so many questions in her mind. "She didn't love him, but I think he might have come to love her. I went over after she disappeared, and Rich seemed about to fall apart." She smiled faintly. "It can happen. Terry and I have become very fond of each other as we grow older together."

It was entirely possible, I guessed. Marriages of convenience had often led to love in centuries past. Shared concerns, shared confidences, shared lives. What else did love need? Honesty, maybe?

Marie was still at the window, and she smoothed her silver-blond hair absently. "I'll have to go back to the house again after the funeral. Rich will need his friends."

Hopgood even had his friends fooled, at least, that was my conclusion. He was good at deception.

Turning to me, Marie said, "I'm sorry. I haven't been very helpful. What did you want to ask me?"

"I'm looking for Eddie." *One word left.*

She seemed surprised. "No one's seen Eddie since June." She stared at me for a moment as if putting things together. "If he showed up in Beulah, you'd let Rich know, wouldn't you?"

"Yes." I said, rising to go. One of these days, I would. With no more words, I extended a hand, gave Marie a smile, and went to the door. She was still looking at me, an odd expression on her face, when I closed the door and hurried down the sidewalk.

Marie Chevrolet had been helpful, and I liked her. I believed she didn't know where Eddie was, and I was sure she didn't know that Rich Hopgood might have killed his wife. I got into my very hot car, turned up the A/C, and left the development, glad Nadine had had a friend who understood her, someone she could talk to about her past.

Still, my visit raised more questions than it answered. Her son, her husband, and now, her best friend said Nadine didn't drink. Something had changed her long-held behavior, or someone had forced her to change it.

Before I could go back to GoodRich Lodge and find answers to my questions, I had more shopping to do. I told the GPS to find the nearest Home Depot. Once I'd purchased some tools, I turned my mind to photography. Again asking the GPS for guidance, I chose the camera shop closest to me, which wasn't a camera shop at all, but a chain store that sold cameras along with TVs, computers, and smart phones. I bought a digital Nikon D, a single-lens reflex camera that allows the long exposure times needed for night photography without a lot of digital noise. It wasn't cheap, especially since I let the guy talk me into the accessory package. Bert insisted I didn't have to pinch pennies, so I didn't. I stopped at a park and took some practice shots to familiarize myself with the camera, and then I was ready. I finished off the M&M's, eating them in sequence until I had one left of each color. I don't know why I do that, but it certainly isn't my only oddity.

As I munched, I thought about my plan. If a return to GoodRich Lodge didn't lead me to Eddie, I didn't know where to look next. I'd have to try again to get help from the police, which meant I needed evidence that the inner compound, double-fenced and well-guarded, existed. Surely that information would need to be investigated, and pictures would go a long way toward proving my case. If I wasn't able to tell the police what I'd seen, after tonight I could show them.

Chapter Fifteen

EDDIE

Bronson was a pretty cool guy. We spent most of the day going to places he thought Loser might look for me. We went to the dealership, but it was closed, I guess so Rich could pretend he was grieving. We went by the house several times. Every time, I scrunched down in the seat while Bronson went to the door, but Rich wasn't there.

Finally Bronson insisted on going to the police. When I begged him to leave me out of it, he made up some story that he was supposed to meet an associate who hadn't shown up. He asked if they'd had any reports of an accident involving a woman in a silver Envoy. They hadn't.

After that he drove around for a while, slowing at drug stores and any park we happened to pass. "She might hang out somewhere like this while she thinks about what to do next," he said when I finally asked what exactly he was looking for. "It might remind her of Richmond."

I figured Alex Bronson has a crush on Loser or something, cuz why else would he spend so much time and effort trying to find her? I didn't complain though, cuz I wanted to find her too. I was getting a little worried, thinking she might have told Dickweed she was Nadine's friend and got killed just like my mom did.

Bronson was also worried. He tried her phone a bunch of times (I didn't even know she *had* a phone), but it was turned off. He got a little irritated every time, but his grin was kind of crooked, like he expected it from her. Definitely a crush.

"She could've gone to the house before I hit town." I'd told Bronson my trials on the trip down from Beulah. "Maybe Loser didn't have so much trouble with Murdock's Law."

"I think you mean Murphy's Law." Bronson looked at his watch. "Let's go back and see if your stepfather's home yet."

He wasn't, and I could see that Bronson was getting frustrated. "He could be up at the lodge," I suggested. "He spends a lot of time up there."

"The lodge?"

"Dickw—I mean, Rich has a hunting camp up in the mountains," I told him, taking another handful of the greasy but tasty potato chips I'd talked him into buying. "It made life easier when he went up there, cuz Mom relaxed for a while. Plus, we ate take-out when he was gone, which is cool."

"How far is this lodge from here?"

"An hour, maybe." I was guessing, having never been up there myself.

"Did Beth know about this place?"

I wiped my hand on my pants. "I guess Mabel could have told her."

"It's worth checking out then." He looked at the dashboard clock. "Quarter to four. If he isn't up there, we can be back here by seven. He should be home by then."

"Long as I don't have to see him," I reminded Bronson. "Either here or at the lodge."

"No problem. You can stay in the car."

"Okay," I said. "I guess it can't hurt."

LOSER

By four o'clock I was ready. I'd donned my black clothes and loaded bottled water, two ham sandwiches, and my new camera, wrapped in a hotel towel, in a backpack I'd bought. I'd chosen one that had buckles, not noisy Velcro or zipper closures. I was pretty sure I could avoid the surveillance cameras in darkness, though I knew the men monitoring them would be more vigilant after my first visit. I told myself Eddie was up there, alive. Even if Hopgood had killed Nadine, he'd keep Eddie safe until they figured out who I was and what I knew. For now, I was the kid's lifeline.

I drove through Cranville, where the gas station was open, though the pumps were idle. I took Kalcutt up to the first fork and turned onto the road I'd explored earlier that dead-ended a short way down. It was a long way from the lodge entrance, but I didn't want to take the chance of being heard or seen approaching. When the road ended, I backed the car into the trees where it wasn't easily visible, heading outward in case I needed to make a quick getaway. Once I'd done that, I crawled into the back seat and took a nap, waiting for full dark.

EDDIE

After I got us lost a couple of times, Bronson and I found GoodRich Lodge. The gate was closed, but he parked the car and got out. I'd crouched down in the passenger seat, but I peeked out just once to take a look. A guy in a cowboy hat was clearing weeds around a crummy old building, making lots of noise. He looked up when Bronson signaled he'd like to talk, and I ducked back down as he checked out the fancy wheels. I didn't recognize the guy, but I was taking no chances he might recognize me.

"I'm looking for a friend," Bronson said when the man shut off the weed-whip. "Have you seen a woman in a silver Buick today, or maybe yesterday?"

At first, I didn't think the guy was going to answer, but finally he said, "Dave—he's the boss—might know the woman you're lookin' for." I heard a creak as the gate swung open. "Come inside where it's cooler, and I'll call him."

Bronson followed the guy up to the lodge. I heard steps on the wooden porch, the jingle of a key ring as he unlocked the door, and the wooden echo as it closed behind them. I waited for what seemed like forever. When the lodge door opened again I wanted to look, but I didn't. When the car door opened beside me, I expected Bronson, but instead I heard, "You're Eddie, ain't you? Dave says you're to come inside."

My first instinct was to run, but he was blocking my way, and right about level with my eyes was the pistol he wore on his hip. It was black, shiny, and as far as I could tell, well-oiled and ready. I crawled out of the car, embarrassed to be caught hiding like a five-year-old but definitely more scared of the way Dickweed's man looked at me. How'd he know I was in the car? Bronson wouldn't have told. I realized he must have seen me peering over the dashboard. That was twice today I hadn't been as clever about staying out of sight as I thought I was.

The guy didn't say anything more but turned and started for the lodge. From the gun he wore and the coldness in his stare, I knew he wouldn't put up with explanations or excuses. I didn't want to go inside Dickweed's territory, didn't want to face Dave, but I didn't have a choice. Telling myself that at least I had Bronson for protection, I followed the guy inside.

The place looked exactly like you'd expect. Knotty pine everywhere, heads on every wall, mostly deer but a few other animals, all dead and dusty-looking. There was too much furniture, as if Rich, or maybe his old man, had kept bringing stuff up the mountain every time he bought new down in the city. It smelled like dust with mouse droppings thrown in.

Bronson stood in the middle of the room, and beside him was Dave, my stepfather's manager. Even though he'd always been friendly in an offhand way, I wasn't sure how the guy felt about me or my mom. While he was telling you how great you did in your race last week, it was like he was thinking something else behind those cold blue eyes.

Bronson looked uncomfortable. "I'm not sure my client would agree," he said, looking at me and flexing his hands like he was making an effort not to wring them together. "The woman my firm is working for has taken an interest in this young man's welfare. I'm not comfortable leaving him here."

"It's what Mr. Hopgood wants, you can bet on it," Dave said smoothly. The man who'd come outside to get me stayed near the door, as if he thought I might turn and run. His presence at my back made my shoulder muscles spasm, like when you think there's a spider back there.

"If he's here," Bronson said in a voice that was higher than normal, "I'd like to discuss the situation."

"He's at a funeral." Dave glanced at me. "Mrs. Hopgood died a few days back, and Mr. Hopgood has commitments in town until at least nine o'clock tonight."

"Yes, we're aware of Mrs. Hopgood's unfortunate accident," Bronson said. He actually did wring his hands, something I would never have imagined him doing. "I'm upset that this young man has missed his mother's service." He turned toward the door. "We should return to Romulus, Edward. We will get in touch with your stepfather tomorrow morning."

Dave hooked his thumbs in his belt and spread his feet, balancing his weight. "Mr. Bronson, how about if we call Mr. Hopgood and ask him what he wants his son to do?"

"Stepson," I said with a pleading look at Bronson. "I don't want—"

"Ed," Dave interrupted. "We've spent the last three months looking all over the state for you. Don't you think you owe it to your dad to explain yourself?" Before I could think of an argument, Dave turned back to Bronson. "And you, sir. If you're a lawyer, as you say, then you know you have no legal standing in this matter. You don't want to get between this boy and his legal guardian."

"I assure you, I have no intent to do any such thing." Bronson huffed like a leaky balloon, and my opinion of him took a dive. "I am attempting to do my duty as I believe my client would see it."

"Well then." Dave pulled out his phone and punched a few buttons. We all heard it ring, and when the click that signaled an answer came, he said, "I'm sorry to bother you at this time, Mr. Hopgood, but we have a lawyer up here who's brought Eddie home." He made the word *lawyer* sound like a curse. "He'd like you to verify that you want me to take custody of the boy until you can come and get him."

He handed the phone to Bronson. "Mr. Hopgood? My name is Alexander Bronson, and I'm concerned about Eddie's welfare. It seems he's got objections to being in your care, and I—"

Rich interrupted at that point. I could hear his voice, but not his words, but I saw Bronson's expression change. "Oh, he did." He glanced at me. "And that's why your wife left Romulus?" He listened some more. "I understand. Yes, of course. I will contact you in a few days to see about returning the boy's things to him."

When he closed the phone, Bronson was apologetic. "I'm sorry for the misunderstanding," he told Dave. "I wasn't aware of the, um, circumstances."

"What circumstances?" I saw a look pass between Dave and Bronson. "I didn't do anything!" I was shouting, but I couldn't help it. Rich had somehow made me the bad guy, and Bronson had bought it.

He looked at me like I was a piece of toilet paper attached to his shoe before turning back to Dave, all polite and businesslike. "I'll inform my client of the facts of the case and explain that Mr. Hopgood has Eddie's best interests in mind. I'm sure she'll understand."

Did nobody but me see the satisfaction on Dave's face? My hands clenched and unclenched in spasms. I wanted to smack him, and I wanted to smack Bronson too. Like every other adult in the world, he took the word of another adult over the word of a kid. It was crap. Total crap.

"Gentlemen, I'll be going." Bronson brushed at his jacket sleeve as if getting rid of the last speck of concern for me. "If we meet again, I hope the circumstances are more pleasant."

In a move that surprised me, he stopped as he passed and gave me a hug. I almost pulled away, but at the last second, I realized he was whispering something in my ear. "Tell the truth," he said as he patted my back like a fond uncle, "but as little as possible."

Letting go, he turned to Dave and put out a hand. "Thank you for your help in resolving this matter."

"Happy to do it, Mr. Bronson." As Dave shook hands, he had what seemed to be a sudden thought. "You know, sir, you could do us a big favor if you don't mind."

Bronson paused, cautious as we all are when a stranger asks a favor.

"I was just about to drive Ben here down to Romulus. He's supposed to pick up a vehicle at the Hopgood Dealership and bring it up here. It's only a few blocks off the highway, and it would save me a trip if he could ride with you."

Bronson seemed relieved that the favor wouldn't cost him anything. "I can do that."

"Thanks so much. I'll get him the papers we need to get signed while you get your car turned around. We won't hold you up but a few seconds." Dave was all Mr. Nice Guy. He even opened the door for Bronson, who left without another glance at me.

As soon as the door closed, Dave said softly to Ben, "It's your call. If he's the dipshit he seems to be, let him go back to Richmond. If he's the least bit likely to make trouble for us, kill him. Take his wallet so it looks like a robbery."

"Right." Ben touched the knife at his belt.

Dave took a couple of sheets of paper from a desk in one corner of the room and handed them to him. "That'll do for the papers you're supposed to be delivering."

171

Ben folded the sheets into thirds, put them in his shirt pocket so they stuck out, and left without another word. It was unbelievable. Their calm discussion of offing someone left me stunned. Was that what my mom's death had been, something on a list of things to get done?

I stepped away from Dave a little, tensing to run after Alex and warn him. I didn't know what he'd do about it, and Ben would probably shoot both of us, but I had to try. I was stopped by an iron grip on the back of my neck. "Come on, kid. We'll put you upstairs for a while." Twisting my shirt collar in his hand so that I was choked and guided at the same time, Dave escorted me under the deer antler chandelier and up the bumpy pine stairway. I heard the sound of Bronson's car starting down the mountain, and I pictured Ben in the passenger seat, making polite conversation while he waited for the right moment to plunge a knife between Alex's ribs.

When we reached the second floor, Dave steered me down a long hallway lined with identical wooden doors, each with a metal number nailed to it. When we got to #4 he reached past me, opened the door, and shoved me so hard that I stumbled a few steps forward. By the time I turned around the door had slammed shut, a key had turned, and I was locked inside. I raised a fist to pound on the door but stopped myself after one blow. What good would that do? I was in trouble, and my last hope, Bronson, was as good as dead.

I wondered where Loser was. Did she believe what I'd told her about Mom's death? She hadn't disagreed, but that could have been simply because she didn't like to talk. Had she gone to Hopgood's house and asked about me? Had Rich's men caught her and killed her? If so, it was my fault. I hadn't thought about the danger of coming back to Romulus or guiding Bronson to this deserted spot. I guessed the only reason they hadn't killed us on sight was they couldn't very well stage a second accident on the mountain in such a short time.

I searched the room for some way to escape, but it was as bare as the old monk's cells they tell about in books: a bed, a washstand with a kerosene lamp, a chest of drawers, all empty, and a wooden chair. I couldn't even set the place on fire; there were no matches with the lamp. The only window was covered by a wooden shutter fastened shut on the outside. Sunlight filtered through the boards, making shiny lines across the gray wool blanket on the bed. I thought I might get a hand between the slats and open the fastener, but the window slid up only a few inches before it stuck. I could have kicked out the glass, but the shutter didn't wiggle when I pushed on it. I doubted I could reach the hardware and open it without making noise that would bring someone up to investigate.

After only a few minutes, I heard the key in the door. Stepping away from the window, I took a stand in the middle of the room, trying not to look scared. Despite my intentions, I took a step back when Dave entered. He was pretty scary now that I knew he was the Dark Side's Chuck Norris. I remembered Rich bragging about Dave's skill and strength in their army days, and I felt like a cornered animal with nowhere to run.

He closed the door and leaned his back against it. "Where you been all this time, boy?"

Remembering Bronson's advice I said, "Motels. All over." I wasn't sure why I should do what Bronson told me to, but I wasn't in much of a mood to talk anyway.

"I see. And who's this woman that's so interested in you?"

How would Bronson answer that one? *The truth, but as little as possible.* "Mom's foster sister."

I could tell my answer pleased him. "Comes from Beulah, does she?" When I nodded he went on, "When you all first went missing, I went to see if your mama'd run to ground up there. Didn't look like nobody lived in that house no more."

The truth. "We didn't go there till just lately."

Dave's head bobbed as if I'd said exactly the right thing. "So why's she looking for you?"

The truth. "She cares what happens to me." It felt good to say it, even though I didn't think I'd ever see Loser again. I had to hope she'd given up and gone home, where she'd be safe from guys like Dave.

"It's nice she cares," he said. "But she shouldn't stick her nose in our business."

I looked around at the dried-up wood floors and the spider webs in the corners of the room. "What's so secret about this old place?"

He smiled. "This place is just window dressin', son. The secret's farther on, and you'll get to see it as soon as your dad gets here."

"Rich is not my dad." It sounded childish and lame, but it was the best thing about my life right now.

Dave's smile turned nasty. "You're right. Your dad was some one-night stand your mother had where she forgot to use a condom. You're just like her—all looks and no brains."

I went at him then, but he reacted before I even got close, punching me in the face so hard I flew backward and landed half on the bed and half on the floor. Dave didn't wait to see how badly I was hurt. I heard the door close behind him as I lay there, my head spinning.

After a while I pulled myself to a sitting position and used the blanket to soak up the blood coming from my nose and mouth. Dave's assumption that I was the result of Nadine's mistake was no doubt true. His belief that it made Dickweed better than me was wrong. Dickweed was what I'd always thought he was, and much, much worse.

I felt like crying for the second time that day, but this time it was from fear and frustration. They'd probably kill me, but I guessed that was Dickweed's decision to make. I might be allowed to live a little longer, at least until the grieving-husband show was over.

Waiting for good things to happen is hard, but at least there's anticipation. Waiting for bad things is the worst. If they'd said, "We're murdering you at midnight," at least I'd have had a timetable. As it was, I didn't know when I'd die, I didn't know if Loser and Bronson were alive or dead. There wasn't one thing I could do about it. I stretched out on the bed and pictured the ways I hoped Dickweed would get his, from Karma or God or a real smart cop. I didn't care which.

CHAPTER SIXTEEN

LOSER

From six until a little after nine I sat in my car, waiting for darkness to cover my incursion onto Hopgood's land. As my body rested, my mind conjured scenarios for the night. I tried to concentrate on ones where success came easily, but I also considered what I'd do if that didn't happen.

When a quarter moon was all that lit my way I exited the car, pushed the door closed with a soft click, and set out. At the library I'd checked the weather, the phase of the moon, and the time the sun would rise the next morning, preferring to travel by natural light rather than a flashlight that might draw attention. Planning paid off, and as I made my way back to the main road and started toward GoodRich Lodge, I could see me way easily, though trees shadowed large patches of road. The way was steep, and my leg muscles soon let me know about it.

I stayed to the right, where the gravel ended and the road turned sandy, my neck muscles tense and my ears straining for sounds of a vehicle behind me. Halfway up I remembered the phone in my backpack. I'd brought it to summon help if needed, but I had one of those weird moments where I couldn't remember if it was on or off. Reaching around awkwardly, I dug it out and checked. It was off. I dropped the phone into a side pocket of the pack, relieved that I wouldn't be getting a call from some telemarketer once I'd settled into my hiding spot.

I crossed the rustic outer fence easily, hiking my body over the splintery boards about twenty yards down from the gate. Following the fence in order to keep my bearings I moved along, stopping every few minutes to listen. Finally I saw the lights of the main gate ahead of me. I stopped again, noting there were more lights than I'd expected.

Someone was in the old lodge. Beside it were two newer vehicles instead of the old pickup that had been there the day before. One looked like the truck that had sat across my path yesterday; the other was a black Hummer with a grill like a big, toothy grin and a bar of lights across the roof for chasing woodland creatures through the night. Possibly a clone of the one I'd seen in Beulah a few months back, but I'd have bet it was the same one.

I moved cautiously around the yard, keeping the woods at my back and watching for threats: people, dogs, even a bird that might startle at my passing and make a noise. Nothing moved. I watched the house for several minutes, but there was no movement inside. Curious, I finally crept up to a window and peered inside. I saw no one.

Whoever had come in those trucks had left them there and taken the old truck down to the inner compound. What better way to continue the fantasy that the lodge was all there was to this place than to have different vehicles in the yard from time to time?

I touched the hood of one truck. It was warm. Even more cautiously than before, I started down the road to the compound. Tracing the road but staying off it, I made my way to the second fence and followed its line into the woods until I was out of sight of its security camera. There I dropped the backpack and dug out the things I'd bought to make my illegal entry easier. First, I had a pair of heavy-duty metal snips. Using them, I cut the bottom links up about a foot. The sharp clunk of severed metal seemed loud to me, and it wasn't easy work. I stopped after each cut, listening for the calls of alarm I dreaded. There was nothing.

Taking my tools into the woods, I hid them under some leaves. No sense carrying all that weight now that I was done with it. Returning to the fence, I bent the sides out of my way, slid through, and pulled them back into place, fastening the edges with green Velcro strips bought for the purpose. The slit wouldn't be obvious to the casual eye, especially at night.

That got me thinking. How would I find the hole myself? It's difficult to pinpoint a location in the woods, where one tree looks pretty much like the rest. Looking around, I located a Y-shaped tree branch on the ground nearby and laid it against the fence a few feet down from the cut I'd made. I set it aslant, so it looked like a natural fall. It would point me toward the spot when I came out, and that would be a big advantage if I had to leave in a hurry.

If you've never traversed dense woods at night, I don't recommend it. I moved with agonizing slowness, stepping carefully to avoid cracks and crunches underfoot. Branches caught at me as I passed, and I couldn't see well enough to avoid all of them. I walked with hands up, as if surrendering, which protected my face somewhat but left my ribs exposed to pokes and scratches. The swish of foliage settling back into place sounded like small explosions in my ears, though I knew better.

I thought gratefully of my years with Marta. A city girl before my time with her, I'd found bricked alleys and concrete underfoot more familiar than pine trees, scrub brush, and ferns. But the lessons I'd learned on the hills outside Beulah came back to me as I walked. I knew from stealing through the woods for a glimpse at a deer that it was best to walk slowly, toe-to-heel. I knew to stop periodically and listen to the night. It all came back now as I made my way, if not gracefully, at least competently, to the fence around the inner compound. It was my high school reading of *Macbeth* that gave me the idea for the last bit of concealment. Breaking off a leafy branch, I stuck it down the back of my shirt. The woods, at least a small part of them, were coming to the castle.

As I neared I looked upward, locating fence supports that loomed overhead. They told me where the cameras were, and I adjusted my path. Choosing a spot midway between posts where there was plenty of undergrowth, I got down on my belly and I crawled forward, keeping my face low and pulling my sleeves over my hands. A camera can't pick black out of blackness, and the branch at my back concealed my head and shoulders. Peeking out from under my leafy disguise, I could see into the compound: the guard house, the tower overlooking it all, and the men with guns who waited, alert for interlopers like me.

Looking in, fear hit me a second time, as if a giant hand descended to slap my face and stop me cold.

What do you think you're doing, Loser?

Do you know how lucky you were to get away with this once?

Do you really think you'll avoid detection a second time?

Loser!

Putting my face to the ground, I gasped air into my lungs. Yes, I'd planned, I'd prepared, and I'd got this far, but the moment had come when I recalled who the mastermind of the scenario was. Loser.

I lay there for a long time, forehead against the fence and body shaking as I resisted the urge to crawl away like the insect I was. Eddie wasn't my son. He wasn't even my responsibility. He'd run away from me, probably with no intention of returning. I might be risking my life for a kid who was, at this moment, hitchhiking to California to become a surfer dude. If I went back to Beulah and told Mabel that Eddie was fine, no one would ever know I'd abandoned the search for him.

Go home, Loser. Home, where you almost belong.

I didn't. After a few minutes I started wriggling my way out of the backpack and getting the camera ready. My jaw was tight. Sweat ran down my forehead, but I stayed.

The compound was unlit except for some recessed lights at ground level along the main building. I guessed the camouflage covering was heavier there, so indirect lights were permissible. The guards might have some sort of night vision capability, but I'd heard that was a little clunky, like wearing Coke-bottle glasses. I hoped if they had it, they didn't use it without a good reason.

I took pictures of everything: the fence, the main building, and the guard towers. I got a good shot of one of the men, a hefty guy in tight-legged jeans and a rumpled linen shirt, crossing the yard with his automatic rifle slung casually over his shoulder. The whole thing was surreal, something one might expect to see in satellite footage of some remote location Pakistan or some embattled African nation. But in West Virginia?

It got even weirder. The door to the main building opened, spilling light and sound across the compound. Out stepped two people, a man and a woman who hurried after him. He looked to be about fifty, wore dull-gray clothing, and carried himself proudly, with the same military bearing I'd noticed in the guards. He was unarmed, however, and seemed to be at leisure.

The woman wore a red sari. I thought she was the one I'd seen yesterday, perhaps the mother of the two younger women. In a language I didn't understand she said something to the man, who was probably her husband and the girls' father. I sensed excited anticipation in her tone. His answer was terse and guttural, but his impatience seemed false. He was pleased she was happy, though he wasn't the type to show it.

They walked the length of the building, turned, and walked back, the man gesturing from time to time as he answered the woman's questions. After three trips back and forth, they went inside. When the door opened, I caught a glimpse of a brightly lit foyer with sand-colored walls. An elderly woman dressed in black greeted the couple with a bow as they entered and closed the door after them.

What is this place?

I backed away from the fence, crawling on hands and knees and ignoring the damp my clothes had soaked up from the ground. From the cover of the trees, I began making my way around the fence. It took a long time, but I finally got to a point where I could see the back of the building. There was a swimming pool, lit along the bottom and edged by a few beach chairs. In one corner was a small bar where a woman in shorts and a tank top served drinks to two men sitting on stools facing her. They were muscular and confident, and they flirted with the woman, whose smile was more professional than amused. She looked Latin, and while it's hard to tell a person's national origin when he's wearing swim trunks, I got the impression the men were American.

What is this place?

It was about eleven-thirty when one of the men left the bar and swam lazily around the pool for a while. I sensed he was giving his companion some time with the barmaid. Though she showed little interest in talking to him, the woman tolerated his playful comments and even a few caresses. When the swimmer emerged from the pool with a careless splash and began picking up the possessions he'd left on the bar, the other man whispered something. The barmaid nodded, but her expression remained blank. When they were gone, she stared into the turquoise water for a long time. Finally, she sighed, tidied up the area, and went inside. In a few minutes, the lights went out. I checked my watch. Midnight seemed to be curfew.

I'd intended to make a complete circle of the perimeter, but the fence took an outward jog ahead of me, edging a second road out of the compound. Without knowing how far the bulge went, I decided to go back the way I'd come, where I knew how to get out. As I retraced my steps, I tried to figure out what GoodRich Lodge was for. The people I'd seen were either employees or guests. Nobody acted like he didn't want to be there, except maybe the barmaid, and who wouldn't hate fending off the advances of horny men and pretending to be okay with it?

From what I'd seen, the security system was designed to keep others out rather than keeping inhabitants in. Hopgood offered his guests—clients, according to the guards I'd overheard—the ultimate in privacy, since no one outside the place even knew it existed. The woman at the gas station had mentioned war veterans and celebrities visiting, but why did they need men with guns to protect them? There was more to this place than giving veterans a break or celebrities some time away from the paparazzi. Something illegal was going on, but I didn't know exactly what. At least I had pictures that should launch an investigation.

It was almost one a.m. when I finally reached the compound gate again. It was a relief to move away from the cameras and to think that in only half an hour I'd be back to the old lodge. From there, I'd quickly be off Hopgood's land, and it was a matter of making my way down the mountain to my car. The sky had clouded, obscuring the moon, but I didn't mind. I'd done what I came to do. Before I started along the road, I stopped and listened to make sure no one was coming.

It was a good thing I did, because a vehicle approached the gate and stopped not ten feet from where I crouched in the trees. I recognized the pickup that had blocked my way down the mountain yesterday, the same one that had been at the old lodge when I came in a few hours ago. I also recognized the driver. Worst of all, I recognized Eddie's pale face as he looked apprehensively out the window on the passenger side. I wasn't out of trouble yet.

EDDIE

When Dave came to get me, my lip felt like a balloon, and I had a couple of teeth that felt loose. He didn't seem to notice.

"Come on, kid."

I wanted to ask where we were going, but I didn't want to let Dave know I was the least bit concerned. I figured it wouldn't change anything, and it might give him satisfaction.

"We got a place for you that's more secure than this old barn." His eyes went cold as he added, "Once your friends leave, you and your dad can settle your differences."

182

It was clear what the settlement would be. Grabbing my neck, Dave escorted me outside, led me to the passenger side of the green pickup, and then got in the driver's side. When he backed it away from the building, we headed not down the drive, as I expected, but along a road that led away from the back of the lodge. Wherever the "secure" place was, it was in the opposite direction from any help I could think of.

CHAPTER SEVENTEEN

LOSER

Eddie was in trouble. If they were taking him into the compound, they didn't expect he'd ever tell what he saw there. The guardhouse was dark and empty, but the driver got out and went to a keypad on the left gatepost, presumably to disarm an alarm system and open the gate.

I had only a moment to decide what to do. Once Eddie was inside that fence, I saw no chance of rescuing him. I had to act quickly.

Using the truck as cover, I left the bushes and approached, tapping lightly on the window. I saw the look of surprise on Eddie's face, quickly replaced by a split second of joy and then apprehension. He glanced at the man, who was as far away from us as he would get and intent on his task.

Opening the door, I motioned for Eddie to follow. The driver had left his door ajar, so the interior light was already on and the alarm pinged its warning. The irritating, repetitive tone was for once an advantage, covering the noise we made. Grabbing Eddie's arm, I pulled him into the woods.

We had only seconds before the driver would realize his prisoner was gone. Hoping they'd assume Eddie would run up the road, I headed into the woods, returning to the spot I'd occupied earlier. It was outside camera range, there were bushes for concealment, and we had no other choice. I recalled, thankfully, that I'd seen no sign of dogs anywhere on the property.

The driver shouted, "The kid took off!" and several voices answered. I took Eddie's arm and pulled him into the leafy center of a clump of shrubby growth. He resisted slightly, clearly ready to try to outrun pursuit, but I held on, and he finally crouched beside me, trusting my decision. He looked into my eyes, searching for assurance I couldn't provide.

Someone shouted, "Which way did he go, Dave?"

"Had to be east, or I'd have seen him."

A strategy session followed. To my immense relief, the man named Dave, who seemed to be in charge, was certain Eddie would head for the front gate. "He doesn't know these woods," he told the men who gathered around him. "He'll have to follow the road."

"The fence will slow him down," someone said.

"Get the Rhinos and the rest of the men," Dave ordered. There was relative silence for a while, and then we heard engines starting up. Lights flashed in the compound. The hunt was under way.

Rhinos turned out to be enclosed ATVs with bar lights mounted on top. Two of them sped out the gate and around Dave's truck, one coming into the woods our way and the other taking the opposite side. They headed away from the fence, however, on the misguided assumption that Eddie was running. I hoped it wouldn't occur to them that he might lie low just outside the fence. Dave turned his truck around, and we saw it start up the road, adding light to the chase. His taillights disappeared around the first curve, but the ATV's, each with two men inside, wove in and out of the trees, hoping to catch sight of a fleeing boy.

The compound went quiet again, but a few minutes later, two pairs of searchers exited the gate and began a circuit of the fence's exterior on foot, traveling in opposite directions and shining extra-bright flashlights into the trees. They were covering all the options.

Looking around, I touched Eddie's shoulder and pointed. Twenty feet back from the fence was an old maple with a massive trunk and branches fairly low to the ground. He got the idea right away, and we moved to it, taking care to move quietly. I gestured for him to go first, and he started upward, lips pressed together. The tree was solid; it didn't move an iota as I followed Eddie up. He soon disappeared, having the advantage of youth and no encumbering backpack to catch on protruding branches as he wove his way upward.

When we'd climbed about fifteen feet, I touched Eddie's foot. We were high enough to be invisible unless someone stood directly under the tree and looked up, which I doubted they would. Searchers tend to focus on the ground, not above their heads. We were as safe as we could be for now.

Within minutes a man and a woman passed below us. From our viewpoint they were merely dark shapes and murmurs of sound, but I held my breath until they'd moved on.

Once they were out of sight, Eddie touched my shoulder in a silent question. I put a cautionary hand on his arm, guessing they'd come back the same way. I was right. A half hour later, the two passed below us again, walking faster and searching less diligently, convinced they'd see nothing in territory they'd already covered.

When they were gone, we climbed down from the safe but definitely not comfortable tree. As we did, a squirrel we'd disturbed began an irritated recitation of our crimes. It seemed endless, rising and falling in tones of complaint, and continued even after we reached the ground. Luckily, the patrollers must have thought they were the ones who woke Mr. Grumpy. They didn't return.

On the ground outside the fence we sat absolutely still, watching what went on inside the compound as if it were a life or death matter, which it was. Neither of us dared whisper, though my mind raced with questions. For once my silence was imposed from the outside. Inside, I longed for conversation.

After what seemed like days but was probably an hour, we heard the truck returning. A man on the inside opened the gate, and Dave jerked to a stop before the main building, where he conferred with his men, obviously unhappy. We heard bits of conversation. "If he gets to that lawyer—"

"Ben left with the lawyer. He won't be talking to nobody."

I glanced at Eddie, raising my brows in a question.

His answer was mouthed, not spoken, but it shook me as much as if he'd shouted it. "Bronson."

I was shocked. Bronson was in West Virginia? In Romulus? He'd been to GoodRich Lodge? How had he and Eddie met, and how did these people know about him? When the meaning of Dave's comment sank in, it made me cringe. Had Bronson come here to help me and died because of it? If so, he paid a terrible price for feeling sorry for a client.

A loser.

I told myself there was no sense fretting over things I couldn't change. I had to concentrate on getting Eddie out of there and maybe living through it myself. I figured we were safe where we were, at least for a while. In a couple of hours, when our pursuers concluded we were gone and gave up the search, we could make our way to the hole I'd cut in the fence and escape. I was used to waiting, but when I nestled into a fairly comfortable spot on the ground, Eddie looked at me as if I were crazy. After a few seconds, he seemed to resolve himself to waiting and did the same. I slept a little, but I don't know if Eddie did. Every time I opened my eyes, he was looking at me.

Maybe an hour later, we heard the low growl of an approaching vehicle. We couldn't see it until it entered the compound, but Eddie tensed at the sound of the engine, and I saw why as it pulled up to the main building. It was the Hummer. When it stopped inside the gate, Hopgood emerged, looking like anything but the grief-stricken man I'd seen earlier. Dave came out of the building to meet him. I couldn't catch every word of their exchange, but the essence was clear enough.

"—find him?"

Dave shook his head. "We looked—nothing."

"—left some men at the house."

Raising a hand in a calming gesture, Dave responded, "He'll go back into hiding."

I turned to Eddie, who was listening as hard as I was. They thought he was heading back to Romulus.

"—about the woman?" Hopgood asked.

"No sign. We think—scared and headed for home."

Hopgood was a pacer. Once he'd been brought up to speed, he turned and walked the fence line, coming directly toward us. Dave fell into step beside him, his face taut with concern. Their closeness allowed Eddie and me to hear their discussion of what to do next. "She knew Nadine?"

"She had the ring you gave Nadine in her car," Dave answered. "Eddie says they're foster sisters."

"So Nadine told her about this place." Hopgood made a sharp gesture. "The bitch swore she hadn't told anyone, not even the kid."

"I thought you got the truth out of her," Dave said. "I guess she was tougher than we thought."

I turned to Eddie, whose eyes had gone wide, and put a cautionary hand on his arm. His lips disappeared as he fought to keep control.

"The kid knows the Romulus cops think he's a juvenile delinquent," Dave said. "If he finds his way out of these woods, he'll most likely head north, to the woman's place."

"Sooner or later, they'll tell someone who'll believe them." Hopgood stopped almost directly in front of us, and I flinched as his gaze passed over our hiding spot. "If you don't catch him here, you'll have to follow him to Beulah and shut them both up."

Dave nodded. "That's doable."

Gesturing at the building behind him, Rich said, "We've got to shut this place down ASAP."

Dave frowned in objection. "We went to a lot of trouble to build all this."

"And we've made good money." Rich turned abruptly. "Now, we need to cut our losses."

"What do we do about the current clients?"

"There's a guy with a ranch in New Mexico who does the same thing we do. We can take the Indians there until their new I.D.'s are ready."

Dave thought that over. "How do you want to do it?"

"Wake them up and say we've run into a small problem. In order to assure their safety, we're going to move them. Once they're gone, tell our people to scatter until we contact them. I want everybody out of here by daylight. And warn them not to talk about this place."

"My guys know how to keep their mouths shut."

"Keep all the men you can spare searching the area until full daylight. The kid could still be up here somewhere. He hasn't got a car." His eyes raked the landscape again as if he might find us just by wanting to. "We should be okay if we find Eddie and shut him up, but the woman bothers me. Why didn't she go to the cops if she knows something?"

"The lawyer said she just wants to be sure the kid's okay. If she does get the local cops out here, how do we explain this place?"

Hopgood turned to look at what I now suspected was a half-way house for rich criminals who'd escaped punishment by disappearing from their homeland. "We make sure there's nothing for them to find."

At that moment the front door of the building opened, and one of my fears materialized. The Indian woman I'd seen earlier stepped out, wearing a shapeless nightgown and holding a fluffy little Pekinese in her arms. Closing the door behind her, she set the animal down. He ran around in a circle, stopped with his malformed nose in the air, and headed straight for Eddie and me. *I had to bring ham sandwiches!*

"Hey," Dave said, turning to follow the dog's headlong path to the fence. "Someone's out there!"

Giving Eddie a push, I whispered, "Run!" He didn't wait for further urging but took off into the woods, moving quickly and staying low. I followed, though I knew there wasn't much chance we'd outrun Hopgood's men now that they had an idea where we were. They knew the terrain, had superior numbers, and drove machines that could catch up to us in a matter of minutes.

We hadn't gone far before the ground sloped sharply ahead. We stopped, uncertain. Should we try to climb the steep embankment or run along the side of the hollow?

Taking Eddie by the shoulders, I turned him toward the bank and ordered, "Go. My car's at the end of the old logging road."

He got the idea right away and shook my hands off. "No. I'm not leaving you."

"Get help. I cut a hole in the fence, east of the gate."

Like a stubborn horse—or a stubborn teenager—he shook his head. "No. We stay together."

"Together, we're caught."

Alarms went off in my head, as they always did when my word count went over twenty. My chest tightened, and my jaw clenched. Words. I had to find the words! I slouched out of the backpack. "Pictures. Proof."

"They'll kill you," Eddie said. "They were gonna kill me. Bronson believed their lies. He just drove away and left me!"

The roar of an approaching ATV sounded behind us. It was like a blow to my chest, but sometimes such blows are necessary. The knowledge of certain capture solidified my decision. I didn't have time to think about Bronson or what he'd done or what had been done to him. Nothing mattered except getting Eddie out of here, not even the fact that I'd uttered my twenty-ninth word. "Go."

Thirty words: a whole day's supply, and the sun wasn't up yet.

190

"No," Eddie insisted. "I can't leave you, can't let them catch you—"

In answer, I turned and ran back the way we'd come. "Don't shoot!" I called. "I'm coming out! I give up!"

EDDIE

I found a skinny ledge of land halfway up the hill that was hidden by leafy plants. Squirming out of sight, I jammed my arms into the straps of the backpack and waited, trying to take breaths that weren't out-loud groans. I heard commotion below, in the spot where Loser had last called out, and knew they'd caught her. They didn't realize I was only a few feet above them, clinging to the steep wall of the hollow and trying not to jiggle the shrubbery.

The few minutes of confusion after Loser's capture were all the time I'd had to find a hiding place. Soon they'd remember they were after me, not her, and return to the hunt. I couldn't blow the chance she'd given me, no matter how much I wanted to go back down there and scream at them to leave her alone.

It wasn't long before I heard them calling to each other as flashlights searched the hillside. I stayed real still, hiding my hands under me and pressing my face into the dirt as I thought about how lucky it was that I never wear anything but black clothes.

Somebody passed fairly close, and I imagined the light raking over my back, but he didn't see me. It took a long time before they moved on, and I cringed at the thought of what they might be doing to Loser. Were they beating her up? Killing her? Was she already dead?

There was nothing I could do down there except die with her, and I knew the pictures she'd taken were my way to get help. If Loser was still alive, I had to do what I could to see that she stayed that way.

When the woods quieted around me, I left my hiding place, checking every direction a hundred times to make sure there wasn't some guy with a gun waiting to pick me off. Nothing happened, but I guessed they'd keep circulating through the woods. My short trip in Dave's truck had been downhill, so I knew I was in some kind of valley. Loser had said something about cutting a hole in a fence, and I remembered we'd come through a gate on the way down. First, I had to find the fence and then find the hole. Jostling Loser's backpack to a balanced position, I began to climb.

The next hour was pure hell. Jumping at every noise and scurrying for cover a couple of times at the threat of what turned out to be little animals, I made my way out of the hollow. When the ground leveled a little, my legs felt better, but that's when I came to a fence so high it made me cuss. Was the hole Loser had made to the right or the left? The moon was on my left. That had to be west, so I turned right.

When I came to the gate, my heart almost stopped. There was a guy guarding it, gun drawn and ready. Crouching, I told myself I should have expected that. They knew, at least they thought they knew, that I had to leave by that gate. I hoped they hadn't found the hole. If it was on the east side of the gate, I had to get past this guy.

Backtracking through the woods, I moved away from the fence, keeping an eye on the moon so I wouldn't lose my sense of direction. Once I was out of sight of the guard, I darted across the road, looking both ways more carefully than I'd ever done before, and continued east. When I was down the fence line a few hundred yards, I made a ninety degree turn and worked my way back. I faced another choice when the fence appeared in the dim light before me: right or left? After maneuvering past the guard, was I on the far side of where Loser had made the hole, or did I need to go east some more?

I got a little panicked, and for a few minutes, I couldn't suck it up and make a decision. When everything you do means your life and maybe the life of someone else too, it's hard to make yourself take action. I kept thinking if I just stayed where I was, someone would come along and rescue me, tell me what to do, make everything all right. I'd never felt so much pressure, and the choice of turning one way or the other was more than I could handle. I stood there, holding myself upright by holding onto a couple of saplings, barely able to make myself breathe, much less move.

Then I heard an ATV passing somewhere behind me. As the sound got closer, I knew I had to do something. A couple dozen feet away was the only cover I could see, an old tree that had been hit by lightning and broken completely off. Its stump stuck jaggedly about eight feet up, but most of the trunk lay on the ground, rotting into compost. I slid under it, feeling Loser's camera equipment poke me in the back, and waited for the ATV to pass. It didn't come that close, but I was terrified anyhow.

When I finally crawled out of my hiding place, I saw the branch lying against the fence. It could have gotten there naturally, but I didn't think so. I shined the flashlight from Loser's backpack ahead, holding it close to the ground and shielding its ray with my T-shirt. There it was, a manmade something that caught my eye. Bending close, I saw a Velcro strip and the shiny edges of metal recently cut. Removing the strip, I bent the fence outward, shrugged out of the backpack, shoved it through, and then dragged myself to the other side, using my elbows like oars. I put it all back, hoping that what Dickweed's men didn't know could hurt them.

Being on the other side of the fence made me feel a little better. Using the slope as a guide, I stumbled through the woods until I found the old wooden fence that was the outer boundary of GoodRich Lodge. I slid through between the middle and top slats, paused briefly to see if anyone was hanging around watching for me, and entered the woods on the downhill side. I was off Dickweed's property, not that it would protect my life if they caught me. Dickweed and his men couldn't afford to let me live now, though I didn't understand what I'd seen. Whatever it was, it was a big secret, so they'd be going all out to catch me. I hoped they hadn't found Loser's car yet.

The route downhill was treacherous, through thick undergrowth and often straight down so I had to sort of skid along. The bad guys owned the road and the gentler slopes. I was okay with skidding if it meant they didn't find me, but it's hard to be quiet when you're crashing into tree branches and piles of dead leaves. I was lucky. They really did think their fence would keep me inside.

As I went I drank a bottle of water from Loser's backpack. It made me think of her again, wondering if she was okay. If I couldn't save her, I promised myself, I'd make sure Dickweed and his men paid for killing her. And my mom.

When I finally came to the road, I didn't even realize it. I was staggering by then, and suddenly the ground firmed beneath me, and I stumbled into the open. I crouched instinctively, afraid I'd be seen, but there was no one near. I couldn't tell where I was since trees all look alike, but I could see by the moonlight that the road sloped down to the right and up to the left. I started right, peering ahead at every turn to see if anybody waited up ahead to pounce on me.

Another half hour and the road got a little wider. To my right, a smaller fork disappeared into thick trees. That had to be the spot where Loser hid her car. It was barely a lane, but the hope of faster transportation than my tired feet sent me that way.

The little two-track took a sharp curve and ended in an open space. I turned, flashing my light at nothing but trees, and I'd seen enough f those lately to be totally sick of them. Then I saw a glint of chrome to my left. Loser's silver car was there, its front end barely sticking out from a clump of birches. She'd done a good job of hiding it, and shadows did the rest.

Slinging the pack off my back, I dug around until I found the keys and pressed the button to unlock the doors. There was a satisfying click and a double beep. I hurried to the car, anxious to be on my way. If I could get help fast enough, maybe Loser would be okay.

As I touched the latch, a hand grabbed my shoulder. "We've got to stop meeting like this, Eddie," Bronson said. "But I'm glad you brought the keys."

Chapter Eighteen

LOSER

They were the kind of men who prove how tough they are by pushing others around. I was shoved, poked, and kicked back to the compound. I was called nasty names too, but nothing I hadn't heard on the streets. I kept my head down and my mouth shut, even when I came face to face with Dave.

"Hello again," he said. He took off my hat, and I made a reflexive grab at it. After examining me for a few seconds, he returned the hat, shoving it into my hands. "How's the berry picking goin' for you?"

I didn't answer but put on the hat again, pulling it down around my face in what I hoped was a defiant gesture. Unimpressed, Dave turned to the two men who'd brought me to him. "Rich wants to talk to her, so keep her somewhere until he gets to it."

"Where should we put her?"

Dave gave the guy that can't-you-make-one-little-decision look, but after a moment's thought said, "That little storage cubby in his office. She won't get out of there."

"There ain't much room," one man commented.

"She'll survive." Dave took a small notepad out of his pocket, the kind with its own pencil, and scribbled something on a piece of paper. "That'll get you into the office," he said. The guard took the paper and put it into his shirt pocket.

Replacing the notebook in his own pocket, Dave touched my chin in a teasing manner. "It's what you get for bein' nosy, lady. It ain't like the box they got in prison, but it's close enough." He looked like a man who might have first-hand knowledge of such things. Turning back to the guards he said, "Once you take care of her, get back out there and find that kid."

I tried not to think about the confined space in my immediate future. I concentrated instead on Eddie, hoping he was on his way down the mountain by now. I also hoped he'd send help, even if it meant revealing his presence in Romulus and facing the possibility of coming under Hopgood's control. Would Eddie take that chance for a woman he hardly knew? I thought he'd at least try, but with Hopgood's connections and the fact that Eddie had been missing for the last few months due to supposed theft of his stepfather's money, it would be difficult for him to get anyone to believe his story. Even if he talked the local sheriff into sending men up to GoodRich Lodge, they were likely to be too late to save me. Eddie's best bet might be to get off the mountain and keep going. The possibility that he'd live through this was the most I could hope for.

I thought again of Bronson, who must have come to Romulus to help me. The guards seemed to think they'd dealt with him. I wished I'd used that fancy phone to tell him what I was up to, so he hadn't walked blindly into a den of criminals. Bronson hadn't treated me like a crazy person. If I'd told him the situation, he might have helped me talk to the police, like he'd helped me at the DMV. It was too late now. My phone was in the backpack I'd given Eddie, and Bronson might already be dead.

With my escort prodding me at every step, I entered the compound. Torn between dread of what was to come and interest in what lay before me, I tried to ignore the former and concentrate on the latter. Homelessness had honed my powers of observation. On the streets, a person might become oblivious to what goes on around her (which I had been at times) or she could become highly tuned in. A state of alert observance was helpful in avoiding confrontations with cops, conflict with the more dangerous of my companions, and encounters with so-called "normal" people bent on harassing street people to amuse themselves. I'd learned to see while seeming to ignore, to hear sounds missed by most, and to sense a dangerous situation.

But this dangerous situation was already upon me. I was captured and on the way to a locked room, a prospect I faced with rising panic. I tried to breathe normally so my brain got the required amounts of oxygen for logical thought. I needed Loser's ability to appear helpless and defeated, but I couldn't let her fears hold sway. I also needed Beth's police training. A chance for escape would come, and when it did, I would take it.

We marched toward the building, my guard sticking his gun in my back more for fun than necessity. When we reached the oversized, dignified entry doors, he stepped ahead, gesturing for me to enter.

As I took a step forward, the Indian couple I'd seen earlier came out, their faces pinched with anger. I had a moment of hope. The men who'd taken me prisoner couldn't very well attack me in front of guests. How would they explain locking up a defenseless woman?

The man looked at me briefly then turned to the guard, distaste evident on his face. "This is the problem which has forced us to leave?"

"Yeah."

Dark eyes focused on me, but he spoke to the guard. "I paid a good deal of money in the belief that you people were in control of this site. I hope this sloppiness is not typical of your services."

"We got it covered," my guard said firmly. "We caught her on the property, so we're moving you as a precaution." I noticed he didn't admit there was a teenager out there somewhere who'd eluded them so far.

The couple moved on, a sniff from the man the only acknowledgement of the guard's statement. I got an extra-hard shove forward, apparently for causing a client to feel that his safety had been compromised.

The room I stumbled into was impressive. Think *Beauty and the Beast*, a haven in the middle of the forest with no expense spared to invite you to "Be Our Guest." The ceiling of the lobby went all the way to the roof, with intricately designed lighting and patterns of color. To the right and left, wings curled around the center space, each with a wide staircase rising to the second floor, where walkways led around the circle and disappeared into the wings. At the back of the lobby was a dining area that might have graced the finest hotels in Europe, though this one seated no more than thirty people. To the right was a lounge with a movie screen, a bar, and comfortable seating. Every piece of furniture was luxurious, from the dining room chairs to the framed artwork on the walls. A place for people with money. Lots of it.

From a hallway to my right came high, petulant voices, and I looked up to find the two Indian girls coming toward me. They looked as if they'd dressed hurriedly, and they spoke in tones of complaint as they passed in a cloud of expensive scent. Neither so much as glanced at me.

Behind them came two dark-haired women in khaki pants and red polo shirts, each with a fully loaded luggage cart. They noticed me, but their faces remained blank as they bent their bodies against the weight of their burdens. One of them gave me a brief look of sympathy, and I saw in her eyes the hopelessness I'd seen so often on the street. *You're not okay, but I'm not okay either.*

A blond woman followed, giving the baggage-toters sharp commands. The guard asked, "Are they ready to move?" Nodding, she moved ahead to hold the door open for the girls and the baggage carts to pass. The Hummer pulled up outside the door, where the old couple waited. The man issued orders to his family with gestures, telling them where to sit. They all obeyed, the girls ceasing their complaints in their father's presence. I heard the sounds of luggage being loaded and car doors closing, shutting out the father's commanding voice. The guests were being moved out, as Hopgood had ordered, but they weren't happy about it.

The blond held the door until the two workers returned inside, and an order given in Spanish sent them scurrying back to where they'd come from. Inclining her head toward them, the woman asked my guard in English, "What about the help?"

His jaw bulged briefly. "They'll be handled. Get your gear packed. We leave in fifteen." She didn't salute, though she might as well have. Turning smartly on her heel, she left.

I felt a jab to my shoulder. "Upstairs." Obedient for lack of a better option, I took the staircase on the right. At the top we turned right again, skirting the open space for a few steps before entering a hallway. As we passed along it, I glanced into an open doorway and saw a living area with a wide-screen TV, a short couch, and two recliners. Along one wall I glimpsed a sink, a small refrigerator, and a cook-top with a microwave oven mounted above it. The next door was open too, revealing a woman who was making a bed. She worked quickly, spreading a colorful, flowered comforter over plumped pillows and squarely tucked sheets. It seemed odd that the rooms were being cleaned when the place was shutting down, but I guessed the help was being kept busy until it came time to "handle" them.

The door at the end of the hallway had a numbered keypad. My escort dug out the paper Dave had given him, punched in the code, and opened the door. "In here." I stepped inside an office that combined luxury and practicality, apparently where Hopgood and Dave managed the place. "Over here." The guard opened a door at the side of the room. My eyes left the desk topped with papers and various electronic devices and settled on my prison, a narrow room containing nothing but filing cabinets, some topped with yet-to-be-stored folders. I shrank back, but the man gave me a shove that propelled me painfully into the nearest cabinet. Before I'd recovered my balance, I heard the door close and the bolt lock engage, and I was locked in darkness.

Though it was useless, I rattled the knob ferociously, testing its strength. I pounded on the metal door a few times too, but there was no response, not even a threat of violence if I didn't keep quiet. That meant no one out there would or could help, no matter how much noise I made. I groped blindly, running my hands over metal cabinets and smooth walls, even over the tile floor. There was no way out. The room was dark, it was tiny, and it was secure. I wasn't going anywhere. Setting my back against the side of a file cabinet, I sank to a crouch, trying to calm my mind. I had to escape, but all I could think of was four walls, a ceiling, and a floor. That's when the voices started:

Loser!

You're dead. You're trapped, and you're going to die.

You knew it was useless to try, and now you've lost.

Loser!

I tried to imagine police cars coming up the mountain road. It didn't work. For a long time, it was just the voices.

EDDIE

Bronson's Beemer was hidden even better than Loser's Buick. When he pointed it out to me with a flashlight, I cringed to think what pulling that far into the woods must have done to his paint job.

"How'd you find her car?" I asked.

"OnStar." He frowned. "It took me all night to get back up here, even after I dealt with Ben."

I felt a shiver go up my spine, half dread, half excitement. "Did you kill him?"

"No," Bronson said grimly. "He's tied up in the trunk."

"Cool." Bronson was back to being Tom Cruise in *Mission: Impossible*.

"It's been a mess." He rubbed at a bandage on his hand that covered the web between his thumb and fingers. "Ben tossed my phone out the car window, so I had to find an all-night drugstore and buy a pre-paid one." He grunted as he pulled it from his pocket. "More suited to the nineties than now. Then, Mr. Suggs, my boss, was at some event and had his phone turned off, which almost drove me crazy. When I finally got hold of him, he thought of locating Beth through OnStar, but it took him a while to convince them it was an emergency. When I finally got the location and realized she was up here, I went back to the drug store, bought some clothes for crawling around in the woods, and located the car. I was about to change when I heard you coming." Taking a bag from the front seat of the BMW, he emptied it onto the hood of Loser's car. "Now, start from the beginning and tell me everything that's happened since we last saw each other."

I would've laughed if we'd been in a less desperate situation. Bronson put on the cheapest-looking pair of black sweatpants I've ever seen, the kind with elastic around the ankles that makes absolutely everyone look like a tool. After that came a black sweatshirt he had to turn inside out because the words *Foxy Lady* were sewn on the front in sequins. I guessed it was a woman's XXX, and it was every bit as wide as it was long. Those sequins would be nasty against his skin, but what can a guy do?

As Bronson dressed for action, I told him what had happened to me. When I finished, he quizzed me on the compound: where stuff was, how many guards, and what kind of equipment they had. I knew my description wasn't great: "big" guns, two "high" fences, and "scary-looking" guys, but Bronson fine-tuned his questions until I remembered some specifics: the guard tower, guns of the kind soldiers but not deer hunters use, and how I'd found the hole Loser made in the middle fence.

Bronson still wore his own black socks, which were now the most expensive items in his outfit. He shone the light on the loafers he'd set on the ground. "I couldn't find shoes. They only had flip-flops." Eyeing my feet, he said, "What size are those?"

"Eleven."

"Hmm." He stuffed the parts of his business suit into the plastic bag the cheap stuff had come in. I heard change jingle in the pants pocket, but Bronson moved only one item to his sweatpants, a small jackknife. If he thought it was going to help against men with guns, he wasn't thinking very clearly.

I had some questions of my own. "How come you acted like you believed Dave and Rich when they said those things about me?"

He smiled that funny smile that makes him look younger than me. "I realized right away those guys were ex-military, the kind that never get over it. Ben was on high alert, kept his hand near his holster the whole time I was there even though there was no reason for it. I got the distinct feeling he'd have shot both of us if I made a fuss. The gun was odd too, a forty-five caliber ACP, which isn't a weapon used for hunting."

It was a relief to know Bronson hadn't abandoned me, but I couldn't help asking, "So you acted like a wimp on purpose?"

"If people don't see you as a threat, they tend to get careless. Just ask Ben." He threw the bag with his suit in it into his car and closed the door gently. "I knew you thought they were killers," he said, turning back to face me. "I guessed Beth did too, or she'd have contacted Hopgood directly when you took off."

"You pretended to believe them so you could get away."

"Yes, but I specifically told Hopgood I'd bring your things in a few days. I hoped that would keep you alive until I figured out what to do."

"What do you think he's doing up there?"

He frowned. "I'm not sure. I thought they might be survivalists, but given what you saw that doesn't seem right." He shifted his shoeless feet. "We need the police up here, but we have nothing to convince them you were held against your will." He glanced at his car. "Even Ben here doesn't help. He's a local. I'm not. Hopgood would no doubt back whatever story Ben told, and he's already spread the lie about you stealing money from him. We're on our own until we get proof."

Peg Herring

That reminded me. "Alex, Loser took pictures." Slipping out of the backpack, I unbuckled the flap and took out the camera. Once we figured out how to work it, we huddled together, me advancing the images while Bronson pointed his pocket flashlight at the screen. There were shots of the compound from three sides: the front with the guard tower on the left; the side, where a guy swam in a pool; and the back, where a road almost directly opposite the front gate led away from the compound.

"There's the proof," I said, "but how do we get it to the cops?"

"One of us has to take Beth's car and get these to police." His tone changed as he added, "That has to be you."

"No way! Loser's in this mess because of me. Besides, the cops will believe a lawyer way before they believe a kid!"

"Head to Cranville. Find a computer. Email the pictures to the state police. Then call and explain what the pictures are about. I'll find Beth, and she and I will be waiting to guide them in when they arrive."

"Alex, shouldn't you and me go up there—"

Bronson scrunched down a little and looked me in the eye, as if to say this was important. "I know you want to help her, but wanting isn't enough. You've got no experience with things like this."

"Come on! You're a lawyer, not Jason Bourne!"

"A lawyer who did two tours in Afghanistan to pay his way through law school." That shut me up for a few seconds, and he added softly, "I've been shot at, Ed. Have you?"

That was a shock, but kind of a good one. At least Loser and me weren't stuck on this mountain with a wimp. Alex Bronson didn't come on like a tough guy, but confidence flowed out of him like heat from a toaster. He was concerned, but he wasn't afraid. Still, I didn't want to head for safety while my friends suffered who-knew-what dangers. "I could help you. I'll create a diversion—" I'd heard that in the movies. I had no idea what it would be.

"Beth made it possible for you to get away, Ed. If they catch you, what she did will be wasted." He put a hand on my shoulder. "I promise, I'll do whatever it takes to get her out of there."

One man against a bunch of criminals didn't sound like good odds. "What if you can't?"

He didn't sugarcoat it. "If I can't, it's because she's already dead. But we need the police up here."

"All right," I said, opening the door of the Buick. "One more thing," Bronson said as I jiggled the right key into my hand. "Trade me shoes."

"What?"

"I'm an eleven and a half, but your shoes aren't new. They should be stretched out enough to fit me, and they'll work a whole lot better in the woods than these."

In a few seconds we'd traded, and I was wearing Italian loafers that felt like I wasn't wearing shoes at all. He knelt beside the car, tying my Nikes in tight, double knots.

"Once you call for help, go back to that IHOP in Romulus and wait for me and Beth to come get you, okay?"

"Okay." Actually, I planned on turning around and coming back as soon as possible. If there was something I could do for Loser, I wanted to be there to do it. It's better to keep some things to yourself, though, so I gave Bronson Smile #9 (Obedient Young Man). Gets 'em every time.

LOSER

I don't know how long I cowered in a corner, holding my hands over my ears and trying to shut out the voices of despair. When some sense of sanity returned, I rose on shaky legs, telling myself I might have missed an air duct I could crawl out. I didn't find anything like that, but my fumbling fingers found a bump between a cabinet and the wall that turned out to be the light switch. Being able to see my prison helped a little. I was still closed in, but I wasn't trapped in darkness.

I looked up at the simple, one-bulb fixture. No way out there. In fact, there was no way out at all except the door, which was firmly locked. I turned my attention to the files that lay on top of the nearest cabinet. Opening one, I paged through the papers inside. The first few didn't make sense to me, but gradually, a pattern emerged. Each folder was a dossier on a client. There was background information on the person, including a long list of their "activities" (crimes). Notes made by Hopgood or DP, which I guessed was Dave, determined how the person would be "transported" (smuggled) into the United States using the automobile dealership as a front. Other documents showed that new identities had been created for the client and for family members he brought along. Last were final resolution documents, showing the clients had been relocated to places where they could start new lives.

The fourth folder seemed likely to be the people I'd seen downstairs. The client was an arms dealer who'd made a fortune but attracted the interest of Interpol in recent months. He wrote to Hopgood through an intermediary, saying he'd heard that he, his wife, and their two daughters could be "reinvented" and take up residence somewhere safe. Other documents finalized the arrangements, and the arrival date had been set for the second week of August. There was no final resolution, and I concluded Hopgood hadn't yet received the documents he needed to help them disappear. That explained why no one else at the dealership was allowed to get the mail. He couldn't have them opening envelopes that looked like they contained advertising copy and finding fake passports and doctored birth certificates instead. GoodRich Lodge was an Underground Railroad for criminals.

Nadine must have stumbled onto Rich's secret, or at least some part of it that scared her into running. He'd killed her, and now he had to kill me too. They wouldn't have let me see these documents if I had any chance of living past tomorrow. Closing the file with a snap, I wedged myself into a corner and waited in a kind of limbo, refusing to let myself feel anything at all. If you feel nothing, death doesn't seem so bad. Dread turns to resignation, to a feeling of let's-get-it-over-with. At times in the past, I'd wanted to die, but something inside hadn't let me end my own life. Now, the option was no longer mine. One less soul tortured into madness was probably a good thing.

In spite of that, the Beth part of me held onto sanity, repeating that there's always hope. Beth wanted to survive.

CHAPTER NINETEEN

EDDIE

I'd driven a car before, but never on my own and never in an emergency. I started Loser's Envoy and drove carefully out of the trees as the branches squeaked along the sides. Leaning into the car, Alex warned, "Someone will be watching the road, but it probably won't be their best man. You put your weakest link in the spot he's least likely to screw up." He'd rubbed at his neck, obviously wishing things were different. "Here's what you do: drive right at the guy. Most times, he'll jump out of the way, and you can get by him." He added grimly, "If he starts shooting, hit the gas and keep going."

That was scary advice, but I tried to appear confident. With a final nod to Alex, who waved with the hand that wasn't holding the half sandwich I'd given him from Loser's backpack, I took off.

"Keep going" wasn't an option. A few hundred yards down from the last fork, a pickup sat sideways in the road, its nose pointed downhill on the right while its tailgate hung over the narrow ditch on the left side. Behind it was a guy who looked younger than Bronson but a few years older than me. If he wasn't their best man, he wasn't stupid either. He'd chosen a spot where trees made it impossible for me to go around, and Loser's car was not going to move that pickup out of the way. I stopped, about to ram the car into reverse, but he stepped forward, pointed a rifle at me, and called out, "We thought y'all might could have a car hidden up here somewhere."

Bronson hadn't anticipated a completely blocked road. I had to improvise, which wasn't easy with a gun aimed at my face. *I've been shot at*, Bronson had said. *Have you?* Not only was the answer no, there was a terrifying corollary: *And I don't want to be.*

Fear calls up old instincts. My life, all fifteen years of it, has taught me to be non-threatening. I'm not big enough, mean enough, or even connected to anyone big or mean enough to be taking bad guys head on. I've always got by, and often got what I wanted, by being just the opposite. I rolled the window down and gave the guy my best Smile #6 (Sad) and said, "I guess you caught me."

He was taken by surprise. Men who work for the Rich Hopgoods of the world are probably used to tough talk and the use of force. He couldn't believe I was giving up so easily.

"Once they caught my friend, I didn't figure I had much of a chance." I let Smile #6 turn into Smile #3 (Hopeful). "Rich won't hurt me, right? I mean, I'm family."

The guy nodded, but it was pretty fake. "Nah, he just wants to talk to you."

I switched to Smile #4 (Bashful Embarrassment) and waved at the trees around us. "I never drove a car before. I don't think I can turn around on this skinny road."

The guy surveyed the situation, trying to decide how he'd manage the gun, the car, and me all at once. I hoped it was beyond the abilities of a low-level, hired goon. "Scoot over," he ordered, opening the driver's side door.

I scrambled over the console into the passenger seat. Leaning in, my new buddy waited until I was settled. "Fasten your seat belt."

Giving him Smile #3 again, I made the buckle click into place.

Satisfied that I was secure, he considered what to do with the gun. He didn't want it within my reach, but it was too long to lie on the floor under his feet. Setting it in the back seat would make it hard for him to reach quickly. In the end he set it on the rear bumper of his truck, giving me a look that said not to try anything. I summoned up Smile #5, which is more of a sick grin (Not An Alpha Male). At the same time I released the seat belt, holding it in place with my left hand.

Climbing into the car, the guy shifted into reverse and backed up a few feet. Another shift and a turn of the wheel to the right, and we paralleled the pickup. Putting it in reverse again, he backed as far into the ditch as he dared, the taillights glowing red against the tree trunks we almost touched. He pulled forward again, positioning the car directly across the narrow road. Backing again toward the trees, he turned the wheels to the right this time, angling the car uphill. One more trip back, almost touching the rear of the truck this time. The gun was briefly lit in a red glow, and I imagined it was evil, even magical. But it was the guy beside me I had to worry about. Maybe guns don't kill people, but people with guns do.

The moment I'd waited for came. The guy was as far from his gun as he was going to get, with the car between him and it. I was close to it, but since I'd never fired a firearm before, this was no time for experiments. My goal was the truck. Shoving the car door open, I jumped out and sprinted toward it. As I passed the tailgate, I grabbed the rifle and, holding it like a javelin, flung it into the woods. Without slowing, I jumped into the pickup, locked first the driver's door and then the other one, and sighed with relief. The key was in the ignition.

By the time I got the truck started, its former driver was pounding on the window, his furious face inches from mine. He was shouting, and suddenly I realized I was too: some sort of primitive yell, a mixture of terror and victory. I slammed the gearshift into drive and gunned it. The truck lurched forward, scraped a couple of trees, and dug in, the wheels spinning for a moment before finding solid ground and shooting me forward. I twisted the steering wheel to the left, heading for the trees on the other side of the road.

I scared myself, but I scared my unwanted passenger more. He let go of the door handle to avoid hitting a pine tree and launched himself off the running board, spinning to the ground. As he sprawled at the edge of the road, I got control of the car again and beat it out of there.

LOSER

I jumped when the bolt on the other side of the door slid aside. The battle I'd waged between wanting life and wishing for death had ended in a surprise. Neither Loser nor Beth was willing to die, so despite my despair, I'd begun plotting ways to keep on living.

Richard Hopgood stepped into my little cell. I was still in the corner, buttressed by file cabinets, and he took advantage of my position, moving quickly to block me in. It was an interrogation technique known to cops everywhere: make the prisoner feel trapped, invade her space, loom over her like doom itself. Make her feel like a loser.

Already there.

Up close, Hopgood showed signs of stress. His perfectly barbered hair was grimy-looking, his expensive suit was streaked with dust, and one of his shoes had a long scratch down its side. I noticed his watch, one of those over-kill brands that's a pound and a half of precious metal and extra dials. It read 6:45. I had no idea if that was a.m. or p.m., but I was pretty sure it was still Friday.

"You're Nadine's foster sister?"

From my spot on the floor, I was looking up his nose. It didn't help my situation, but it did make it a little easier to ignore the threat he posed. I turned away and said nothing, wondering why gut feelings don't reveal who's a good guy and who isn't. Hopgood had fooled a lot of people, including me.

"It doesn't matter," he said. "Whoever you are, you're dead."

The inside pocket of his suit chirped, and he turned away, pulling the phone out. "Yeah?"

We both waited.

"He's a kid. How'd he manage that?" After listening for a few seconds he swore, and I hid a smile. It sounded like Eddie was still free, which made my terrible, very bad day one iota better. "Okay. Are the Indian clients in the air yet? ... Good. Send Ben to take the Texans to

211

Miami. ... What? Where is he? ... Oh. Well, send someone else then. Get them on a boat to Mexico. When I get their papers I'll send them along, and from there they can go wherever they want." He listened again, glancing at me. "I'll take care of her."

My worst fears were confirmed with an offhand, mildly irritated comment. Killing me was the next thing on Hopgood's to-do list.

"Send someone up with a bottle of something." He glanced at me. "Any liquor you're particularly fond of? No?" Into the phone he said, "Anything will do." Hopgood ended the call and put his phone into his jacket pocket. "I'll have a lot of trouble repairing the damage you've done, Miss No-name. In return for that, I'm going to kill you."

"Like Nadine?"

His nostrils flared. "Like Nadine. Only we haven't found your car, so you can't have that kind of accident." He considered. "I think you're going to fall asleep on a railroad track, somewhere far enough away from here to keep us out of it."

I heard three quick raps before the door opened. A man handed Hopgood a bottle of vodka. He glanced at the label, took the cap off and threw it in a corner, and handed it to me. "Drink."

When I hesitated, he smiled. "That train is going to mess your corpse up pretty good, so it doesn't matter if I have to smack you around until you do as I say."

He had a point. Besides, that tiny flicker of hope that is the last refuge of the doomed whispered that I had a better chance of escape if I wasn't beaten bloody. I took a drink from the bottle. Hopgood nodded as if to say I was a good girl. "What'd Nadine tell you about what she saw here?"

He gestured, and I took another swig. A little spot of heat started glowing in my center. "Nothing."

"You're lying, but it doesn't matter." He took a step back. "Drink." As I obeyed, he spoke, maybe to me, maybe to himself. "It was bad luck

212

for both of us when she came home just after I stuck a knife into an employee who drank too much and then talked too much."

That explained the bloodstains that made Eddie think his mother had killed his stepfather. A dramatic conclusion, but Nadine's terrified flight from Romulus had fed the boy's fears. I imagined Nadine, dumbstruck to find her husband bent over a bleeding corpse. What had Rich threatened that kept her from calling the police?

"Drink." I took another drink, managing to drizzle some down my shirt. "Spill all you like," he said. "We've got more." With a gesture, he indicated I should try again. I did.

Watching to make sure I swallowed, he said, "I thought the money was enough to keep her quiet, but when I threatened the kid, she took off."

"No more happy home."

"Nadine was the perfect wife for a corny car dealer, beautiful but not too classy." Hopgood's comment revealed surprise that he could possibly have been mistaken. "My money kept her under control, at least until this happened."

Be careful what you wish for, Nadine. Aloud I said, "I saw your man in Beulah."

Hopgood grinned. "My wife thought she hid her slutty past, but I'd never marry a woman without knowing everything about her."

That was how they'd known where to look for her. They'd simply come too early, before Nadine was desperate enough to beg help from the foster mother she'd rejected.

Hopgood rolled a hand to encourage me, and I took another drink. My gut burned as the liquor hit my empty stomach. "Why'd she come back?"

"She called me a week ago from some little town. I promised if she me, I'd give her enough money to get started somewhere new." He huffed disgustedly. "The greedy bitch believed me."

213

I was feeling a little dizzy but a lot disgusted with myself for falling for his act. "You seemed sad."

He chuckled and made a theatrical little bow. "Tragedy's easy."

"She was your wife."

"I'll get another one." A wave of his hand dismissed Nadine completely. "How are you feeling?"

"Fine," I lied. "I took pictures." The last word sounded slushy.

"Did you." He was unconcerned. "*If* they ever come to light, I'll be incensed at the invasion of my privacy. I've gone to great expense to provide a retreat for my friends, and I'll be upset they weren't allowed the peace and quiet I'd promised them."

"They're criminals."

Hopgood glanced at the files lying out. "You've been reading. Yes, our guests have trouble with the law. We help them relocate, and they pay us well. A good deal for everyone."

"Except the law." I was going to die anyway. I could use all the words I wanted.

"What the law doesn't know won't hurt them. Drink."

I drank. "Eddie?"

"He's an overly dramatic teen who sees intrigue where there is none. The sheriff knows the kid has a troubled past, and he's distraught due to his mother's recent death. Drink."

I drank. Hopgood reached down and took the bottle from me, judging its contents before handing it back. It was half empty.

"With you gone and my logical explanation, Eddie's story will be unbelievable. I'll even beg the sheriff not to arrest him for stealing my truck." He scratched his head in a comic portrayal of a stressed parent. "I'll probably have to send him to a facility equipped to deal with problem kids. After asking how he's doing once or twice, people will forget him. They won't even notice when he never comes back again."

A knock sounded on the door. "Finish that bottle," Hopgood ordered. "If Dave's got things under control, you and I are going to take a ride."

EDDIE

Cranville was a burg with no police, but there was a sign on the scrapbooking store that advertised Wi-Fi. I banged on the front door, got no answer, and went to the back, where a light shone in a neat little kitchen and a coffeepot sent steam into the air. As I peered in, a lady in a homemade sweater and those glasses that sit down on your nose peeked around a corner, decided I wasn't scary enough to hide from, and bustled over to let me in.

I explained there was an emergency up on the mountain, and I needed to contact the state police. When I asked if I could send pictures to them by email, she said it was possible. "We have the Net, so we can share our stuff on Pinterest," she told me proudly. "What is it the police need to see?"

I gave her Smile #2. "If you don't mind, I'll explain as I go. It's kind of urgent."

"Fair enough," she replied. "Let's get the PC booted up."

I followed her into the storefront and dug the camera and the little cord that connected it to the USB port out of the backpack. As I did, I noticed a phone that had to be Loser's at the bottom of the bag. It was turned off, and I sighed at her lack of technical smarts. If she'd used the phone to take her pictures, the quality wouldn't have been as good, but we could have sent them from the mountaintop and saved me the drive down.

I attached the camera to the computer, located the state police website, and sent the pictures. The woman watched over my shoulder the whole time, her coffee cup so close to my head, I could smell the hazelnut creamer she'd put in it. I guess she was afraid my emergency might be an overwhelming desire to find a porn site.

"What is that place?" she asked when the pictures came up.

"It's what's hidden up at GoodRich Lodge."

"You're kiddin' me."

Squashing a sarcastic answer I replied, "Ma'am, I've never been more serious in my life."

Once I'd sent the pictures, I called the state police post. Trying to keep my voice from jumping three octaves like it does when I'm stressed, I said, "I need to report criminal activity."

"What is it, son?" Great. The guy already pegged me for a kid. I explained a little of it, but whoever I'd reached interrupted. "Who is this?"

"My name is Eddie Forsythe."

There was a pause. "Aren't you the young man who's been missing all summer?"

"Yes, but—"

"Son, you might be mad at your stepdad and all, but it's a crime to make a report that's—"

That's when the scrapbook lady took the phone out of my hand. "Listen," she told the guy on the other end of the line. "This boy has proof of what he's telling you. I suggest you listen to him, but first get some patrol cars on the way over here. Once you've seen these pictures, you ain't gonna want to be sitting around on your thumbs!"

CHAPTER TWENTY

LOSER

As soon as Hopgood left, I went into action. Opening one of the file drawers as far as it would go, I stuck my finger down my throat, gagging as I emptied my stomach into it. I poured the rest of the vodka in and laid folders over the mess to absorb the liquid and cover the odor of vomit. When the door opened again, I was back in the corner, the bottle lying on its side between my spread legs.

Dave put his head in, saw me apparently legless, and stood aside. Four women entered the room, looking as unwilling to be there as I've ever seen anyone look. Two were the ones I'd seen hauling baggage to the Hummer, and one was the barmaid from the night before. The fourth might have been the woman who'd been making beds; I'd only seen her backside. All were Latino in appearance. No one was smiling.

Brought you some company," Dave announced. He sniffed suspiciously. "Did you puke in here?" Following his nose, he opened drawers until he found one that made him recoil. "Not quite clever enough, bitch." He pulled a bottle of liquor from his jacket, the pint size Bubba used to call his "pocket-rocket," and handed it to the closest woman. "See that she drinks every drop of that."

When the woman looked at him blankly, Dave scowled. "How long you been here and you still got no English!" He pantomimed with exaggerated actions. "She. Drink. All. Get it?"

"Si." The woman nodded, smiling in a placating manner. "Si. She drink. Si."

Giving us an irritated look, Dave left. I heard the lock snap closed again, followed by the sound of his retreating footsteps.

We stared at each other for a few seconds. The women, all in their twenties and attractive, nevertheless had that air of hopelessness I'd sensed earlier. Finally, I said, "Who are you?"

Silent conversation passed among them and tacit agreement was reached. The barmaid said, "They took us from our homes in Mexico after the hurricane called Karl made things...(She twirled a hand)—upset, crazy."

I must have looked surprised at the complete sentence, because she added with a tiny smile, "We all speak English a little, but we pretend like we don't."

"Why?"

"We are slaves here. They bring us to do the work of this place. We cook, we clean, we take care of the guests. If we don't do it, they hurt us." Her expression shifted. "It is bad, what they do."

"I'm sorry."

She rejected the pain with a shrug. "We let them think we are stupid. They almost forget we are here."

Except when they want a woman, I thought, remembering the scene the night before and the reluctant resignation I'd seen in her body language when the man at the pool touched her.

One of the others said something in Spanish, and the barmaid asked, "Do you know why have they brought us here?"

I sighed. "They're going to kill me. You too, probably." My corpse would be found somewhere close to Beulah. I guessed these women's bodies would never be found.

Their eyes told me they understood. After a moment of silence, the barmaid gestured at the bottle. "If we all drink a little, none of us will be drunk when they come back for us, eh?"

EDDIE

The cops took way too long, and I couldn't stand to sit there sipping at the Sprite Miss Candace brought me. Thinking about the pictures, I asked, "Have you lived here a long time?"

She was adding decorative stickers to a page of photographs of her dogs. "All my life, dear."

"Is there another way to get up to the lodge?"

She adjusted her glasses, and I noticed red marks on either side of her nose where they sat. "We used to use an old logging road to get to some of the best berry patches." Her eyes squinted at the memory. "Then Mr. Hopgood bought the land and fenced it so we couldn't get in anymore. I'm not sure the road is even passable these days."

Ten minutes later I was on my way. I'd got her to draw me a map, promising with my best #1 smile that I'd simply drive up the old road a little way to see if the cops could use it to approach the lodge from two directions and keep any of the criminals from escaping. She didn't think it was a good idea, but what was a little old lady going to do, get the drop on me with her glue gun?

LOSER

When Hopgood returned I was in my corner, the second bottle empty beside me. The four women huddled in a different corner, ignoring me as if aware that I was bad luck to be around.

"Let's go," he ordered.

"Listen," I said, slurring the word. "I can keep quiet. I'll disappear."

"You will," he answered as he pulled me to my feet, his fingers pinching the soft underside of my arm. "I intend to help with both."

He led me out of the room. I didn't look at my new friends, but I felt their eyes on me. I could almost hear their desperate plea: *Get away! Come back and help us!*

Great. More voices in my head. More lives to be responsible for.

Partly faking and partly not, I stumbled down the hallway and stairs to the front door. Some of the alcohol had entered my bloodstream before I was able to expel it, and with the fact that I'd had nothing to eat in a long time, I was feeling the effects. Still, I faked more drunkenness than I actually felt, knowing I had the classic chances for escape: slim to none.

At the bottom of the stairs, the woman who'd overseen the departure of the Indian guests waited with a younger man. Beside them sat four five-gallon gas cans, their strong smell revealing they'd been filled hurriedly. "Burn everything," Hopgood said. "The kid will take the blame."

The woman nodded smartly and picked up a can in each hand. The guy took the other two, and they headed off in opposite directions.

I had a moment of dread, imagining Hopgood might leave the Mexican women upstairs to burn, but turning back I saw them coming down the stairs, sandwiched between two guards.

"Out in the woods," Hopgood ordered. "Do it right. We don't want critters digging up the remains."

One guy's jaw looked tight. I guessed he hadn't signed on to kill innocent women, but he didn't argue. "Got it."

All four women kept their eyes down, no doubt trying to hide their fear. They understood more than Hopgood realized, so at least they knew they had to make their break as soon as possible. Magglia, the barmaid, had feared they'd simply open the door and shoot us all, but I guessed they wanted our blood inside our bodies until we reached our final resting places. Then we could bleed all we liked.

"If we get out of here, I will run," one of the women had said. "I will not wait to be shot like a sick dog." The others had nodded agreement, though we all knew running wouldn't help. The gate was guarded, and there was no way we'd get over the fence before they caught and killed us. Still, I told myself, a chance, however small, might arise. Once before, when someone meant to kill me, I'd found that Loser wasn't willing to give up and let it happen. Someone inside my head, either Loser or Beth, whispered: *When the chance comes, take it!*

It was almost dawn. Black still covered the camouflaged compound, but streaks of gray light showed around the edges. I looked longingly at the hills around me, wishing I were out there. Running I knew I could do; disarming a killer with a gun I wasn't so sure about.

The chance came as we exited the main building. The whine of an engine revved to full speed came to my ears. My first reaction was dread: they'd caught Eddie and were bringing him in. That idea disappeared when an ATV came barreling up to the gate.

Coming at the gate.

Crashing through the gate!

The sound of metal straining, bending, and letting go rent the air. For an instant, everything stopped, at least, everything but the ATV, which ground forward, gaining speed.

The compound yard was deserted except for our little party and a single guard in the front tower. Hopgood's other people were occupied, searching for Eddie, moving their guests, and setting the place on fire. The guard in the tower took aim at the interloper, but surprise slowed his reaction. The ATV hit the tower squarely, bouncing backward from the impact. The wooden support that took the hit buckled, and the guard was thrown forward. I saw one hand leave his weapon as he tried to keep from spilling out like a pebble from a pail. The ATV shifted gears, backed up, and roared toward the tower a second time. This time the gun jolted free and glanced off the framework before hitting the ground with a rattling thud.

Whoever the gate-crashing maniac in the ATV was, he'd given me the chance I'd hoped for. Hopgood, surprised by the newcomer and convinced I was inebriated beyond action, loosened his grip on me. Wrenching my arm upward at the gap where his thumb and fingers didn't quite meet, I pulled away, smacked him once just above the cheekbone with my elbow, and took off at a dead run. I heard Hopgood shout, "Get her!" and knew that the two men guarding the Mexicans would be coming after me. At least I'd given them a chance to escape.

They tell you to zigzag when people shoot at you, but I can testify that true panic calls for a straight shot. I headed for the ruined gate like a cat in a thunderstorm, hoping if I got past the fence, they'd cut their losses and run rather than spending time looking for me.

Behind me was chaos as the ATV zoomed around the compound, its engine revving to a high whine and then dropping to a growl as the driver turned and gunned it again. I hoped my pursuers had lost sight of me as they evaded the unpredictable vehicle, but Hopgood shouted, "She's heading for the gate!"

The guard from the tower had scrambled to the ground, and he hurried to the gate to intercept me. He hadn't stopped to retrieve his gun, but he was still more than I could handle. I could either try to duck past him or run directly at him, hoping to bowl him over with sheer determination. The guy crouched as I approached, and I saw that he relished the confrontation. He was bigger, stronger, and had a relatively small space to defend. A confident grin spread over his face as I raced toward him. Suddenly, the grin disappeared. I didn't realize why until the ATV roared past as if I were standing still. Dirt pelted my face, but I didn't mind. The guard jumped out of the way, losing his footing. He hit the ground with a grunt and lay sprawled and dazed.

The ATV made a circle, sending the two men behind me scattering for cover. It pulled up beside me, and the canvas passenger door opened. "Beth!" a familiar voice shouted. "Get in!"

Alex Bronson! My body responded before my brain fully understood, and I launched myself into the ATV. Alex took off before I could close the door. "Head down!" he ordered, gunning the engine again. He ducked too, as one of the guards scrambled to pull the twisted metal gate into some sort of barrier. We hit it full force, sending the man flying as the gate swung open. We roared through the opening and up the sloping roadway. Shots sounded behind us, but we rounded the first curve and sped away.

Neither of us said a word for a while. Alex was focused on driving, and I tried hard to stay in my seat. The vehicle seemed to have a mind of its own, veering wildly in one direction and then in another. It made a terrible noise too. Finally, Alex shouted, "I think I broke something." In a grim attempt at humor, he added, "No idea if the gate did it, or the tower, or the gate again, but I think we're screwed!"

As if in support of his words, the machine chugged, chugged, and died. "I guess we're pedestrians from here." We got out, and Alex threw the key into the trees, assuring that whoever came after us couldn't start the machine again.

"Alex, we have to go back."

"What?"

"There are four women in there who'll be killed if we don't do something."

He puffed out his cheeks. "Wow."

"Yeah."

"Well, they think we're gone. That's a plus. And Eddie went for help, so it shouldn't be too long before the police arrive." Though his tone was hopeful, I didn't think he had any more illusions than I did about our prospects for success. At this point, Hopgood was operating in desperation mode. He'd kill us if he could and make up a plausible explanation later.

EDDIE

Scrapbooking must be good for visualizing, cuz Miss Candace's map was great. I followed the highway past the Kalcutt Road turnoff and went on for about three more miles. The land started to rise, and houses became fewer and fewer. There was no sign for the old logging and/or berry-picking road, but I was watching for a creek she'd penciled in. When I saw it flowing alongside the road, I slowed down and stuck my head out the window to be sure I didn't miss the back way up the mountain.

The road looked like there'd been traffic on it, but like a lot of old roads, it went just a few hundred feet and disappeared. At least that's what I thought at first. When I came to what looked like the end, however, my headlights (well, my stolen truck's headlights) revealed a narrow gap in the trees. Figuring I didn't have anything to lose, I pushed through to see what was beyond. Branches scraped the sides of the truck for a ways, making creepy metallic cries, and then the road opened up again like a highway. Except most highways don't go almost straight up, like this one did. A road that didn't look like a road. Another way Dickweed hid what he was doing from the world.

A glint of light ahead of me sent my foot to the brake. Reflected off the trees above, the light was moving. Fumbling for the switch, I turned my headlights off and sat for a moment, trying to decide what to do. Back up? It would be tricky, and whoever was coming might get to me before I could get to the main road again. The trees around me were small for the most part, and the truck's back bumper was the solid, reinforced kind. I put the gearshift into reverse and swung the wheel to the right. Gunning the engine, I backed directly into the trees. There was a lot of cracking and some resistance, but I kept going.

The ride wasn't smooth. I ended up tilted way over to one side, stopped by a tree the size of a fencepost. But I was far enough off the road that the other vehicle's headlights wouldn't reach me.

It was the Hummer. I saw its wide grill as it passed. I didn't know the man who was driving, but I glimpsed others inside. Women, it looked like. When I couldn't see their taillights any more, I started the engine and prayed the truck hadn't been damaged by my little detour. It's possible to rupture a gas tank or oil pan when you back over things like tree trunks, but luckily, the truck started easily and pulled back onto the road like those pickups in commercials that warn you not to try this at home. Like you wouldn't be an idiot if you did.

The road had been graded and graveled, but it was real steep and the curves were sharp. Not a road for a Sunday ride. After a while, I passed through an open gate that had to be part of the middle fence. I silently thanked the Hummer driver for leaving it open for me.

When the ground leveled, I turned off the lights again. It was scary not knowing what I was driving into, but surprise was the best chance I had of helping Loser. The truck was my secret weapon. I'd find her, ram through the gate, and pick up Alex somewhere along the escape route.

After a sharp turn the road went flat, and steep walls rose on either side of me. I'd come into the hollow on the opposite end, and the compound was below. A gate hung open before me, and beyond it, flames lit the side of the building I'd seen earlier. I stopped the truck, rolled the window down, and listened. At least one vehicle was moving around out front, but it didn't seem to be coming my way.

What was coming, or rather who, was some women speaking very excited Spanish. They came around the building at a dead run before I had time to decide what to do. There were four of them, and two helped a third who staggered along in a daze. They kept looking back, as if expecting somebody to come after them. I knew right away that these weren't dangerous people. They were running away from the compound, and they were scared to death.

Rolling down the window I said, "Hey." They jumped. One of them let out a little yelp. "I'm looking for Loser." Three of the women stared at me blankly, but the fourth, whose eye was starting to swell shut, lifted her head and looked at me through the other one.

"The woman in black?"

"Yeah. I think my stepdad's men have her."

I immediately wished I hadn't identified myself with Rich, because her eyes turned cold. "She got away in one of the little cars, but they are chasing her, many of them."

"Cool!" It was the best news I'd heard in a while. I could turn around and go back to Cranville if Loser was safe, leaving the cops to handle Dickweed.

"We will go." The women shifted their feet, and it was like a threat. I wasn't going to stop them from leaving the compound.

Knowledge came to me from somewhere. "You were prisoners?"

The leader gave me a look that made me uncomfortable. "Your father keep—kept us to work for him."

"He's not my father. And I hate him."

The woman almost smiled but stopped, putting a hand over a cut on her lip. "That is good," she said. "Because we beat him a little bit so we can get away."

CHAPTER TWENTY-ONE

LOSER

As Alex and I tried to decide what to do, we heard ATVs roaring up the road like angry hornets. I looked at him, a question in my eyes. We could run or we could fight. Fighting probably wasn't smart, since our opponents had guns, but running wasn't such a great option either. Their vehicles worked; ours didn't. They'd easily overtake us on the road, and attempts to scale the steep slope would make us easy targets for a shot in the back as we struggled for handholds in the scrub brush.

"Give me your hat."

Surprised, I pulled my toque off and handed it to Alex. He laid it in the center of the road, a few feet in front of the disabled vehicle. He pointed to a clump of sumac directly beside it on the uphill side. "Hide in there. They'll stop, and one of them will probably get out to investigate. When he gets to the hat, hop into his machine and go."

"What about you?"

"If it's possible, I'll jump in with you. If I don't, keep going and get help."

He didn't have to say it would in all likelihood be too late for him if I did locate the police. Still, there wasn't time to argue. I slid into the brush, maneuvering to find a place where I was concealed but able to make a quick exit. When I looked out, Alex had disappeared.

There wasn't time to wonder where he'd gone. Two ATV's rounded the curve at top speed, spitting dirt as their wheels skidded on the sandy shoulder. They stopped abruptly, and I saw Dave, the friendly killer, park next to the disabled ATV and get out, crouching to look at the undercarriage. The other man, who got out of his own vehicle more cautiously, was Rich Hopgood. He had what looked like fingernail scratches arcing down his forehead and cheek. He limped a little too, like he'd been kicked. Both men carried pistols, and I saw a rifle on the seat next to where Dave had been.

"Oil pan's ruptured," Dave said, sitting on his haunches as he looked around. "They're on foot."

Rich limped forward and picked up my hat. He too looked around, and I lowered my face. Day had arrived, but the shadows in the hollow were still deep. My black clothing would hide me if no pale skin caught the light.

My mind raced. When should I make my move? Rich was a few steps ahead of his machine, which idled only fifteen feet away. I wished Alex had thrown the hat a few feet farther down, but he couldn't have known where they'd stop. As it was, Rich and I were about the same distance from the vehicle. I'd have to count on surprise freezing him long enough for me to get there ahead of him.

Surprise did freeze him, but it wasn't my appearance that did it. We were all surprised to hear a vehicle coming, one much bigger than an ATV. Headlights showed first as a pickup rounded the curve. Crowded on the passenger side were the four Mexican women, their faces serious and their arms a tangle as they held on to whatever they could find. In the driver's seat was Eddie.

The truck was coming too fast to stop. It crashed into the ATVs, first hitting the hindmost machine, which lurched forward and hit the disabled one. That one rolled forward and to the side, leaving the road and crashing down the hillside, where it slammed into several small trees before turning on its side and sliding to a stop. Rebounding from the impact with our machine, Dave's ATV popped backward and hit the truck a second time. With a crash of metal the axle gave way, and it came to rest listing badly to one side.

Hopgood and his foreman jumped out of the way, one to either side. Both reacted like the military men they were, pulling their pistols and readying for a counter offensive as they scrambled for cover. Probably the only thing that stopped them from shooting Eddie was fear of hitting each other.

Eddie kept his foot on the gas, and the truck continued forward, hitting the third ATV and sending it into the bank on the opposite side. I heard the women scream a warning and looked up to see Dave moving into position on the other side of the truck.

"Stop, Eddie!" I heard Rich shout as he raised his gun. "You've done enough damage."

In response Eddie threw the truck into reverse. I didn't know if he planned to back down the road and escape or get up speed for another attack, but from the determined look on his face, it was the latter.

I was out of my hiding spot before any sort of plan came to mind. All I could think of was stopping Rich from shooting his stepson. A blur of movement from the other side of the road told me Alex had the same idea. Good. One on one. They had guns, but we had surprise on our side.

Hopgood's back was to me, and I left my feet a short distance away, hitting him with my full body weight square in the back, as high as I could manage. He went down with a grunt, but so did I. My shoulder felt like it had collided with a bridge abutment, but I rolled to my feet and scurried toward Hopgood. He'd rolled too, but the good part was he'd dropped the pistol when he fell. I picked it up, found the proper end, and pointed it at him. "Stay down!"

I heard sounds of a struggle behind me. Pointing the gun at Hopgood with both hands and stepping sideways, I saw Alex and Dave engaged in a contest over who would control Dave's gun. Alex had a death grip on his opponent's gun hand, trying desperately to keep Dave from pointing the muzzle at him. With the other hand, he held Dave off, throwing a punch to the man's midsection or face when the opportunity arose. Although both men had the disadvantage of fighting one-handed, Dave's advantage was meanness. He kneed Alex in the groin, gouged at his eyes, and head-butted him, causing blood to flow from Alex's nose like water from a faucet.

"Shoot him!" Eddie had got out of the truck and stood in the road, his eyes wide. "Loser, you got to shoot him, or he'll kill Alex!"

It wasn't that simple. Yes, I can shoot a pistol. I was trained as a cop. But Beth wasn't holding the gun. It was Loser, who feared she'd miss Dave and kill Alex. Beth, unaware of loss, might have done as Eddie urged. All too familiar with the mistakes someone like her could make, Loser could not.

A mighty grunt, followed by one even mightier, banished my hesitation. Alex had landed a punch squarely on Dave's jaw. He stumbled backward, arms wind-milling and feet moving rapidly as he struggled to maintain balance. His path brought him directly at me, and I whacked him soundly above the ear with the pistol. That even a loser could handle.

Dave went to the ground, eyes unfocused. But when I turned back to Hopgood, he was gone.

Alex stood in a crouch, hands on his knees as he fought for breath. Eddie, who'd been focused on the struggle, looked in confusion at the spot where Rich had been.

We all reacted a moment later as two shots rang out. One whizzed past my ear; the other was farther away but not far enough. Grabbing my arm with one hand and Eddie's sleeve with the other, Alex pulled us behind Dave's bent and useless ATV as a third shot hit a tire with a muted clunk. At least one of the women in the truck screamed, and a second later they spilled onto the ground, lining up on the downhill side of the vehicle in a frightened crouch.

Dave's rifle lay on the seat in front of us, and in a frantic attempt at defense, Eddie picked it up and fired several shots into the hillside overhead. "Leave us alone, Dickweed!" He shouted. "Leave us alone!"

"Ed, no." Alex pushed the muzzle down and took the gun from him with a gentle hand.

"He's getting away!" Eddie objected. "The cops will be too late, and he'll be gone."

Alex's eyes met mine. The boy was right. Hopgood had lots of ways to get out of the country, and we couldn't stop him. Pointing at Dave, who lay on the ground, awake but dazed, Alex ordered, "Let's tie this guy up so he doesn't run off too."

We dragged Dave behind the truck, keeping our heads low. I took a coil of rope from the ATV and moved to his side, where I went to work securing Dave's hands and feet. He didn't seem to care what I did, though he grunted a little when I tightened the rope around his feet.

Pulling a cell phone from his pocket, Alex said, "I doubt this will work up here." Opening the cheap plastic phone, he squinted at the screen. "That's what I was afraid of. No bars."

"Wait!" Eddie ran to the truck and got the backpack I'd given him. "Loser's phone is in here. It should have better service."

"Call the police and give them directions." Alex scanned the hillside. "I'll circle around and see if I can get behind him."

Eddie opened his mouth, but Alex added, "Someone has to be here when they arrive."

Dave's eyes had begun to focus, and he regarded us with unmitigated hatred. "You ain't gonna catch Rich. He knows this land, and no city boy's gonna hunt him down."

Alex ignored him as if he hadn't spoken. "If I can, I'll push him toward the gate. If the police leave a couple of men there, they can intercept him."

I was surprised when Eddie nodded agreement, but I was also surprised at Alex's air of command. This wasn't a guy who was making it up as he went along.

As soon as Eddie was busy with the phone, I turned to Alex. "I'm coming." He looked at me for a second then, shouldering the rifle, he

231

ordered, "Okay, Officer Lousiere, bring the pistol. It might be useful at close quarters."

Climbing the hill took all our energy, so we were silent for a while. I was thinking about Hopgood's chances of getting away with his crimes, which were good. He knew these woods better than any of those who'd be tracking him. If we caught him, he'd hire lawyers and spin stories that would keep him from ever getting the punishment he deserved.

Glancing back at the black smoke rising behind me, I guessed the compound was a pile of ashes by now. Hopgood's men were scattered. A clever lawyer would confuse the women he'd enslaved and offer believable alternatives to their story. I considered with dread the certainty that I'd be called to testify against him, and I imagined being cross-examined. *And where did you live, Ms. Lousiere, during the months between March of 2010 and June of 2012? On the streets of Richmond, isn't that right? Talking to yourself and crying, sleeping in parks and missions, correct? Yet, you ask this jury to take your word against the word of a decorated military veteran, a successful businessman, an upstanding citizen?* I pictured his smug smile at the jury. *Why should we believe you, Ms. Lousiere? Explain to us why.*

It was a disheartening image, but it disappeared as we reached the crest that ran along the edge of the hollow. There was Richard Hopgood, the man who'd murdered his wife, tried to murder us, and intended to murder his stepson, half concealed in a clump of laurel, a gun just out of reach of his hand.

I turned to Alex, whose expression revealed doubt. He'd been ready for a manhunt. He wasn't sure how to deal with a corpse.

For once Loser made a confident decision. Taking the rifle from Alex, I aimed in Hopgood's general direction and fired a single shot. It echoed loudly across the hollow, getting fainter each time but striking me like a series of blows anyway.

Hopgood lay sprawled, his head turned to one side, his eyes open but sightless. Using my shirttail, I picked up his pistol and fired it once into the air. Setting it back beside the body, I looked to Alex questioningly.

He nodded. We were in complete agreement.

Hearing cars pull up below us, he turned and shouted down, "We're up here, and it's over. He's dead."

EDDIE

I won't ever tell anyone, but I saw what Loser and Alex did. There were binoculars on the floor of Dave's ATV, and I watched as they climbed the hill. I couldn't see where Rich was, but I saw Loser stop and point at a spot in some bushes. She and Alex looked at each other for a few seconds before Loser took the rifle, aimed, and fired once. Handing it back to him, she stepped forward, bent down for a second, and came up with Rich's pistol, holding it with her shirt over her hand. She fired again, this time into the air. She bent down again, and when she stood up, the pistol was gone.

Loser killed Rich, but he deserved it. That's why I asked the question at the beginning: If you're pretty sure someone you like a lot killed somebody you didn't like at all, what are you supposed to do about it?

LOSER

Arriving with the state police was the sheriff of Remus County, who'd been called when the pictures I'd taken came in. Once he got his head wrapped around the idea that Rich Hopgood had for some time provided aid and comfort to criminals from both inside and outside the country, he started asking intelligent questions. Alex provided the answers, explaining that he served as my legal counsel and would speak for both of us in the matter. It wasn't quite the truth, but it was close enough. He told the police we'd happily give depositions covering what we knew of the matter. That wasn't true in my case, at least not the "happily" part. Alex suggested that Magglia and her companions could provide details of the operation as a whole.

Dave was given his Miranda warning and bundled into a squad car, still a little fuzzy about things. Fire trucks screamed by as we waited, but radio reports indicated there wasn't much left to save.

"Rich and Dave grew up together and served in the army that way too," Sheriff Garms told us as we waited for his men and the state officers to go to the compound and round up whoever was left. "I suppose they hatched this scheme then." He squeezed his chin in one hand. "I should've known, because Rich was never much for hunting as a kid. His daddy lived for it, but Rich and Dave? Those two were into raising hell."

"Usually, the military helps a man grow up," Alex commented. "But every once in a while, it gives him the skills to do the wrong thing."

The sheriff sniffed disgustedly. "I thought it was good they'd settled down and got to be productive members of society." He spit on the ground as if banishing that idea forever.

"I'm willing to bet Rich kept at least a few files at the dealership," Alex suggested.

"Probably," the sheriff agreed. "Those containers they ship cars in woulda come in handy for smuggling people in and out of the country."

"The clients who were up here must be on the move. If you alert the FBI, they might catch them before they leave the States."

"Miami," I said. "And a ranch in New Mexico." I was so far over my word count I couldn't even keep track, but it was okay. My lungs functioned normally; my blood didn't flow hot and cold. They were just words: thirty-one or one hundred thirty-one. Just words.

That sounded like Beth talking. Loser wasn't sure, but it was kind of good not to count. For now.

When the sheriff went off to arrange transportation back to Romulus, I turned to Alex, raising my brows in a question. A deputy had put Eddie into a patrol car, where he slumped as if exhausted.

"Once they know we're who we say we are, and once they have some proof that what we've told them about Rich is true, I think we can tell Sheriff Garms the truth." Alex glanced in the boy's direction. "But I don't think Eddie should know his shot killed Hopgood."

I hesitated. I'd been lied to in the past, and I'd hated it. Now I was going to lie to Eddie? It felt like the right thing to do, but it also felt wrong.

Alex read my mind. "If I'd thought of it, I'd have done it myself and saved you the stress." He focused on the kid's future. "Mabel says Eddie could live with you until he graduates high school."

I raised my brows, wondering when we'd discussed that topic at any length. He chuckled, which must have hurt, because the chuckle was followed by a wince. Alex wiped at his battered face, and I realized belatedly that the friendly thing to do was clean him up a little. Using the sleeve of my shirt, I tried to wipe away the grime and blood from his struggle with Dave.

"Are you okay with it?" he asked as I swabbed. "I mean, I could find him a good foster home in Richmond, maybe—"

"It's okay."

He nodded. "That's what Mabel said you'd say." Enduring my ministrations patiently he added, "She's really quite a woman, that Mabel. And being with you has done wonders for her."

I realized it was true, at least a little. Mabel would never be a "normal" woman, whatever that term means to society as a whole. But having a place to live and someone to care about her, and to care for, had gone a long way toward revealing the real Mabel.

"I think your yardman's sweet on her," Alex went on. "They were having coffee on the porch when I got there, and he had that look, you know?"

I was flabbergasted at the thought of Calvin and Mabel as a couple, but Alex had another zinger. "She also told the real estate lady the property won't be for sale any time soon."

Wow. Mabel takes charge.

"So when she said Eddie could live with you, I figured you two had talked things over and had your future all planned out. If I can convince the sheriff to leave the question of who actually killed Hopgood up in the air, I think it will all work out okay."

I looked over at Garms, who was calmly telling his people what they needed to do next. Maybe he would understand why I'd done as I had. Maybe he had a teenage boy of his own.

CHAPTER TWENTY-TWO

EDDIE

The judge let me go live with Loser and Mabel. Loser had to fill out a bunch of papers and stand up in court and say she'd be my guardian, but she did okay. The lady who talked to me before the hearing said I could stay in Romulus, where I knew people and the school, but I said I'd rather go to Beulah. When she told that to the judge, he banged his gavel and said it was a done deal.

I think Mabel is glad to have me around. She talks about boys like she knows how they are, but if she ever had a boy, it was in the Dark Ages. She's good to me though.

As far as Loser killing Rich, maybe I saw it wrong. Maybe he was waiting there, ready to shoot them and Loser just shot him first. I know she's a good person and he wasn't, so I'm cutting her some slack.

I miss my mom every single day. Mabel talks to me about it sometimes, and believe it or not, it helps. "When it came down to it," Mabel says, "your mamma chose you. She gave up everything that man could give her to keep you safe." Her good eye turns away then, like she's thinking about someone else. "A mother will do anything for her son."

I thought about that for a long time. My mom wasn't perfect. Neither are Mabel and Loser. I think that's how everybody is: not perfect. If that's true, then you have to judge people by what they do when things get bad. I think Mom did okay for what she got dealt in life. I'm not perfect either, but I'm going to try to make sure she'd be proud of me.

When Mabel talks about moms and sons, I listen. I said to her one time, "I guess you're right."

"Sure I am," she replied. "Now, take a look at this elbow. It used to be double-jointed, but now only one of 'em is working. You think maybe I got fiber mytalgia?"

Beth

This time when the BMW came up the driveway, I wasn't surprised. Alex Bronson must have liked the peace and quiet up here, probably because it was so different from the city.

"It's my twenty-ninth birthday," he announced. "I decided what I wanted for my present was the view from your front porch. Something about looking down on treetops for miles and miles puts pushing thirty into perspective, don't you think?"

Twenty-nine? I'd thought I was older than Alex, but I was two years younger. *Not where it counts*, Loser whispered inside my head. *You're old as these hills in the places where it matters.*

As we sat on the front porch drinking iced tea, Alex caught me up on recent events. The government had seized Rich Hopgood's assets. Happily, Nadine had a life insurance policy that would give Eddie a start in life when he was ready for college or whatever else he chose. Dave had turned state's evidence, providing names and places so the authorities could locate a long list of fugitives, domestic and foreign. That meant, Alex contended, that I wouldn't have to testify in court, which relieved my mind a great deal.

"Oh, and I called those people you told me about at the Meldero Center. They're working to get Magglia and the others the help they need, either to get back home or to stay in this country." He turned to look at me. "How'd you know about that place? I've lived most of my life in Richmond, and I'd never heard of it."

"A friend," I murmured. More like the father of a friend, but my relationship to Bryn and Nick Saraff wasn't easy to explain.

Alex sipped his tea, swallowed, and turned his eyes to the treetops below us, tinged with vibrant yellows, reds, and oranges. "We make a pretty good team, Beth. Maybe we should do it again sometime."

I gave him a friendly swat. Reliving that terror was not something I looked forward to.

He turned to me, his expression serious. "I admire you, you know."

Yeah, right, Loser said before Beth could start bathing in the glow of the first compliment she'd had from a man in years. Part of me wondered why Bronson had followed me to Romulus, climbed a mountain to rescue me, and supported me when I lied to the police—or at least didn't tell them the whole truth. Looking at him, such a nice, normal guy, I knew it couldn't really be admiration. Alex Bronson had a little white knight in him, and I was a damsel in all kinds of distress. Bert had convinced him that Loser needed watching, and Alex had gone above and beyond his duty to help.

I stood up. "Do me a favor?"

Alex looked a little disappointed, but being a nice, normal guy, he rose too. "Sure."

I took him to where a large basket of apples sat by the back door. They'd been carefully selected and polished until they shone. "Take these to the All-Aid Drugstore on Broad Street. Give anyone standing around outside the store as many as they want, from Loser and Mabel."

I'd gone way over thirty words for the day, but who's counting?

If you enjoyed *Killing Memories*, there are two other Loser Mysteries.

Killing Silence (Book #1): Loser sleeps on the streets of Richmond, Virginia. She washes up in gas station bathrooms, eats when an opportunity comes along, speaks less than thirty words per day, and spends her waking hours in front of a local drug store, watching the world pass by. When the father of a child Loser is fond of is accused of murder, she wants to help, but can Loser the Loser pull herself out of her own pain to help catch a killer?

Killing Despair (Book #3): When Loser receives word that new evidence has been uncovered in the murders she has long been suspected of committing, she returns to Richmond to investigate. What she finds is peril, but if she can survive, she'll find the answers she's wanted for so long: Who hated her enough to kill her husband and daughter?

Website: http://pegherring.com

OTHER BOOKS BY PEG HERRING

The Simon & Elizabeth Mysteries *(Tudor Era Historical)*
Her Highness' First Murder
Poison, Your Grace
The Lady Flirts with Death
Her Majesty's Mischief
***

The Loser Mysteries *(Contemporary Mystery/Suspense)*
Killing Silence
Killing Memories
Killing Despair
***

Clan Macbeth Historical Romance (medieval Scotland)
Macbeth's Niece
Double Toil & Trouble
***

Standalone Mysteries
Somebody Doesn't Like Sarah Leigh (contemporary cozy mystery)
Her Ex-GI P.I. ('60s-era traditional mystery)
Not Dead Yet... ('60s-era paranormal mystery)
***

The Mercedes Mysteries (thrillers)
Shakespeare's Blood
Charlie Dickens' Documents
***

Writing as Maggie Pill

The Sleuth Sisters Mysteries (cozy Michigan)
If you like lighter mysteries, and if you have sisters, had sisters, or know a little about sisters, you'll love Maggie's series.
The Sleuth Sisters
3 Sleuths, 2 Dogs, 1 Murder
Murder in the Boonies

Sleuthing at Sweet Springs
Eat, Drink, & Be Wary
Peril, Plots, and Puppies

Maggie's Website: **http://maggiepill.maggiepillmysteries.com**